MUST READ WELL

A NOVEL

bancroft
press

ELLEN PALL

Cover Design: Christine Van Bree
Interior Design: tracycopescreative.com

978-1-61088-542-3 (HC)
978-1-61088-543-0 (PB)
978-1-61088-544-7 (Ebook)
978-1-61088-545-4 (PDF)
978-1-61088-546-1 (Audiobook)

Published by Bancroft Press
"Books that Enlighten"
410-358-0658
P.O. Box 65360,
Baltimore, MD 21209
www.bancroftpress.com

Printed in the United States of America

ONE

Wrapped in a blanket, mainlining coffee, I sat in the cold light of dawn at the table in Petra Smolnikov's kitchen scrolling grimly through the morning's crop of housing ads on Craigslist. It was February 2011—for me, a February of the mind, the soul, the heart, and the wallet as well as the calendar. Ten days before, Tim Gunderson, the man whose life and apartment I'd shared for two years, had announced without warning that he'd fallen in love with another woman. An hour later, I was out of his place and installed in Petra's.

God bless her, Petra had insisted I come to her at once. We've been friends since we were toddlers growing up across the street from each other, both of us only children, in Flyspeck (technically Fleissport), Pennsylvania. I spent a substantial portion of my childhood at the Smolnikovs' house, eating dinner in their kitchen, watching TV in their den, sleeping in the twin bed across from Petra's. Irina Smolnikov became a second mother to me—a second mother I sorely needed. And so Petra had no hesitation in offering me refuge, and I had no hesitation in accepting.

The night I arrived and every night since, I had slept on the foldout sofa in her tiny living room. Each morning, I sat down in her similarly tiny but beautiful kitchen (Petra designs kitchens for a living) and opened Craigslist. Unfortunately, though hardly surprisingly, ninety-six percent of the offerings were beyond what I could afford. More than nine years after I'd started at Columbia, a fearful, watchful visitor from another world, I was still at Columbia. I had scraped through on odd jobs, summer jobs, the paltry wages paid to financial aid students for work-study gigs, and as a graduate student, teaching. The rest I had borrowed. By that February morning in 2011, I had a B.A., a Master's, four years as a Ph.D. candidate, and such a mountain of debt that I wondered if I could live long enough to repay it.

Not only that, I had recently learned that it might be impossible to finish my dissertation.

My heart sank as I plunged through the ads. There were a few bargains. For example, the "Free room and board for fulltime care of dementia mom." The man who "just wanted someone to cuddle with—a girlfriend-type situation." There was also the confounding "sublet in sunny jungle loft" and the "laidback" guy in Flatbush. His place I'd seen. He had opened the door in a red velour robe, then sat down with his crotch very much on display. At least he was honest; he was laidback. By the time Petra came into the kitchen, I had closed my computer and set my cheek down on it. Petra placed a hand on my back.

"French toast?" she asked.

"No thanks. Not hungry."

I sat with my head still down, eyes closed, as the kitchen filled with the smell of butter and eggs and cinnamon. Ten minutes later,

---

Petra set a laden plate beside my computer and sat down across from me.

"Eat," she said, and I ate. She was washing the dishes when I reopened my laptop and saw the miraculous ad that transformed February into May.

> Private room and bath with river view in pre-war doorman Greenwich Village building. Kitchen privileges. Available now. Advantageous terms for quiet female willing to read aloud to purblind landlady one hour a day. Reply with brief work/educational details to ATW1301922@ juno.com. Must read well.

Must read well. A shiver ran through me. I took a deep breath and studied the ad with more attention, but I already knew who had placed it. No psychic powers were needed, only a sharp eye and four years of research. "Must read well"? And "purblind"—purblind was the word of a writer. An elderly writer, probably, since her vision was so poor. Then there was the pre-war doorman Greenwich Village building with river view. How many such buildings were there amid the Village's quaint townhouses and six-story walkups? A handful, no more. But these clues wouldn't have been enough on their own. What sealed it was the email address. As I looked at it again, the letters and numbers dropped into their slots. ATW—Anne Taussig Weil. 1301922—January 30, 1922. Her birthdate.

You know that dissertation I mentioned, the one I might be unable to finish? I had titled it "Inadvertent Feminists: Three Mid-century Popular Female Novelists Who Advanced the Cause of Women," and it was to be a close study of the work and lives and sociopolitical importance of three very successful authors of so-called "women's fiction" in the late 1950s and early '60s. My thesis was that although these and a handful of similar writers had been dismissed by critics as mere providers of light entertainment for lady readers at the very moment when other writers, writers of nonfiction, were launching the second wave of feminism, they had in fact had a significant, empowering impact on the lives of at least some of the women who read them.

Of the three authors I'd chosen to focus on, two had proven only too happy to help me. They showered me unstoppably with private and professional correspondence from fifty years before, the phone numbers of their children, siblings, and friends, unpublished manuscripts, ancient appointment books; in brief, more information about, and documentation of, their lives and thoughts and intentions than I could ever use. But the third and by far most important author was Anne Taussig Weil. And she had refused to speak with me.

I knew from the start that Weil, who wrote the 1965 blockbuster *The Vengeance of Catherine Clark*, must be central to my thesis. Derided by all but a few reviewers, *Vengeance* nevertheless ignited a brushfire within weeks of its publication. The blaze soon exploded into five-alarm flames that spread across America, then jumped the

Atlantic to burn through Europe. It was a bestseller in half a dozen countries there; in the U.S., it soared to the top of the *New York Times* list, reigned supreme for seven months, then floated up and down in the lower ranks for more than a year. A paperback version amplified its fame and doubled its sales, and when these finally started to slow, the book was produced as an off-Broadway play.

Four years later, it returned to the public eye in the form of a successful Hollywood film. The scene in which Catherine Clark saws her marriage bed in half continues to inspire and delight angry young women today. With its near ubiquity and spellbinding tale of a woman's drastic revenge on her unfaithful and abusive husband, I believed *Vengeance* did as much as, if not more than, any other book of its time, highbrow or low, to awaken, energize, educate, embolden, and liberate its readers.

This being the case, as soon as my dissertation topic was approved, I naturally made it my first order of business to set up an interview with Weil. I could have chosen to go through her literary agency (*Vengeance* was, and is, still in print) but I preferred to start with a personal, woman-to-woman appeal. So, having learned from a 1965 *New York Times Sunday Magazine* profile that she then resided in a large Greenwich Village building called the Windrush, I visited it on the off chance that she lived there still. And, against all odds, she did, as a casual inquiry to the doorman confirmed.

I went home at once and wrote her a letter explaining my project. With elaborate deference, I asked if I might meet with her. Her input would be so valuable, I admired her style so much, wished so fervently to understand what had most influenced her writing, how she saw the fiction of her contemporaries then and now, whether she considered herself a feminist, and why, in her opinion, her books had had the tremendous and lasting impact they did. (For diplomatic reasons, I said "books" rather than "book" even though all of them except *Vengeance* sank from view shortly after publication.) The letter might have been a bit on the fawning side, but my admiration for her was sincere. Grace Paley she was not; but whatever her gifts as a writer, her great success had happened. She had published a book that pulled women forward with a mighty lurch. I dropped it into a mailbox and waited for a reply.

None came.

After three weeks, I sent another letter, saying the same things in a different way.

Nothing.

A month later, I wrote once more. Maybe she'd been away; maybe she'd been unwell. This third letter did receive an answer, though not the one I hoped for: A person named Kenneth Fitzhugh, who had the honor of representing Anne Weil as her literary agent, informed me that, while she appreciated my interest, she had nothing to say on the subject of her influences or the impact that her work did or did not have on American gender politics, literature, or female empowerment in the second half of the twentieth century. She did not wish to contribute to any study on this subject and requested that Mr. Fitzhugh communicate this to me. If he himself could be of any help, however, I should not hesitate to let him know. Best of luck with your dissertation, Yours truly, Kenneth Fitzhugh.

After that, I turned to the farfetched hope of catching her as she went into or out of the Windrush. For this purpose, I made a series of visits there. The building was a tall one—tall for the Village, anyway—a few blocks from the Hudson, with a crisp green canopy announcing its painfully appropriate name. During those wintry pilgrimages, I stood by the hour in the icy gusts off the river, gazing up at its façade like a pining lover, willing her to come out. I stopped every elderly woman I saw on the sidewalk with a tentative, "Anne?" But no such luck; no Anne ever appeared.

Stymied and half mad with frustration, I finally gave up. I would have to make do with the recollections of the few willing former colleagues and acquaintances I could round up for interviews and the secondary sources available to anyone: microfilmed articles from *Vengeance*'s heyday, contemporary essays and articles about the reaction it provoked in the U.S. and abroad, subsequent novels by other women that (I believed) were spawned by *Vengeance*, book reviews and essays she herself had written, cameo appearances in biographies of other authors of her time whose work had been recognized as "important," reviews of her novels, and, of course, the novels themselves.

As I began to move from research to writing, I was keenly aware of the lack of fresh material on Weil. With no choice, however, I soldiered on, and by December of 2010 believed I had closed in on the end. Before the holiday break, I gave my dissertation advisor, Professor Gwendolyn Probst, what I believed were the final two chapters of my dissertation. As I went in to discuss them with her soon after classes resumed, I felt triumphant, elated, certain she would tell me it was ready to submit.

An hour later, I was another woman. Having reviewed the chapters I'd imagined would be my last, Professor Probst felt herself obliged to inform me that she could not recommend I submit my manuscript to the committee as it was. It simply wasn't substantial enough; it wouldn't do. The material on Anne Weil was too "skimpy." I must get more.

I sat listening, sucked deeper and deeper into a vortex of flame-cheeked humiliation. How sure I had been of my imminent success, and how disastrously wrong! By the time I got home, however, self-reproach had turned into desperation. Getting "more material" on Anne Weil was impossible, as Professor Probst knew full well. And on the success of my dissertation hung my future.

While it may not have the glamour, say, of betting your future on becoming an Olympic champion, going for a doctoral degree is a high-stakes game. I had gambled more than $100,000 borrowed dollars—not to mention the irretrievable years since college graduation—on earning my Ph.D. If I failed, I would still have the debt, but not the qualifications for a job lucrative enough to pay it back.

A Ph.D. degree may not be a matter of life and death, but for me, it was certainly the fulcrum upon which balanced one kind of life or another: on the one hand, the life of credentialed prestige that I hungered for, with time and license to defend the work of neglected female writers, to document the power of their impact on their readers, to teach and mentor younger women, and to pursue the highest levels of study and research; on the other hand, a far more circumscribed, less solvent one spent in a world of community colleges and private high schools, if not permanent exile from academia altogether.

That Anne Weil, of all people, had chosen to stand between me and the life I'd worked so hard to achieve maddened me. Yet I could see no way around her. I was by turns furious, terrified, and despondent—and, in retrospect, likely not very good company for Tim in the weeks before he broke up with me.

And so, as soon as I read that little ad, I opened my email and typed in the address given. Gone, for now at least, was the heartsore, homeless waif who had, just minutes before, declined (then inhaled) a plate of French toast in her old friend's kitchen. In her place sat an energetic, self-possessed woman with hope and a very clear goal. I would tell her who I was and share with her my delight that chance had brought us together in such a way that we could help each other. What an extraordinary boon to each of us! I would happily read to her as long and as often as she liked, and at the same time, I would get to know her, fill the gaps in my knowledge of her life and work, and restore to her the attention, respect, and appreciation she deserved.

Within seconds, I realized what a terrible mistake such an approach would be. Weil had made it more than clear that she wanted nothing to do with me or my dissertation. Why should a chance crossing of paths, an accidental concatenation of needs, change her feeling about that? The correct, the smart, the necessary course of action was to make sure she had no idea of my identity, my interest in her, even my awareness of her. I must present myself as a complete stranger, one who happened also to be her ideal tenant.

A moment later, almost without thought, the text of my reply to her ad appeared in my head in its entirety. I set my fingers on the keyboard and wrote that the room she offered sounded ideal for me. Without naming the college I'd attended, I told her I had a B.A. in English and loved to read. I said that, as it happened, my mother was blind, and that growing up, I'd often read to her. I noted that I had a part-time job with flexible hours writing marketing copy for a small, online business, and that I usually worked at home.

I thought this stable if unimpressive employment would reassure her as regarded the matter of the "advantageous" rent. It was also a little bit true, since I did get an occasional assignment of this sort from a friend whose online store sold imported leather goods. I said that I hoped very much she would consider meeting me, and that I looked forward to hearing from her. I thanked her for her attention. Then, after a brief hesitation, I decided to send the message from my .edu address, to which Columbia graduates are forever entitled. This, I believed, would reinforce the suggestion of literacy, intelligence, modest accomplishment, and trustworthiness. All this I did calmly, steadily, as if my computer and I were one machine.

I pressed send, listened for the little "whoosh" sound of the message on its way, then made it to the sink just in time to puke. I stared at the still recognizable fragments of French toast in disbelief. Who was I? How could I lie to Anne Weil to get her to do what I wanted?

I knew I was capable of dissembling. I had had to dissemble regularly—pretend, lie, hide my true feelings—when I was a child, or I wouldn't have lived to be an adult. But I had become an adult, and since then, I'd worked hard to learn it was safe (usually safe, at least) to be my true self, to be honest. I'd spent a year seeing a psychotherapist at Student Health twice a week. I'd attended Al-Anon meetings on and off since freshman year. I thought I had left my days of hiding behind me, yet here I was again. What kind of scholar—what kind of person—was I?

———

I washed my mouth out, emptied the sink, scrubbed it with Comet, threw away the sponge, and then, although I wanted to sit at my computer refreshing my email every two minutes, made myself get in the shower. Petra left the apartment just as I was toweling off, calling out a cheerful "See you later!" through the bathroom door. It flew through my head that I must tell Tim about this incredible turn of luck! Then reality returned. It's quite convenient to cry in a shower.

You almost don't need tissues.

Clean and dry-eyed, I spent a sobering ten minutes with my reflection as I blew my hair into some kind of acceptable condition. My hair is fat. Thick, savage, willful—and as if that wasn't enough, a particularly brilliant coppery red. I keep it long so I can brush it all back and clamp it into a braid or ponytail, something less menacing than what it looks like when it's on the loose. That day I coiled it into a big, conservative bun at the nape of my neck, watching myself as I did so. At the best of times I am pale, but that morning I was even paler than usual. My eyes had a weird, glassy look, partly caused by the Shower of Tears, partly by the strain of the last ten days and the tense, desperate hope that when I got back to my laptop, I would find a response from Anne Weil.

Which I did.

Mercifully, she had answered my email less than half an hour after I sent it. Her reply, in very large font, was brief: She had received my note and would like to speak with me by phone. I could reach her today between 11 a.m. and 2 p.m. at—and then a 212 number. There was no greeting, no "please" call, no "thanks for your reply," no closing salutation, no name.

It was now 9:45. I forced myself to make up the sofa bed, sweep and tidy what little of the apartment wasn't inaccessible thanks to my own belongings, then sit down on the sofa with a batch of student essays from the class I was teaching that semester, a freshman course on social activism during the 1960s. These particular papers, if I recall correctly, were about the 1968 student protests at Columbia itself. In spite of everything, I was soon fully absorbed in what my students had written. I loved teaching, loved to see the uncurling of young minds as they encountered other minds, loved getting a classroom full of students to mix it up with each other, the bracing, competitive, collaborative excitement of intellectual engagement.

All the same, some part of me must have been ticking off the minutes, because at 11:04, I put down the paper I was reading and picked up my phone. I fought a pulse-quickening fear as I dialed the number Weil had sent me. I'd been quite diligent about combing through the Craigslist ads, but I only did it once a day, in the mornings. When had she posted hers? Had someone else gotten in ahead of me? Had she answered my email, only to line up a fallback tenant?

She picked up the phone on the fifth ring with a slow, interrogatory "Hello?" Strikingly, her voice gave no hint of her age. It was low and vibrant, with a slight mid-Atlantic accent. Knowing that she'd grown up in Brookline, not far from the center of Boston, I wondered when and why she'd decided to start speaking this way. Though it struck me at first as ridiculous, when I met her, I realized how provident her resolve had been. A voice can remain alluring long after other charms have fled.

"Hello!" I squealed in my excitement, then heard my tone and hastily reined myself in. Squealing with excitement suggested a personality far from the one her post had stipulated. Calm, stable, trustworthy, intelligent, mannerly, pleasant, sensible, competent, quiet—quiet above all—such was the impression I needed to create.

"This is Beth Miller calling," I went on more evenly, grateful for once to have so forgettable a surname. Had it been Freud or Rockefeller, Weil might just have remembered me from the letters I'd sent so long ago. As for "Beth," I had signed them with a professional "Elizabeth Miller." To my ear, "Beth" suggests a given name of its own, not a shortened form of a longer one. No one ever calls me Beth; I am always Liz. But there's no law, I told myself, against using a different nickname.

"We exchanged emails about a room you're offering for rent?" I went on, fiercely reminding myself that she hadn't yet given me her own name. "Or—am I speaking to the right person?"

"Yes. Thank you for getting back to me. Do you have time to chat for a moment?"

"Certainly."

We chatted, as she called it.

What sort of room are you looking for?

A quiet one; I needed quiet to work.

That I would surely have, she said. And when would I like to move in?

As soon as possible. (The ad said "available now.")

And, if she might ask, how old was I?

I thought for a moment. "Twenty-four," I decided. Twenty-four seemed young enough still to be renting a room in another person's house, but old enough to be mature.

"Well, I'm afraid you'll find most of the people in my building quite a bit older than yourself," came the cultivated voice, "but the neighborhood is lively. Do you know the Village?"

"A little. I mean, I went to Columbia. I've lived in the city for—" I hesitated, flummoxed by the elementary math. "—for six years now. So, of course I know it. Just not very well."

"Six years," she echoed, as if thinking this over. "And where did you live before college?"

"Well, I grew up in Brookline," I said. I made it sound like a question—"in Brookline?"—to signal that I wasn't sure she would ever have heard of the place. "Just outside Boston." I had no hesitation in giving this answer. As it happens, my father's sister used to live in Brookline. When I was little, before my dad died, my folks would drive me up there each summer and leave me for a few weeks with my cousins.

I had expected Weil to exclaim, "So did I!" Instead, "Oh, did you?" she replied.

I repeated that I had.

"Ah."

Can a single syllable be spoken dryly? If so, her tone was dry. I noticed later that she quite often spoke this way and began to wonder if, like her low voice and mid-Atlantic accent, this hint of archness might be a deliberate affectation. It put me in mind of Lauren Bacall's cool, insinuating drawl; maybe Weil had picked it up from her as a young woman, in a bid to suggest a certain blasé sophistication.

"Now let's talk for a moment about my need for a tenant who can read to me. If I remember your email correctly, you said you have a job with flexible hours?"

If she remembered correctly! My heart flip-flopped. How many answers had she received?

"Yes. I only have to go into the office on Tuesday and Friday afternoons." This was when I taught. "Other than that, I can easily be with you whenever you like."

"That's handy." Again, her tone was flat, cool, almost bored.

"I believe you mentioned that you've been in the habit of reading aloud to your mother," she went on. "But I wonder—forgive my asking, but someone of your generation, you probably haven't had to deal very often with handwritten documents?"

The question caught me off guard. I'd assumed I'd be reading books to her. Luckily, though, I could address this matter with no trouble.

"As a matter of fact, I have. I didn't have my own computer until I was fourteen," I said. "And I was taught penmanship in school. I still write lots of things by hand." A moment later, I realized I was holding a genuine ace.

"Also, in my senior year of college, I wrote a long paper on the letters of Dorothea Carstairs," I went on. "No one's ever heard of her, but she was the sister-in-law of—well, of a nineteenth-century novelist no one's ever heard of either—and they had a correspondence.

Dorothea kept her sister-in-law's letters, and they're what I wrote my paper about.

"Those letters," I continued, as she said nothing, "were what are called—I'm sorry, this is kind of complicated, but they were 'crossed,' which means that to save paper, which was expensive, the person would write across the page the way we do, but then turn the paper sideways and write over the lines at a ninety-degree angle."

I could hardly believe Anne Weil was letting me explain this—surely she knew what a crossed letter was. She had written the preface for an edition of *Pride and Prejudice*!

"Anyway, Carstairs's handwriting was tiny and kind of a mess even when she didn't write across it, so—so yes, I'm very familiar with reading handwritten documents."

After this, she finally gave me the name and address that I knew were hers. She asked when I would have time to come look at the room and I told her I could be there in half an hour.

"I mean, you know," I added lamely. "New York real estate."

"I see. Well, I'll need a few hours myself," she said, "but later today is fine. There's just one other thing I should mention. If you do want the room, we'll have to have a little—a little audition, you might call it. I must have an excellent reader."

"Of course."

We set the time for 2:30 and I hung up almost trembling.

What handwritten documents?

Two

Three hours later, I sailed into the Windrush with the assurance of a queen.

"Anne Weil," I conjured at the doorman's desk. "She's expecting me."

"Yes. She called down a little while ago," the doorman—Frank, according to his nametag—answered promptly. "Tenth floor. Take that elevator." He gestured toward the left side of the lobby. "10A will be on your right."

I trotted off in the direction he'd indicated and, glancing behind me, saw to my surprise that there were indeed two elevator banks in the Windrush, one to the west and one to the east. For all my mooning at its brick face, I hadn't realized this before. Between the building's two sides, perceptible from here only as muffled light behind a row of stained-glass windows, lay a courtyard of some kind.

Beyond the lobby, I passed a mailroom, and around a corner came to the elevator, its heavy brass doors figured with an ornate geometric pattern. Here I paused a long time before pushing the button. The day was sunny but the cold knife-sharp, and I had been walking around the Village since coming up from the subway station shortly after two o'clock. Now I let my nose thaw, blew it, blotted it, rubbed it warm. I took off my gloves, scarf, hat, and coat, the better to display the tastefully conventional black cable-knit turtleneck and gray wool slacks I had unearthed from one of the suitcases cluttering up Petra's place. I was still arranging myself when the elevator startled me by opening to disgorge a couple in late middle age, bundled up as if for an Arctic expedition. The woman gave me a vague smile as we passed each other.

The elevator was small and wood-paneled, with a tiny velvet seat in a back corner and a mirror in which I checked my reflection. I am green-eyed, lightly freckled, and tall for a woman. Assuming my hair cooperates, I can look quite pretty when I try. But that day, I didn't want to look pretty. I wanted to look ordinary—a sparrow, not a parakeet. The woman I saw in the mirror seemed to have achieved this goal. I'd parted my hair in the middle, put only a tiny bit of blush on my cheekbones and a couple of swipes of unremarkable lipstick on my mouth. My clothes looked respectable, decent, neither cheap nor expensive. If you'd come to apply for a mortgage at a midwestern bank, you would have had no trouble recognizing me as the junior functionary who would start the process by taking your information.

I pulled my turtleneck up to my jaw and made sure my slacks hung straight before pressing the tenth-floor button. The elevator vibrated ominously as it rose. Emerging, I found that only two apartments shared the dim, tiled vestibule. After a pause to compose my features, I pressed the doorbell of 10A. In the brief interval that passed before it was answered, I caught myself holding my breath. Here was a moment I would never forget, the moment when I would finally meet Anne Weil.

When the door opened, however, it wasn't Weil who greeted me. Instead, it was a smiling woman in her middle forties, with a broad face, short blond hair, and a slight Eastern European accent. She wore jeans, a sweatshirt, and red sneakers. Housekeeper? Home health aide? Whoever she was, I hoped she didn't live here.

"Come in," she invited, stepping back into a vast, gloomy foyer. "It is so cold out! Too cold! The wind!" She gestured at a coatrack beside the door. "Hang up your things while I tell Mrs. Anne you are here," she said, disappearing through a light-filled archway into the depths of the apartment.

Having spent so long shut out of Weil's place, I gazed at my surroundings with as much amazement as if it were the Land of Oz. "Pleasant, capable, reserved, quiet," I chanted to myself as, heart skittering, I made myself turn away from the light to hang up my coat, stuff my gloves into one of its sleeves and my knitted cap into the other. "Pleasant, capable, reserved, quiet." It was my new mantra. I didn't even think of the word "misleading," nor the phrase "false pretenses." Such was the tenant Weil was seeking, and such—for her own good, I now told myself, as well as my own—I must be.

Unbundled, I turned back to survey the dim, cavernous foyer. As my eyes adjusted to the light, I saw that the parquet floor was highly polished, its center covered with an old, once-lush Persian rug. I knew that the woman who'd let me in expected me to stay where I was, but I couldn't resist drifting toward the archway to peek into the next room.

This, I found, was a living room too narrow for its great length but with three grand, very tall latticed windows at its far end. Outside these, as I would see a few minutes later, lay the rooftops of the westernmost Village, a long reach of the Hudson beyond them, a jumble of buildings strewn along the Jersey side of the river, and above all this a boundless atrium of white winter sky. Red toile drapes had been pulled back from the windows, so long that they pooled luxuriously on the floor. This too was parquet, but in a different pattern from the foyer. Again, its center was dominated by a thick, if somewhat timeworn, Persian rug.

It was an immaculate room and almost too full of tasteful antiques: delicate little tables inlaid with mother-of-pearl or banded with marquetry, gleaming copper lamps with pierced parchment-shades, a pair of red velvet love seats with rolled, sloping arms. But like the carpets, it was no longer at its best. Dingy white paint peeled off the ceiling in curls, and the worn upholstery had been bleached by years of too much sun. On the walls hung eight gilt-framed oils, several of the Hudson River School variety as well as a pair of unsentimental portraits taken, to guess by their style and the clothing of the subjects, in the early years of the twentieth century.

At the very end of the room, directly in front of the middle window, a cherry-wood Biedermeier desk faced the river. Drawn up before it was a black, throne-like chair of carved wood, ball-and-claw footed, distinctly non-Biedermeier. (For the record, everything

I knew at that time about marquetry, or parchment shades, or Biedermeier furniture, I had learned from reading novels; there were no gilt-framed paintings or velvet love seats in the house where I grew up.) I had gotten this far in my survey when the sound of a doorknob turning some distance away warned me to scurry back to the shadowy foyer. There I stood, hands folded, trying to calm myself.

"Pleasant, capable, reserved, quiet..."

Several minutes passed before Marta, as I learned to call her, came back to me. In the meanwhile, I heard the murmur of voices and a slow, intermittent thump—presumably Weil's halting progress down some long hall to the living room. When Marta finally returned and conducted me to the living room and "Mrs. Anne," I saw that this personage was now seated in the dark throne, presenting her back to me. Her hair was surprisingly thick and long, a shiny silver curtain descending to her shoulders. A black metal cane with a foam grip and a trio of rubber-tipped feet stood close to her right arm.

I hesitated, doubting that she would stand and turn to greet me, but waiting in case she did. Then Marta pointed me to a small, old-fashioned armchair I had failed to observe during my surreptitious look around. This sat catty-corner to the desk, its oval back to the window, so that, after seating myself, I was facing Weil. The chair's back and its round seat were stiffly upholstered in brocade, its curved blond wooden arms and legs glossy with varnish.

I hadn't reckoned on sitting down to introduce myself to Anne Weil. In my imagination, she herself would shuffle to her front door, let me in, and offer me her hand to shake. Instinctively, I had known just how I would tilt my head and shyly, deferentially smile at her. She would say a few words, then lead me to the room for rent so I could look it over.

Now, as I took the oval-backed chair across from her at her desk, the situation began to remind me of a job interview. After the puking incident, I had dared to have a slice of dry toast and a scrambled egg for lunch. These now began to stir uneasily in my stomach. I felt myself heating up and realized there was a small but powerful radiator a few feet to my left. Despite the fierce river wind that rattled the latticed windows, the living room was very warm. I soon regretted my turtleneck.

For a few seconds, I simply stared at her, overcome by my thirst to take her in. So many years had gone by since the time the last photo I'd seen of her had been taken. It was one of a flurry of pictures that appeared in the many articles provoked by the success of *Vengeance*. The Anne Taussig Weil of those articles, like the one on her long-ago book jackets, was a severely beautiful woman with dark, blunt-cut, shoulder-length hair and thick bangs that brushed the black brows over her bold, hooded eyes. Now I faced a tall, very thin, very old lady wearing a white silk blouse, a cream-colored cashmere cardigan, and loose crêpe pants.

Aged as she was, though, she was not without beauty. The silver hair that hung to her shoulders differed only in color from the hair of the woman in the publicity pictures; she still had the same high cheekbones and the elegant hollows (albeit no longer unlined) that accompany them. Her posture was remarkable for a person of any age; it must have been the work of a lifetime.

But her mouth had collapsed, her lips showed no trace of the fullness they once had, and the flesh above them was deeply corrugated. Her chin had lost its definition, her neck its ivory smoothness. The eyes behind heavy tortoise-shell glasses retained some of their youthful, sharp challenge, but their color had faded from deep brown to a dull amber.

All the same, the remnants of her youth caught the eye at least as much as the passage of years. She put me in mind of a silent-film actress, one long gone from the screen but whose ghost still lives in her face, her gestures, her carriage. Even now, she looked commanding enough to have been the notorious author of a book that galvanized a generation. (I say "galvanized" even though in my own view—the view I argued in my dissertation proposal—Weil had been propelled by the force of feminism's gathering second wave no less than she helped to forward it.)

As we started to talk, I saw that the faded eyes behind the glasses were still capable of a steady, considering gaze. The collapsed mouth came alive, curling into a smile—a smile of genuine pleasure, it seemed to me. In fact, old as she was, she looked a bit like a child who has just been given a toy. I wondered how often she had visitors these days.

"You'll excuse my not getting up to shake your hand," she informed me. Her voice was lighter, less studied, than it had been on the phone. "I'm enjoying some of the maladies that are the reward of long life—brittle bones, uncooperative joints, a soupçon of heart disease."

"I'm so sorry," I said, neither too warmly nor too casually, I hoped.

"And, as you know, impaired vision," she went on, ignoring me. "In the past seven years, two exciting events have occurred in my eyes, first the left, then the right. In each, a sort of ocular explosion took place that was caused by—well, never mind the exact cause, the result is that I've entirely, permanently, lost my focal vision. My central vision, that is. Whatever I look at isn't there. Words have blank spots in the middle. Straight lines curve. Only my peripheral vision is intact. I have to look sidelong to see anything at all clearly."

With this, she turned her head slightly and briefly eyed me aslant. I realized now that the terseness of her reply to my email reflected not imperious discourtesy but disability.

For a moment, I felt the bitterness of such a loss to a writer. "That must be very hard," I said, as she turned back to face me.

"Well, you know . . ." She paused, smiled, and lifted an expressive eyebrow. "It beats your mother's situation, anyway," she said.

My mother? By February of 2011, my mother had been dead half a dozen years. It was a moment before I understood the reference.

"Yes," I said, recovering. "Yes. She can see a little, she's not completely blind, but she can't really function on her own. She needs a stick to keep from bumping into things, she can't cook or handle money, that kind of thing," I embroidered feverishly. "And obviously, she can't read."

"Not Braille?"

Strangely, Weil was still smiling. It surprised me that she had so little sympathy for a fellow sufferer.

"No, she never learned. She was already in her thirties when her vision started to go," I said, "so I guess . . ."

I shrugged, unable to think of what I guessed. How careless I'd been not to think out the details of my invented mother's case in advance! Afflicted as she was, of course Anne Weil would be interested in them. While I berated myself, she began to explain that she could still read a little, provided the type was large enough or she used a powerful magnifying glass. She greatly enlarged the print on her computer and relied on glare-free Kindles, with their adjustable print, to read newspapers and books.

It was a relief when she changed the subject.

"Well," she said, then appeared to cast about for my first name. "Well, Beth, it's a pleasure to meet you, but I think you'd best see the room I'm offering before we go any further. If you like it, I'll ask you to try reading some of the documents I have in mind. If not, we'll say goodbye."

With this, she turned to reach for a bell I hadn't noticed on a corner of her desk. A silver bell with a long, black, tapering handle. She rang it. The sound was bright and surprisingly loud.

"I'm afraid you'll find this very *ancien régime*," she said, setting it down, "but I can't shout anymore."

Moments later, Marta hurried in, a dishcloth in her hand. Weil introduced us properly and asked her to show me the kitchen I'd share and the bedroom that would be mine. Trying to look as if I couldn't wait to see them, I stood up to follow her.

We walked through a rounded archway into a dining room. This had exactly the same proportions and fabulous windows as the room I'd been sitting in but was bare and neglected. Yellowed voile curtains blocked the view from the windows, and a ragged kilim lay under a long, plain pine table. I suspected it had been many years since the ten chairs around it had last been filled.

There was a swing door opposite the windows, doubtless the entrance to the kitchen, but Marta took me through a second archway across the dining room. Here there was a corridor. The second door on the right was slightly ajar. Marta opened it wide and ushered me in, flinging her arm out in the manner of a game-show hostess exhibiting a prize.

As well she might. Like the rest of the apartment, it could do with a new coat of paint, but the two windows had the same view as the other front rooms and the blue-and-white duvet looked new. There was a small rug—Persian again—to put your feet on when you got out of bed, a small flat-screen TV atop a wide dresser, a mahogany night table and, set in front of the windows, a serviceable wooden desk.

Marta opened a door, revealing a more than adequate closet. "There is plenty of room in the front hall closet," she told me as I peered into this one. "You can put your extra things there if you need to. And—" She crossed the room to open another door, near the dresser, "this is yours, too." Inside was a bathroom, with a second door that I realized opened onto the corridor.

"You can keep it private," she said, moving into the room to turn the bolt below the knob. "Mrs. Anne doesn't use it."

Having researched the Windrush on Zillow, I knew a good deal of its history. The bathroom in 10A still had the original fixtures. The floor was covered in the classic little black-and-white hexagons, the walls in white subway tile. There was a pedestal sink and a small glass-enclosed stall inside of which drooped a showerhead the size of a sunflower. Like the crisscross faucet handles, that showerhead was valuable now, a sought-after antique.

I turned to face Marta. "Everything's so clean!" I thought it wise to exclaim. She gave a modest shrug, as if to say it was nothing, and I leaned toward my growing suspicion that she was a housekeeper, not a home health aide.

"You must live here, to keep the apartment so sparkling," I

ventured.

"Oh, no," came her welcome reply. "I only come on weekdays, twelve till six. I do the cleaning and a little cooking, but Mrs. Anne likes to be alone." She returned to the door into the corridor.

"Does she?" I asked, reluctant to follow her out during this interesting conversation. "Then it must bother her, always having someone in this room."

She turned back, surprised.

"Oh, she never rented out the room before!" She lowered her voice to a whisper, her tone worried rather than gossipy. "I think—I know—she has a health problem. Her heart. So maybe she wants someone here now just in case... Anyway, come. I can show you the kitchen."

We returned to the dining room and went through the swing door into a long galley kitchen at least five times the size of Petra's. Though immaculate, it was depressing. The white Formica countertops were dulled and scarred, the enamel on the elderly stove chipped, and the ancient fridge three-quarters the size of a modern one. A single window faced an empty courtyard across which squinted and winked the many back windows of the opposite side of the building.

I stood a moment looking at them, disappointed that my route to the kitchen would bypass the living room, where I imagined Weil spent most of her time. Still, whenever I left or returned to the apartment, I would have to cross it. As for her bedroom, I had caught a glimpse of it at the end of the corridor, just beyond the room that would be mine. I would have no excuse for intruding there, of course, but she would pass my door whenever she left.

Marta opened the refrigerator and showed me its crepuscular interior. "I cleared a shelf for you," she pointed out. I said thank you, though I was all too aware that I had yet to be accepted as a tenant.

Escorted by her, I returned to the living room. Anne Weil had not moved. She sat at her desk, wearing a different pair of glasses, smaller, with black frames. Reading glasses, I presumed: she was inspecting a Con Ed bill through a large, jade-handled magnifying glass. As I took my chair again, hands demurely folded in my lap, she set this down, changed back to the tortoiseshells, and turned toward me.

"So, what do you think? I imagine you're accustomed to roommates a little closer to your age," she said with her habitual, understated wryness. "I can't say there's a lot of social life around here."

"It's beautiful. Perfect."

"Not too far from work? I think you said you've been living uptown?"

"Yes, but this is actually closer to the company I work for. It's in Chelsea. Anyway, I only go there twice a week. The rest of the time I'm home. And I've always wanted to live in the Village," I added. "This would be—if you're willing to have me, I would love to stay here. But—the rent?"

There was a short silence before she said, "Ah, the rent."

She looked directly into my eyes (but how well could she see them? I wondered) and made a little "hmph" sound. Her own eyes now had a thoughtful, calculating look. In that moment, I had the unnerving feeling that, for all her vision problems, she saw me more clearly than I saw her. Will it make sense if I mention that, just then, my estimation of her as a writer went up a notch?

"How much can you afford?" she asked.

Caught off guard again, I dropped my gaze and scrambled to think of an answer. Too little and she would dismiss me; too much and I really wouldn't be able to pay, no matter how desperate I was to get the room.

I looked up again, still groping for a number, and found Weil's head tilted to one side.

"Tell you what," she said. "If you're able to read my handwriting, and if you're very good at reading aloud, and if you will make yourself available as often as possible to read to me at short notice, even Saturdays and Sundays, I will charge you one hundred sixty dollars a month. I hope that amount will be acceptable."

I nodded, not trusting myself to speak. A hundred sixty dollars a month? In New York, you could hardly rent a storage locker for that.

"And you'll do your best to be within reach when I wish you to read to me?"

"Yes, sure. That won't be hard for me. I work at home, after all. And I'm a homebody anyway."

"Good, because I can't know in advance when I'll feel up to listening for an hour. That is why I'm looking for a tenant rather than hiring a reader." She moved her gaze away from me, toward the long window beside her desk, before going on, "Now let's see if you can do the job. Marta will take you into my study to fetch a couple of notebooks for me. What I want read aloud are excerpts from some of my journals, entries I wrote quite a long time ago. I've kept a journal nearly all my life. There are some three hundred of them. However, there's only one section I want to hear. A—" she broke off, looking for a word. "An episode that took place when I was in my early forties," she resumed. "I wish to...to revisit it."

My mind took off. If she had been in her early forties, then *Vengeance* had come out a year or two after the part she wanted me to read. A moment later, I realized I was missing a far larger point. Three hundred handwritten notebooks documenting Anne Weil's entire life! And I would be reading some of them to her. Never mind that—I would be living with them! It was like telling a four-year-old her bedroom would be located inside a candy shop. My heart started to race.

With an effort, I returned my attention to her low voice as she gave me instructions on how to locate the notebooks she wanted. The journals were stored in chronological order, she was saying as I tuned back in. I was to find one from the very early 1960s—'60 or '61, and another from '66 or so. Their start and end dates were recorded on the covers, and each had been numbered as well. At a guess, I'd probably want to begin my search around number 185.

"You'll need to be very good at deciphering," she added in a tone of warning. "Since childhood, my handwriting has been execrable, almost a sort of private code. For many years, I was ridiculous enough to pride myself on that. It was my imprimatur, proof of my unique, creative nature. I'm a writer," she added. "Or was."

"Or was" indeed. She had published three novels before *Vengeance* and, several years afterward, a last one titled *The Balance*. The first three were what are known as "literary" novels. They had been politely received and respectfully read when they appeared, although more, perhaps, by other writers than anyone else. They generated no money to speak of, and until her marriage—quite late in life for a woman of her time—Weil had worked fulltime as a copyeditor at the then-thriving, now long-defunct, publishing house Dodd, Mead.

The Balance was also "literary," and not dissimilar from its three older sisters, but coming after *Vengeance*, it landed very differently. The great reading public, like dogs fed on the red meat of her sensational bestseller, scorned such literary kibble. Reviewers, too, were rudely dismissive, and *The Balance* died a quick and lonely death.

Vengeance was so different from Weil's other, refined efforts that I had occasionally wondered whether it might perhaps have been written by someone else. Not only was it unlike those well-bred books in its slash-and-burn style and propulsive energy, there was nothing at all in her biography—nothing I could find, at least—to suggest the origin of its plot.

Her marriage had been a happy one, at least to hear her tell it. And there was only her version of events to go on: Her husband, a prosperous malpractice lawyer named Stephen Pace, had been killed in a car crash seven years after they married. According to a short piece in the *Daily News*, one rainy morning in July 1963, a taxi speeding east on 28th Street broadsided the cab taking him up Eighth Avenue. He was fifty-five when he died. Weil was forty-one.

In the various interviews his widow granted to newspapers and magazines after *Vengeance* came out, journalists repeatedly suggested that her own marriage must have given rise to its story. This she steadfastly denied. *Vengeance* was not about her. It was a sustained act of imagination about a set of fictional characters. She spoke warmly of her late husband, emphasized how well the two of them got along despite their disparate fields and personalities. They had bonded over a shared love of hard-boiled mysteries, she told them. They used to read Raymond Chandler and Dashiell Hammett aloud to each other. He admired and took an interest in her work, as she did in his.

It was true that his law practice was lucrative, but equally true that he represented his clients from the heart. He worked very hard. It outraged him that a doctor's careless mistake might forever incapacitate, not to mention kill, a patient. He was a strong supporter of and generous contributor to the civil rights movement. He had no patience with people who wanted women "kept in their place." They skied together, played tennis together. Losing him had shaken her deeply.

She wasn't shy about her enjoyment of the luxuries his income had brought her. It was he who had lived in the Windrush when they met, she mentioned in more than one article, staying on there after his first wife returned to her native Texas. She talked of her awed delight at occupying so large and beautiful a place after ten years in a Hell's Kitchen studio. She said she enjoyed cooking for him, and even that she'd sewn curtains for their bedroom windows. The most interesting statement she made on the subject of her married life was that she'd never wanted children.

"I don't think everyone is cut out for children," she told a reporter. "I like to have my time for myself."

And so she was—or had been—a writer.

"Are you?" I remembered to say. "That's so interesting!"

"Yes, I thought that might interest you," she said, tilting her head and considering me for rather a long time before she went on, "because you majored in English. Sadly, my penmanship only got worse as I got older," she went on. "The result is that my vision impairment has left me unable to read my own journals. You can imagine my vexation," she added after a pause.

There was venom in that last sentence, understated and deadly. I did take a moment to imagine her "vexation." It must be monumental; mine would be. Not that I would ever have kept a journal. In those days, and with my childhood, privacy meant far too much to me. I considered keeping a written record of your thoughts and doings an invitation to disaster.

"So, let's summon Marta," Weil said, ringing the silver bell again. While we waited, she took a small key from her pocket and used it to open the middle drawer in her desk. From this, she withdrew a ring of old-fashioned skeleton keys. Marta appeared and she handed them to her.

"Marta, would you kindly take Beth to the study?"

She turned again to me.

"You'll find all the journals in a glass-fronted cabinet to your right as you walk in. I'd have gotten them myself, but I'd need a new spine and new hips and knees to do it. And new eyes to find the right ones."

I stood and followed Marta into the room that would change my life.

THREE

One sometimes reads of a "book-lined" room. Anne Weil's study was one. Every available inch of wall was chockablock with books, so much so that the room had no color of its own, only a kaleidoscopic rainbow of bindings. Even the windows, shuttered to block out the ugly, lightless courtyard, were all but interred in books—books jacketed and unjacketed, paperback and hardcover, old and new, famous and obscure. Almost all were novels.

It was quite a large room, nearly twice the size of the bedroom I hoped to occupy. There was yet another Persian carpet, this one predominantly dark green, and a long, narrow writing table set back a few feet from the wall on the left. This was old, its surface scratched and pitted; the term "refectory table" floated into my mind—flotsam, no doubt, from some long-ago reading I'd done. On it lay untidy stacks of mail, opened and unopened, another, even larger magnifying glass (this one with a brass handle), a large jar full of pens and pencils, a scattering of paperweights, a jumble of paper clips, and a very big desktop Mac.

Opposite this table sat an armchair covered in moss-green velvet, and beside it a tall lamp with a Tiffany-style shade. (Or, perhaps, a Tiffany shade.) The glass-fronted bookcase, surrounded by less distinguished shelves, was impossible to miss. It was a very wide, beautiful, hip-high piece of furniture made of fruitwood, with an inlaid strip of pale wood winding like a vine around its eight glass doors. Each of these was furnished with a tarnished brass keyhole.

The doors restrained a riot of spiral notebooks, three long shelves of them jammed together so tightly that some of the curly bindings had become interlaced with their neighbors. Many had been turned on their sides and shoved on top of others. A wave of dizziness passed through me. I believe my mouth actually watered. Then, reckoning that of the three hundred, number 185 might be on the middle shelf behind the sixth door, I asked Marta to open it.

She slid the keys around the ring, peering at what I now saw were tiny numbered tags attached to each. Settling on one, she used it to unlock and open the door I'd indicated, then stood and watched as I removed a handful of notebooks; it was necessary to take out this many to make enough room to ferret among the others. With a few exceptions, they all looked the same: five by eight inches, with brown cardboard covers and light green, narrow-ruled pages. It was obvious they'd been handled often. Some were soiled, a few slightly swollen. On two of the half dozen I had selected, the metal spirals had sprung up out of place.

Consulting the fat numerals inked on each of these, I found that my guess at the right location was not far off. The books I'd plucked out, numbers 190-194, dated from the early 1970s. I opened one at random, November 21, 1972-January 12, 1973. Weil wasn't joking about her penmanship. Her writing was execrable, inexcusable, a tangled, barbed-wire mass of misshapen letters, idiosyncratic abbreviations, and words whose vowels had been excised. Still, I really had managed to make my way through the crossed and recrossed letters I'd told her about—all 132 of them—and I was confident that I could read a handwritten sentence as well as anyone in New York. The page I'd flipped to had an entry written on December 4th.

"Yest" (yesterday) "finished rev" (review) "of Breakfast of Champions for the Chicago Trib," it began. "Not my cup of tea—too much skipping back and forth in time—but funny and inventive and—" Here came a word I first read as "whistle" but then saw must be "worthwhile." "The protag" (protagonist) "is a scifi writer, nvr" (never) "my cup of tea either, but he and the lunatic who takes his fiction for truth are entertaining chars, so erred on the side of praise." I flipped the page over and sighed with relief: She hadn't written on the backs.

I returned these notebooks to their place and asked Marta to open the fifth door so I could grab another handful a couple of feet to the left of those from the '70s. This time I guessed right. Number 185 itself (May 3-August 1, 1966) was among the bunch I pulled out. I kept this and put the others away, asked Marta to open the fourth door, and soon found September 24-November 30, 1961. Now, finally, I stood and she returned me to the living room, where I took my designated chair. She restored the keys to their owner, who put them back in the drawer and locked them inside.

"I will be in the kitchen," Marta said, and left us alone.

Weil had resumed her scrutiny of the few papers on her pretty desk. On my way back to the living room, just for a moment, I had a chance to look at her before she noticed I'd come in. The sight of her lax, unanimated face, so different from the social face she had presented to me, alarmed me so much that my heart beat faster. How very old she was! And how precarious her health. I regret to say that it wasn't compassion for a fellow mortal's nearness to death that moved me. It was the possibility that she might die before I learned anything worth knowing.

Although if she died while I was still living here, wouldn't I be able to—

Again, my careful little lunch asserted itself somewhere in my innards, a lurch of queasiness gone the moment it came. *It was a good thing, it was a good thing, it was a good thing* I was doing. This strong woman's valuable diaries should not be lost or forgotten. They should be read and the light they shed on her work shared with the world. It crossed my mind that she might, in fact, have made arrangements to sell or donate the journals to the archives of some scholarly institution somewhere. If she had, perhaps the shipping date was coming near.

Weil sensed my presence and looked up, again setting the magnifier on the desk. I seated myself and reported the dates I'd brought back.

"Well done. Those will nicely bracket the period I'm interested in. If you can decipher those, you'll be able to read what's in between."

I started to say that I'd already glanced at a page and could indeed read it, so eager was I to prove my competence, and so forgetful that I'd looked without license. Fortunately, she was still talking.

"Just to be clear, the question isn't simply whether you can decipher it," she was saying. "There are several other requirements. The first, I'm happy to say, you already meet: I need someone with a pleasant voice who speaks well. You do."

"Thank you. I appreciate that," I said, and meant it. I owed this accomplishment to Miss Hart, my English teacher in junior year of high school, who had recognized my intellectual potential and taken me under her wing. If not for her, I would never have dreamed of applying to Columbia; in fact, I might have skipped college entirely. Miss Hart spoke beautifully, with a loving regard for vowels and a deep respect for consonants. Among many other kindnesses, she taught me to do the same.

"But I also need someone who can read for meaning," Weil was going on. "Do you follow me? There are readers, even professional readers of recorded books, who seem unable to see the shape of a sentence, who don't get its sense. They emphasize the wrong word— 'He turned *around* to look at her.' '*She* lived happily ever after.' Or they make a statement of a question, as if they couldn't be bothered to look at the end of the sentence before beginning to speak it aloud. 'Daddy, what happened to the rabbit after it went back into the hat.' That kind of thing. Do you see? I need someone who can read with understanding."

"Yes. I believe I can do that."

"And the last bit is—"

Here she paused to give me a stern look, a look of warning.

"The last requirement is that whatever you read here must be kept in absolute confidence. You will not speak a word of it to a friend or your family or the newspapers—not that they'd be interested—or whisper it into a bed of reeds, for that matter."

I said "Of course" without thinking—what else could I say?—but inside my chest I felt a mighty wrenching, as if the bottom brick of a tall stack had suddenly been pulled out. If she wanted the journals kept secret, might she be planning to destroy them before she died? Might this revisiting of the "episode" be a sort of last waltz? Even if (as I believed) the prose in *Vengeance* was pedestrian at best, even if Weil was as much propelled by her social moment as responsible for it, *Vengeance* had indeed jolted hundreds of thousands of women forward toward independence, and her journals surely must form a picture of a life of her time—the life of a creative, highly intelligent woman in a particularly transformative era.

"Yes. Of course," she repeated. "And I'll ask you to sign an agreement stipulating that." Another long pause, another minatory glance at me, while I tried to keep the alarm out of my face. "But the first order of business—" With a wave of her hand at the notebooks in my lap, she settled back into her chair. "The first thing is to hear how you read. Start with the earlier notebook. Any entry will do."

I opened the 1961 journal to a page near the middle, scanned a paragraph, and began.

Tuesday October 24, 10 p.m.

Worked all morning on And Sometimes Y, if that's what it ends up being called. Laura needs more backstory. Thinking of giving her scoliosis. Phone rang four times in two hours. I let it. Who are these people who think I have nothing to do but chat?

Lunch at Zouave with Sarah Thacker. She's working on a profile of Norman Mailer. I wish her joy of him.

Weil made a "hmph" sound and I looked up to find her smiling a faintly nostalgic smile. Thacker had been a prolific staff writer at *The New Yorker* for many years. I felt a pang as I realized I might have tapped her as a source for my dissertation. She had died only a year or two before.

I hoped Anne would say something more about her, or about Mailer, but she didn't. As for *And Sometimes Y*, unless she had indeed changed the title, it was never published.

"Go on."

I went on.

Drank a whole vodka tonic before our meal even arrived. So ridiculous of me. Naturally, I couldn't work when I got home. Instead, trotted over to Ottomanelli's and bought a sirloin steak. I made Béarnaise sauce for it—I thought it rather a failure but S. liked it."

"'S.' was my husband. Steve," Weil told me. She had closed her eyes but opened them now. She added, her tone a little dreamy, "We were introduced by a mutual friend." Her choosing to explain how they'd met surprised me, since it was in no way necessary for me to know. "Though I say it myself, he was immediately intrigued by me," she went on. "I was very exotic to him. A Jew! He was a WASP, of course."

I had noticed while doing my research that no article about Weil, and no essay she had written, referred directly to her religious heritage. I supposed she was born Jewish, because of her name, but it was nice to have it confirmed. At the same time, I wondered what being a WASP connoted for her. Officially, though perhaps not culturally, I am a WASP myself.

"Just say Steve when you see an S," she was going on. "Or any other abbreviation, just say the word I meant, assuming you can figure it out. How's the deciphering going?"

"It's a little difficult." Why make it sound easy? Then she would think anyone could do it. Besides, it was difficult. Her handwriting was a combination of print and cursive. The letters leaned against each other and overlapped as if they were drunk, tangling into almost abstract knots. They poked up and down over the narrow-ruled lines. Both *th* and *gh* were rendered as a single curve. All the letters were flattened, the *t* barely taller than the *s*, and the tail of the *g* docked like the tail of a cocker spaniel.

"Nothing I can't manage, though," I added. I took a deep breath before daring to go on, "You know, it occurs to me that if I do end up reading to you, it would help if I knew what sections we'd be looking at next. That way I could spend some time on them in advance and be able to read more fluently."

"You're doing fine," she said. "Go on."

I read.

Steve had much to say at the table (and for half an hour after, as he watched me clean up), about the new partner they've taken on at Lister, Pace. Porter Somebody. He voted against letting him in and he's still not a fan. The man is arrogant, brags about his political connections, already alienated a potential client, doesn't know the law nearly as well as he should, etc.

After he'd unburdened himself of this and gone off to do more work, I spent a couple of hours reading a novel called "The Bell," by Iris Murdoch. It's extraordinary. Such a wonderful writer. I owe Sarah T. a debt for having pointed me to her.

Off to bed now to read until Steve comes in or I pass out.

"That's the end of the entry. Should I go to the next one?"

"No, switch to the other book."

I switched and spent a few moments flipping the pages from June 1966. I would have appreciated a little feedback. Was I reading "for meaning," as she called it, getting "the shape" of the sentences?

Wednesday June 8, 8 p.m.

Wrote this a.m., then took a break to walk to the Morgan Library to see if they had anything special on view that might be of interest to me. No. Came home and was standing in the lobby, dripping wet from suddenly pouring rain, when I had the always miserable experience of catching sight of—"

I stopped here. "It just says 'G.'"

Weil repeated the letter with a querying emphasis. "G?"

"Yes. An uppercase letter *G* with a period after it."

"And what was the year?"

I reminded her.

"I see... G. stands for 'Greg.' You can say Greg. Keep going."

Came home and was standing in the lobby, dripping wet from suddenly pouring rain, when I had the always miserable experience of catching sight of Greg on his way out. I suppose this is something that's going to happen till one of us moves away. Or dies.

He looked purposeful, as if he were on some important errand. As usual, I played my assigned part—pretended not to see him, didn't even warn him it was raining. Also as usual, sank into agitated wretchedness as soon as I was home.

Who could "Greg" have been? An editor who'd dropped her? A critic who'd panned one of her novels? An agent with whom she'd quarreled? Or maybe he had nothing to do with her professional life.

"Skip a few pages," she instructed, her voice somehow hardened, curt. "Go to another date."

I skipped.

June 25, 9:30 p.m.

Worked on The Balance (still very rough but going okay), then a review for Harper's in the a.m. Read (reread) "The Tenant of Wildfell Hall" for pleasure over lunch (buttered bread and olives). Later wrote a long letter to Ginny and met Nina for coffee. Then hared off to Macy's to replace the sheets that turned pink in the wash.

Dinner and out to see "Zorba the Greek" with Corinne. Quite enter-taining, though a little too much joie de vivre *for my taste. Somehow I've never cared for* joie de vivre. *Maybe I'll read the book.*

In those lines about *joie de vivre,* I noticed a similar tone to the archness I'd heard in her voice. She used it to amuse herself, it seemed. A line had been left blank here. I reported this to Weil, then finished the entry.

Is this really to be my life?

Having come to the end of the day, I fell silent. Weil also remained silent for a few long seconds. When she spoke, her words had a listless, faraway sound.

"How did you manage with the handwriting?"

"It's a little difficult in one or two places," I said, "but mostly no problem." As she didn't reply, I went on, "How did it sound? I can make my voice more animated or louder or—whatever you want."

"You did very well. Very well," she repeated, her own voice more vigorous as she came back from wherever she'd been. She smiled at me. "You're hired. The room is yours."

Mine! A rush of excitement flooded me and I had to work hard to keep from grinning as I thanked her.

"You're quite welcome," she replied, then added, "I don't know how long all this will take. I hope you can move in fairly soon. And that you'll stay at least a month."

I assured her that I would take up residence within the week and stay a month, much longer if she would have me. Certainly, I wouldn't leave while she still needed me to read.

"Well, that's very kind, but you never know how life will change. You're young. I'm sure you must have some irons in the fire, some ambitions you haven't mentioned. You're much too smart to be content with a rented room and a job writing catalogue copy."

I hadn't anticipated her raising such a point and cursed myself. In a moment, though, a plausible answer came to my lips.

"I have been looking for some kind of nonprofit where I could work. I'm pretty good at copywriting, and nonprofits always need that. My hope is to work on women's issues," I added in a flash of inspiration, "maybe for Planned Parenthood or NOW." Surely Anne Weil would endorse such a goal.

She nodded, smiling with what I hoped was approval.

"Well, that is an aspiration," she admitted. "Let me know when you're ready to move in. I'll be here."

I left the Windrush feeling as if my blood were carbonated. I wanted to leap into the air, yell, declare myself Liz the Victorious, the Brilliant, the Magnificent. Adrenaline (and maybe some testosterone?) coursed through me, so much so that I strode through the knife-blade winter wind all the way to Penn Station before reluctantly descending to the warmth of the subway. I thought of calling

Petra to tell her the news but decided instead to go to Gourmet Garage and buy some fresh shrimp and asparagus and arborio rice— it was Tim who had taught me to make risotto, but I shoved that memory away—as well as a celebratory bottle of Pellegrino, and cook us up a truly excellent dinner.

I slowed as I passed a liquor store on the way back to her place. Petra drinks; I could get a split of Champagne for her. But I don't drink. And since she never orders alcohol for herself when we eat out together, I decided she'd just as soon share my *acqua frizzante*. I sent a text to tell her to be sure to come home for dinner and left it at that.

About the alcohol thing: I know I've been dancing around about that already, hinting darkly at my background, so let's get it over with. When I was eleven years old and she was twenty-nine, my mother either did or did not kill my father, either intentionally or accidentally, because she was too fucked up herself to realize what she was doing when she shared some heroin with him. My dad, normally an active addict and alcoholic, had been clean for several months before that day, and the dose that was fine for her killed him. This is something that happens pretty often when addicts relapse; they don't have the tolerance they had before they got sober, but they forget that. They slip, they pick up, they use much more of whatever substance they crave than their body can tolerate, and they die.

Two more things before I leave this subject. If my mother was a little careless about my father's wellbeing, you could say she had some reason. He slammed her around quite a bit when he was using, and that tendency to rage didn't magically go away when he wasn't using, either. Also, my mother died young as well, but not because she OD'd. She just got really, really drunk and walked into the intersection of Main and Susquehanna in downtown Fliessport. She was forty. I was twenty-one.

So this is why I do not drink. Don't drink, don't use drugs, don't even like to take Tylenol. (In fact, Tylenol can be really dangerous; everyone should be careful about using it.) Among her other life-saving acts on my behalf, as soon as Miss Hart learned how my dad had died, she took me to a meeting of Alateen, a twelve-step offshoot of Al-Anon, itself a twelve-step offshoot of A.A. There I met other children of alcoholics and addicts and learned I was not the cause of my father's death, nor his anger, nor my mother's various failings (sloth, irresponsibility, occasional wrath, bottomless self-pity), nor, for that matter, any of my parents' problems. I also learned that neither of my parents had asked to be addicts. No one does. They were responsible for their actions, but they were also victims of their own disease. At least that is how I came to think of them and, if not entirely forgive them, then at least understand them.

So that's all about that.

The shrimp risotto turned out better than I'd dared hope—I'm not a natural cook—and Petra was thrilled for me when I told her my tale. (And maybe a tiny bit thrilled for herself, since she'd finally be getting her privacy back.) Naturally, she knew all about Anne

Weil and the dead end to which that lady's coyness had brought my dissertation. Like other people whose life plans weren't about to be completely destroyed by Weil's intransigence, I knew that Petra thought her well within her rights. And she was, of course. I was the idiot who'd assumed without a thought that I would win her cooperation. But Petra had always had the diplomacy and good sense to refrain from pointing that out to me.

When I told her about the non-disclosure agreement Weil mentioned, however, she put her fork down and gave me a sideways, narrow-eyed look. "You're going to abide by that, I trust," she said.

"Am I?"

"You'll have to. She could take you to court if you don't."

I hesitated, torn between the person I usually was and the cunning child reawakened by the prospect of access to Anne Weil. "But when would she do that?" I asked, speaking from some middle ground between those two personae. "What are the chances my dissertation would ever even come to anyone's attention? It's not as if it's likely to be published. And if by some bizarre fluke it were, would she—well, not to be crude or insensitive, but how likely is she even to be alive by then? She's eighty-nine years old, and she has a bad heart.

"Not that I want her to die," I added, as Petra's cool green eyes continued to bore into me. "Besides, it's not as if I'm planning to write anything scurrilous about her. I'm trying to champion her work. I'm trying to carve out a place for her in women's history, for

Chrissake. She's just too—I don't know what, too stubborn, too dopey, too mistrustful? Whatever, she just doesn't get that."

Petra was silent for a little while. She used the fingers of her left hand to shove a few stray grains of risotto onto her fork, chewed them, swallowed. Then she said, "But what if the journals she wants you to read from don't have anything to do with her work? What use will that be?"

"Well, first of all, I think they probably will have to do with her work, because of the timing. Because of the dates she's interested in and when *Vengeance* came out. But also—"

I stopped talking, wondering if I should tell even Petra what was in my mind. Probably not. Remote as the likelihood was, I supposed it was true that there could be legal action against me one day, and if a case were to arise, the less she knew, the better.

"But also because once I get to know her," I improvised, "I'm sure she'll open up to me."

Petra knew me well enough to know I didn't believe this. If there's a sort of person people confide in, I am not that sort of person. I'm not open enough myself to invite confidences from others. But Petra also knew enough to let the subject drop.

Four

I moved into Apartment 10A two days after my first visit there, arriving on a Sunday just before noon. I came prepared with many stories about why I might have needed to move so quickly, from splitting up with a boyfriend (not much imagination there) to having been kicked out of what I'd thought was a legal sublet. But Weil never asked. Nor did she follow up on the work reference I had offered. This surprised me, but I attributed it to the outstanding job I'd done of presenting myself as an ideal tenant—not to mention my skills as a reader. In that capacity, I really did excel; she would be hard put to find someone better.

It was easy to pack up, because I'd hardly unpacked since evacuating Tim's apartment; there was no room in Petra's place for me to put my things "away," so the suitcases had remained nearly full and the boxes sealed. Petra made us oatmeal for breakfast, then helped me lug everything down to a taxi late that morning. Just before I left, with the cabbie's trunk full and the backseat crammed with overflow, we both felt a wave of sadness, the kind that would make sense if I were on my way to a new life on another continent.

Petra leaned into the backseat to give me a hug and our mouths accidentally banged into each other. This made us laugh. But after she'd straightened and slammed the door shut, and I'd rolled down the window so we could call goodbye and I love you to each other as the taxi pulled away, we both had tears in our eyes.

Half an hour later, at the Windrush, the doorman (Frank again) lugged everything out of the taxi and loaded it onto a brass luggage cart. He had been told I was coming to stay and that I should be treated as a resident. During the phone call when we set up my move-in date, Weil had asked if I could be available at two o'clock on the afternoon of my arrival, for a brief meeting in her living room. Naturally, I said I could; I had yet to see a lease and assumed she meant by "meeting" an occasion for me to sign one and pay my rent.

As it turned out, I didn't cross paths with her until the appointed hour that day. It was Marta who let me in when I rang the bell, Marta who helped me carry my possessions to my room, she who gave me a key, she who suggested a nearby grocery store where I could pick up some food for myself. I did this soon after my arrival, coming back with a small stash of thriftily chosen tuna fish, bread, off-brand mayo, yogurt, and bananas. Without a glimpse of my landlady, I made myself a sandwich and, with Marta's blessing, sat down at the lonely dining-room table to eat it. Then I unpacked.

Shortly before two o'clock, I heard the doorbell ring. Soon Marta passed my door and a couple of minutes later repassed slowly in the other direction, this time with Anne. Going into the living room promptly at 2:00, I found her again seated at her beautiful desk. With her, occupying what I already considered my chair, was a short, smiley, ruddy-cheeked man of fifty or so in a shapeless brown suit and a pair of salt-stained Oxford shoes. Emanating vigorous good cheer, he stood to shake my hand. And so I made the acquaintance of Patrick Quigley, who I soon learned was Anne's lawyer.

"Please sit down," he invited, moving toward me and waving me into the chair he'd just vacated. As I sat, Anne nodded amiably at me, even casually, as if we'd seen each other just a few minutes ago. Meanwhile, her lawyer brought in a little wooden chair from the foyer, sat, then reached into a briefcase he'd left on the floor. From this he withdrew several documents, which he set on the desk in front of me.

The first was indeed a lease, a lease of six sentences on a single page. In it, Anne Taussig Weil (hereinafter "Landlord") agreed to rent a room and private bath in Apartment 10A of the Windrush, with kitchen privileges and free internet access included, on a weekly basis, to Beth Miller (hereinafter "Tenant") for the sum of $160 a month. Tenant agreed to pay this rent in four weekly installments of $40 starting on the seventh day after the signing of this lease. She further agreed to conduct herself quietly and to bring no visitors to the apartment.

This was something we hadn't discussed, but it had never crossed my mind to bring anyone anyhow. She also agreed to do all she could to make herself available to read to Landlord no less than one hour of every day during the tenure of her stay. Should Tenant fail to meet these terms, or if for any other reason Landlord should wish to, Landlord retained the right to demand, on a week's written notice, that Tenant move out. As for Tenant, she had the right to move out at any time.

After this, there were signature lines for both of us.

"Oh," Quigley said, as he handed us pens. "Do you have a picture ID, Beth?"

"Yes, of course. In my room. Should I get it?"

"Please."

On my way to my room, I felt a suspense I'd been mercifully spared since getting myself out of Flyspeck—the suspense that comes when a person bigger than you might suddenly explode. My forehead was visibly sweating when I returned and gave the license to Quigley, but thankfully, all he did was look at it, murmur "Oh" again, then take out a pen for himself and neatly alter the tenant's name to "Elizabeth Miller." Given the usual single-spaced lines and squint-worthy font in which the lease was printed, I told myself it was unlikely Anne would be able to make out either my crossed-out name or his printed substitute.

This done, Quigley handed back my license and copy of the lease, gave a copy to her, and asked us both to sign. Anne had put on her reading glasses. Now she scanned her desk, then put out a hand and slid it over the surface. She was searching for the magnifying glass with the jade handle, I assumed, but it wasn't there. It lay on a Chippendale-style end table next to one of the red velvet sofas; I had noticed it earlier, when I came in, but I said nothing. Failing to locate it, she let the matter go and instead merely skimmed over, or pretended to skim over, the lease, pen hovering, until Quigley reached out to guide her hand to her signature line. We both signed two more copies. Then Quigley gave one to each of us and slipped the third into his briefcase.

"There, that's done. And now," he went on, drawing a few other papers from his bag, "I have the non-disclosure agreement you discussed." He riffled through the copies quickly, neatly changing my first name again, then put one before each of us. Reaching again into the briefcase, he produced from it the sort of clamp used for embossing notarized documents. "Please read it," he told me. After a minute, he murmured to Anne, "We'll need our witness soon."

Anne rang her little bell, upon which Marta promptly appeared, driver's license in hand. Since she'd told me she was here from Monday through Friday, I realized now that she must have come in today only to welcome me and to serve as witness.

Quigley took a look at her license, then at her face, and returned it.

I was still reading the agreement, and the others waited in silence until I was done. For better or for worse, I was too nervous to make much sense of it. I tried to keep my face pleasant, businesslike, but inside I was quivering. With a formal, legal document before me and a pen with which to sign it, Petra's imaginary lawsuit seemed less far-fetched.

"Take your time," Quigley said, watching me. "Let me know if you'd like to consult a lawyer before you sign. It is a legally binding document, and I'd advise you to do so."

But I declined. Apart from suggesting that I had doubts about my willingness to observe its stipulations, taking time to see a lawyer of my own would only delay things. Besides, like the lease, the NDA was short and very clear. It stated that I agreed to keep in strict confidence any information pertaining to the personal or professional life of Anne Taussig Weil or other named persons in the material I was to read her. I would not provide or permit unauthorized access to, use of, publication, or dissemination of same. I would not disclose or discuss the information with any person.

Further, I would keep confidential the very existence of this agreement (too late for that!), revealing neither the fact of it nor the nature of the business that occasioned it. This agreement would terminate only with the written consent of Anne Taussig Weil. Failure to observe any or all of these obligations could result in money damages and/or litigation.

It was disturbing, very disturbing, and the more I read, the faster ran my heart. Still, I comforted myself that there was one very good thing about it: The terms applied only to what I learned from the material I read aloud to her. Nothing was said about information from conversations we might have, nor the other 290 or so journals sitting unattended not a hundred feet away. I signed, and as Quigley handed two more copies around, signed both of these as well. One copy for each of us, each with Anne's and my signature, each witnessed by Marta and notarized by Quigley. I look back at that moment now and believe that I both knew and did not know just then that I was determined to examine those journals no matter what. I was like a person burning with fleshly desire, mesmerized by the perverse lure of the forbidden. I wanted them. I would have them.

The NDAs distributed, Marta disappeared while the rest of us exchanged polite smiles (mine sending a quick squiggle of nausea through me) and Quigley tucked his copy of the executed document into his briefcase.

"And that," he said, standing up, "I believe, is that."

He gave a little bow, returned his chair to the foyer, then came back to the desk to say goodbye. Anne tilted her face up at him and, in her most thrilling Lauren Bacall voice, thanked him for sparing her a trip to his office—and on a Sunday at that. He smiled, said it was no trouble, leaned down, air-kissed her, and went away, leaving Anne and me alone.

For a moment, in the vacuum the others had left behind, she trained her eyes on my face with what seemed to me a speculative look. As before, I wondered what she could really see of me, whether she was truly scrutinizing me or, for some reason, merely schooling her own gaze to mimic speculation. I thought it had to be the latter, since she had told me that anything she focused on was blank. She couldn't pretend to walk steadily or, of course, read text without great difficulty, but she could pretend to read my expressions. Diminished as her abilities were, this must have been a consolation.

"We haven't discussed when we'll meet for the readings," she pointed out after a moment. "Providing I'm well enough, I'd prefer ten in the morning. Does that suit you?"

Because the class I taught met on Tuesdays and Fridays at three, I assured her this was fine.

"Good. And seven days a week?"

"Yes, that's no problem at all."

"And if I'm not well enough in the morning, we'll try to arrange it for another time that day? There will no doubt be such mornings. My energy is—" she hesitated before finishing, "—my health is variable these days."

"Yes, I understand. Yes, sure."

"Wonderful. Shall we start tomorrow then? Oh, and by the way," she added, "I'm not sure I'll be able to listen for a whole hour every time. But you won't mind if some sessions are shorter."

"Not at all; whatever works for you." I hesitated before going on, "If you'd care to get started now, I'm free."

She shook her head.

"I'm afraid this afternoon's little ceremony was enough excitement for me for today. I don't know how old you imagine I am, but I'm nearly ninety. Even at my best, I spend many hours a day lying down in my room, recovering from nothing more than the ordinary exertions of daily life. I'm already longing to do that right now."

I jumped to my feet. "Then we'll start tomorrow. Shall I—?"

I gestured at the cane and crooked my arm to suggest my willingness to escort her, but she said no.

"It's best for me to manage on my own, or so my doctor tells me. I must keep my joints and muscles working as best I can. Many people older than I am have less trouble with this, I know, but I am being punished for a lifetime of sedentary pursuits. My only comfort is that I've had enough self-discipline to keep my spine straight. I couldn't bear to be one of those people you see with their backs hunched and their heads irremediably thrust forward."

With this, she reached for her cane and, leaning heavily on it, used it to lever herself upright. Then, each action deliberate, she turned slowly in the direction of the dining room and began a cautious journey toward it.

"Between my shaky pins and my wonky eyes, every walk is an adventure," she remarked as she went. "Still, I try to hobble up and down the corridor every day or two. Dr. Braudy's orders. God, how I loathe exercise," she called back as she neared the dining room.

Out of tact, I stayed where I was until I heard her three-footed steps reach her bedroom door. Then I went to my own room and called Carrie Benson, my roommate freshman year at Columbia.

Carrie is a lawyer.

———————

That night, after nearly two weeks of camping out at Petra's, I slept easily and deeply. At her place, even though I knew it so well, I had awakened every morning with a sense of dislocation. When I came to consciousness, the thought of Tim rushed to my mind—his habit of throwing off all the covers by morning no matter the weather, the way he slept curled up on his side, facing away from me, the march of sharp vertebrae up his curved spine—and a wave of self-pity and exhaustion would run through me.

At Anne's, the mattress was pleasantly firm, the quilt and linens fresh. Despite my deep sleep, I woke up preternaturally aware of where I was—as if, like a bird's, half my brain had been awake all night. When I got out of bed and opened the blackout shades concealed behind the eyelet curtains, it was a delight to see the morning's cloud-dotted blue sky and the bright, flowing river, so different from Petra's courtyard view, not to mention the airshaft outside the bedroom I'd shared with Tim. (Only the living room faced Morningside Park.) A little snow had fallen overnight and lay crisp and pure along the branches of the black, leafless trees below. I checked my phone and found I had slept nine hours, till 7:45.

I washed and dressed before creeping to the kitchen, drawn by a strong smell of coffee. I thought perhaps Marta had already come but found Anne there alone, her thin body canted against a counter while she buttered a slice of toast. Her beautiful hair was neatly brushed, and she wore a quilted, cream-colored, ankle-length robe with a pair of soft tan leather slippers. The robe had lapels and a wide sash; it reminded me of dressing gowns in movies of the '30s. I hesitated in the open doorway—the swing door was flush to the wall, held there by some built-in mechanism—unsure if she was aware of me and reluctant to disturb her, until she said without turning, "Go ahead, come in. Kitchen privileges, you know."

I went in.

"It takes me quite a while to wake up," she continued, still with her back to me, "so please ignore me and I'll do the same. I'm no morning person. Have some coffee if you like."

I thought a morning cup of coffee might become a little bond between us and accepted with thanks. Then, delighted to know Anne shared my own need for time to myself at the start of the day, I stood at the window quietly sipping while, behind me, she dropped the butter knife into the sink and took her toast to the dining room. The muffled thump of her cane marked her progress. I had already noticed a mug of coffee on the dining table on my way in and realized that, needing a hand to hold her cane, she could carry only one thing at a time.

Uncertain whether I was allowed to eat in my room, I delayed my own breakfast and, hoping she wouldn't look up, tiptoed past her with only the coffee. I was sure she'd prefer I not join her at the table. A few minutes later, I dared to return to ask for the password to her internet network. ("Windrush," as it turned out.) Back in my room, I checked my email: Petra, demanding a full report; several students with questions about an upcoming paper; Carrie, confirming our plan to meet for lunch. Nothing from Tim. I wondered how long it would be before I could open my email without looking for his name.

At nine, there was a knock on my open door. Anne poked her

head in.

"I'm good for a reading today," she said. "See you in the living room at ten?"

"Yes, absolutely." It was happening! As she thumped away, my pulses began to throb and my breath quickened. I dashed out to the kitchen again to grab a banana and a container of yogurt, ate them without ceremony at the dining table, then went back to my room to count the minutes until it was time to present myself in the living room.

Anne was already at her desk, dressed in the same sort of clothes as the day before, this time an olive-green sweater and gray pleated pants. Through her magnifying glass, she was looking at a credit card bill. She set this down as I came in and exchanged the black reading glasses for the tortoise-shell ones.

"Today we'll take out all the notebooks we'll need," she said. "The first must include February 1963. If you take the next five or six as well, they should encompass the time period I want, and we won't have to go through getting them out of my study again."

Marta was out shopping, so Anne began the difficult work of rising from her chair—the cane, the business of making sure it was steady, the free hand pressed on the desk for safety as she pushed herself up—while I meditated upon the fact that, with all the pertinent notebooks out, she would never need me to open the magic bookcase on my own. It felt like a move in a chess game, a move against me. In her study, she took the ring of old-fashioned keys from her pocket and handed it over. I knelt down in front of the glass façade of the bookcase, which seemed to gleam at me defiantly, impregnable and smug.

"Look wherever you think they might be. Somewhere between the journals you read from the first time, of course."

I found key number five and opened the door, then began to search for 1963. I realized now what I'd failed to notice before: the shelves had only two vertical dividers. This meant that just three keys would be required to gain access to all of the notebooks. Even a single one would suffice to get to a third of them. The eight doors were merely a convenience. The thought gave me a little flicker of hope. It occurred to me to wonder if Anne might have stashed away duplicate keys somewhere in the apartment.

February '63 was soon in my hand, a short month that also contained the last few days of January and the first five of March. I pulled it out, then the five after it. The last contained May 17 through June 12.

I told Anne the dates and she said I might as well put the last one back; we wouldn't need it. I did so, then locked the door and returned the key ring to her. She thanked me and we left the study. As I followed her halting steps to the corridor, the four notebooks in my arms, my thoughts turned to the nature of this so-called "episode." I was curious about it, of course, had been since she first mentioned it. I reminded myself it might be nothing more intriguing than an account of her father's illness and death, for example—he had died sometime in the '60s, as I recalled—or a burst of creativity at Yaddo. Still, it might be something far more useful to me. My curiosity helped divert me from my frustration.

Back in the living room, we seated ourselves. I kept the February notebook and put the others on her desk.

"Try starting on February 9th," Anne said. "I'm pretty sure that's the day it began."

Just for that moment, she had lost the mid-Atlantic accent and reverted to Brookline. I was already paging through the journal, but I glanced up. Her face was strained, as if preparing for a blow. Looking down again, I found the 9th and began.

Saturday February 9, 11:15 p.m.

Home from an interminable dinner chez Amy and Len Reeves. Twelve of us, six women, six men, three of the latter Steve and Len's colleagues at L.P.

"Bingo," Anne interrupted. "That was the start of everything." She reverted to her cultivated accent. "L.P. is Lister, Pace, the law firm where Steve was a partner. 'Pace' was Steve—Stephen Pace. I think the firm was mentioned in one of the sections you read on your first visit here." She paused for a moment before telling me to keep reading.

The odd man out, whose name I never quite got, hardly spoke. His wife quiet also. She went in and out of the kitchen "helping" Amy, who looked ready to hit her. At the table, the usual segregation of the sexes, men choosing one end, women relegated to the other. Among the lucky—

I hesitated. She had written "atts" and it took me a moment to translate it.

—among the lucky attorneys, there was a discussion of the aftermath of the missile crisis in Cuba. At our end, Beatrice Holloway and Amy talked about the price of meat these days and the rumor that Balducci's was going to open another store. Amy served a quiche Lorraine, forgetting that Steve is allergic to eggs. She made him a sandwich jambon and I wished she had made one for me. The quiche strangely concave and thick, and the chocolate mousse for dessert the same. Eggs again, of course, and Steve relegated to graham crackers, poor man.

A surprise as we were leaving. It turned out that the unfamiliar couple lives in the Windrush. They moved in a month ago. We all took a cab home together, but I didn't learn much about them except that Mrs. Whatsit met Amy through a book club they belong to. She didn't seem to know I was a writer and I said nothing. They live on the C/D side of the building, hence no wonder we haven't crossed paths before.

Steve planning a three-day trip to Cleveland. He'll leave ungodly early from Idlewild on Monday. I'll miss him but am hoping the time will allow me to make some better progress on—

I paused. "It says ASY here. Is that the book you mentioned in the 1961 journal? *And Sometimes Y*?"

"Yes. It took forever and then came to nothing," she said. "But never mind. Scan ahead. I don't need to hear anything until the new neighbors I mentioned come in again. The dinner guests. I'm not sure how I'd have identified them the next time."

Obediently, I ran my eyes over the bumpy lines. Days went by. *"Moderated a panel discussion called 'Whither Publishing' for PEN at Mercantile Lib,"* read one entry. *"Companionable sex w/S"* was recorded a few days later. *"Dad called, said he was feeling well, though I always wonder if he would tell me if wasn't. Mostly talked about the mistake he made in taking his car to a new repair shop, where it has now been for almost a week." "Nightmare last night. Someone (S?) was choking me."* The next day: *"Long phone call with Ginny. She's still going on endlessly about Mike: How could he leave her? Why didn't she see it coming?... I urged her, gently I hope, not to let him take away her joy in life, suggested she focus on her friends, her work, the pleasure she takes in art and books and music and so on and so on, but what I really wanted to do was tell her to snap out of it, for Chrissake. Mike's gone! Celebrate! But she seems to remember nothing of the hell he put her through."*

Finally, the Reeveses reappeared, and with them word of the new neighbors. The entry began with other details of the day and Anne told me to read them as well.

February 18, 2 a.m.

Just woke from another nightmare, this time a classic: Dad crying in his sleep and I couldn't wake him. I remember finding him sobbing once in real life, a few months after Mother died. He was sitting on the back steps after breakfast one morning.

Stayed up late tonight to finish reading "The Makioka Sisters." I don't know why I never read it before. A beautifully detailed and historically fascinating novel, though it surely has the strangest last sentence I've ever encountered. Earlier made a little progress on And Sometimes Y but also deleted several paragraphs, so I guess I came out even. I know this book isn't commercial (big surprise) but I can't seem to set it aside. The characters have a hold on me, especially Bridget.

Now we came to the part she was after. I heard her shift in her chair as I read the first words.

A curious moment today in the mailroom. I ran into the man who came home with us from Amy and Len's. He was fetching his mail on the C/D side of the room and I was fetching ours across from him, so that our backs were to each other. Then I turned around and stood in the middle of the room, eyes on the letters as I flipped through them. At the same time, I guess, he did the very same thing, because it turned out we were facing each other, so close together that our hands brushed. Instant apologies on both sides, instant springing apart, then laughter. After this, I thought he lingered an extra moment, looking as if he had something to say. But he only smiled and hurried off.

Writing this, I realize I must have lingered just a bit myself. I wonder what kind of work he does that allows him to be home at three o'clock in the afternoon on a weekday.

From here, the entry went back to unrelated matters.

In the mail, a letter from Christine Geer. She's going to MacDowell this summer, and much good may it do her. Her paramour Martin Keller will also be there, so at least she'll get something done.

I read this with interest. I'd never heard of a romance between Geer and Keller, both of whose work I'd read and liked. Unlike me, however, Anne was not interested. She soon told me to skim ahead again, keeping an eye out for the Reeveses or the dinner party or the neighbors or possibly the names Susan or Greg.

Greg it was:

Wednesday February 20, 11 p.m.

Oddly—or maybe just that thing where you come across a word you've never heard of before and then see it again the next day—I blundered once more into Greg (the name, as I now know, of the unknown dinner guest chez Reeves that endless evening). This time we met on the downtown 1 train. I was on my way home from the research library, where I found some excellent recipes of the 1920s for And Sometimes Y. He was wearing a pea-coat and had a leather briefcase with him, battered, not suitable for business. I think I boarded the train after he did, but I didn't notice him until we were at 34th Street, even though he was sitting right across from me. The train being crowded, we just waved when we first spotted each other, but at 28th Street, the woman who'd been squashed up against me got off and he dashed over to take her place. Perforce (or not so much? She was a very big woman, and he is not a very big man) also squashing against me. We shouted over the roaring train that it looked likely to snow again tonight, then established that we were both going home.

We disembarked and went up to the sidewalk and walked together along West 12th Street. He said he was coming from a class (teaching or learning? I wondered) and I told him where I'd been, though not why. He's a small man, fine-boned, sharp-featured, with a crooked nose and eyes of two different colors, one blue, one brown. If men can be called jolie-laide (beau-laid, would it be?), that's what he is. Quite attractive, even though the parts don't add up. His face is off-kilter somehow.

As we walked the last block, he very distinctly slowed down, moving the briefcase between us to his other hand. A few yards from the door, he turned, stopped in the freezing wind, and leaned closer, until we were within murmuring distance. Very deliberately he almost whispered, "I hope we meet again." Spoken in such a murmur, the commonplace phrase sounded far more significant than it should have.

"Bound to happen!" I answered heartily. Later, I felt like a coward for having replied as any virtuous hausfrau should, my tone as bright and vague as possible. At the time, though, I was intent on seeming not to notice the emphasis with which he spoke. I smiled a public smile and hurried into the building, making a quick left toward the elevator.

Made some changes to And Sometimes Y after I got home. I love those old recipes. Feather Cake! Who could resist a piece of that? Left my desk feeling less worried about Bridget's argument with her mother, less worried about the book in general. Steve home early and startled me. He just materialized in my study, jolting me out of my work. It's his house, of course he's not going to ring, but I wish I could put the chain on the front door so he'd have to. Still, in the end, we had an enjoyable evening together—went out for a drink and dinner and made each other laugh about the pretentious, ridiculous maître d'. At home, Steve read to me from the Rex Stout we started last week.

This was the end of the entry. I looked up to tell her so. Half a dozen emotions seemed to be flickering across her face—recollection, nostalgia, pleasure, rue, and a hint of the worry you feel when you see a friend about to make a terrible mistake. Clearly, the "episode" was no routine thing, no summer at a writer's retreat or the sad but inevitable loss of a parent. She looked exhausted. Although our session had been very short, I wasn't surprised when she said we were done for the day.

"Or I am, at least," she added, glancing at her cane without moving. She sat silent a while, hands in her lap, face to the window, profile to me, her gaze unfocused. I could no longer see the mix of feelings of a moment before. Now she looked grave, as grave as the woman in her dustjacket photos.

"I'll keep the notebooks here," she said, holding out her hand. She took the journal I'd been reading from, set it on top of the others, opened the drawer from which she'd taken the keys to the glass-fronted bookcase the day we met, put them and the books inside it, locked it, and tucked the drawer key into her pocket. Sadly, I realized that she would always keep the notebooks locked up.

I saw that I should leave her be.

FIVE

few hours after that first reading, I took the train down to lower Broadway, near Reade Street, where Carrie Benson had her office. Contract law isn't her area of expertise—she does family law—but she can interpret a legal agreement.

I called her from the tiny, overheated lobby of her building and waited while she came down to meet me. Then we made our way through the bundled, harried crowds released for their too-brief lunch breaks.

It was a day of ominous warmth, with *CLIMATE CHANGE!* almost written across the sky. The snow that had fallen in the night had already pooled in slushy gray masses at the corners. We leapt over these and a few blocks away wedged ourselves into an insanely noisy sandwich shop. I grabbed a vacant table while she shouted our orders at the counter, returning with a numbered buzzer that would alert us when our food was ready for pickup.

Though we'd been roommates, Carrie and I had never been especially close, and so I normally would have liked to dive immediately into the matter of the NDA. However, I made myself ask first how she was—work, kids (she started early), husband (also an early start). Work was busy, she yelled over the babble of the crowd. She liked her new boss. Emma was only four but had won a spelling bee. "Pretzel" was the word that broke the runner-up. Caleb had started climbing up the bookshelves—they were going to have them bolted to the walls—and her husband, Scott, was singing in the Gay Men's Chorus "even though he isn't gay."

After the buzzer went off and was exchanged for our meals, we sat down again and she asked how I was. I answered as succinctly as possible, brushing quickly over my breakup with Tim and implying that it was a mutual decision—I don't like to be thought of as a victim—then moved on to an update on my dissertation and an account of who Anne Weil was and how I'd come to be reading to her.

"So…" I trailed off, finally taking the agreement from my purse and handing it to her. She read it while finishing her salad, then looked up at me.

"Well, it's binding," she began, speaking in a subdued, lawyerly voice and leaning over the table so I could hear her through the din. "Although I'm not sure what judge would give it much court time, if it ever came to a dispute. You'd almost certainly be sent to a mediator."

"Oh," I said, the remainder of my BLT cooling in my hands. I was glad she thought a formal charge against me unlikely. But mediation sounded expensive, especially if I was found to be at fault.

"Other than the woman's wish to keep her privacy, not much seems to be at stake," Carrie went on, "unless I'm missing something. But I think you said her famous book came out more than forty years ago?"

I nodded.

"So she's not a celebrity now?"

"Definitely not. Not for decades."

"Okay, and not a criminal—hopefully—or, I don't know, someone in witness protection. And you're not a muckraking journalist or a TMZ reporter, so . . ." Her sentence trailed off into a shrug. "I wouldn't worry about it much. I mean, of course you should follow it. Don't breach it. But...I can refer you to a friend who works on non-disclosure agreements all the time if you want a more educated opinion."

"That's okay." For the moment, at least, I'd done nothing wrong. (Nothing except show it to a lawyer, anyway. And surely that was all right; in fact, Quigley had counseled me *to* see a lawyer.) Anyway, I was nearly broke; I wasn't looking for new ways to spend money I didn't have.

"Thank you, Carrie," I said, and meant it. We had always been very different people, we didn't see each other often, and it had been kind of her to use her lunch break to do me a favor.

"No worries. I'm sure you'd—I don't know, check out a quotation from Shakespeare for me if I asked."

"Of course. Just give me a jingle," I said, and we moved on to ordinary topics. The war in Iraq, the protests in Egypt, the rash of cupcake shops all over the city. Eventually, she glanced at her watch and announced that she had to dash.

Off she dove, out of the packed restaurant and into the scrum of scurrying office workers, while I ignored the couple that stood two feet away from me, vulturizing my table. It bothers me that people do that, especially when it's a couple trying to pressure someone eating alone. Only after I'd consumed the last crumb of bacon, and the final shred of coleslaw, did I stand and languidly don my coat, pull on my hat, adjust my scarf, and saunter past them. Then I took the train up to 116th Street and went to the small, somewhat grubby office I shared with two other teaching fellows.

I was happy to find myself alone. The place was crowded enough with one person in it—with no one in it, for that matter. Three little desks—desklets, really—were jammed in there for us, and three little bookcases for our books. Mine was largely filled with the many novels of my "inadvertent feminists," and I spent the rest of the afternoon in my well-worn chair there, rereading Anne Weil's first, *Linda and the Swan*. It's the story of a college student's infatuation with her professor, a man she discovers—with surprise and great disappointment—to be both her intellectual and moral inferior. I read it with fresh interest, thinking now and then of Tim, who was "inferior" to me intellectually only if you took a very narrow view of the meaning of intellect, and morally not at all, though it pleased me to think otherwise at the time.

———————

Petra called me at 5:30, eager to know how I was doing, and offered to come across town and meet me for dinner at the Metro

Diner. But I had insisted on paying for Carrie's lunch as well as my own that afternoon, and there was a perfectly good can of Progresso lentil soup waiting for me in 10A. Because Tim liked to cook, I'd grown accustomed to being fed by him; but for many years before we met, Progresso had been among my best friends. So Petra and I just talked on the phone, me sitting on the uncarpeted floor of the little office, my back against the locked door.

It was good to catch up with her, even though we'd parted less than thirty-six hours before. I told her about what Carrie had said, and that I'd had my first reading session with Anne, but I kept the content of the journal entries to myself. I hadn't thought about it ahead of time, but once we were on the phone, I just felt that it was one thing to contemplate putting Weil's private writings to use in a scholarly work, quite another to gossip about them with a friend.

I waited till 6:15 before getting on the train and arrived at the Windrush half an hour later. The doorman on duty, Gustavo, was new to me, so I introduced myself, waited while he found my name in the book of authorized visitors, then went up and quietly let myself into 10A. Marta was gone for the day, of course, and I'd hoped that, with the house to herself, Anne might have ventured out for a few solitary hours in her living room, where I could run across her as I came in and we could exchange some friendly words. The more relaxed we got with each other, the better for me. Or rather, because I didn't really plan on relaxing, the more relaxed she got.

But the living room was empty and Anne's bedroom door closed.

Through it came faint music. Something baroque—Vivaldi, maybe. Thwarted, I consumed my soup alone in the dining room, reading a months-old copy of *The New York Review of Books* I'd pulled out at random from a stack on an officemate's shelf.

I wasn't sorry to eat by myself. To be honest, I've never quite understood why dinnertime, when your mouth is at its busiest, is considered a good opportunity for company and conversation. But I did miss Tim, missed being able to share with him the extraordinary turn of events that had brought me to this table. It felt weird, wrong, that he knew nothing about this, had no idea where I was. Two years with a man is a long time.

I finished the soup, buttered a slice of bread, ate it, and tidied up the kitchen. Then I went to my room and spent some time noodling through my email before making myself turn to the task of writing down everything I could remember of my session with Anne that morning—not only what I'd read, but her responses to it. I'd begun to keep notes on our interactions immediately after our first interview, titling the file "Letters Jan-June 2008" out of a super-abundance of caution (or perhaps my childhood habit of secretiveness). After that, I ventured again into the living room in hopes of finding her.

No luck. I roamed about the common rooms a little, quietly taking a good look at the lock on the pretty little desk in the living room before retiring to my quarters. Then I had a long, contemplative shower under the porcelain sunflower.

In the course of packing up at Tim's, I had come across a

radioactive shoebox I kept on a shelf in his coat closet while we lived together. Once upon a time, the box had contained a pair of knock-off Nike running shoes my mother had bought and worn (though never run in; the only running she did was toward her problems and away from them again, poor woman).

After her death, it had fallen to me to clear out the place where she'd been living, a small "mother-in-law" apartment over the garage of a house a few blocks away from the tumbledown one where I'd grown up. Petra, angel that she is, came with me. Into this shoebox I had put every item I kept from that unhappy place. I hadn't opened it in the six years since then, but when I'd gone to Tim's with Petra to fetch my things, I wrote "shoebox" on the much larger carton we packed it into. Now somehow seemed to be the time to look through the shoebox again.

So I took the carton out of the front hall closet, where I'd stored it per Marta's invitation, carried it to my room, borrowed a steak knife from Anne's kitchen, sat down with it on the blue-and-white carpet, and sliced through the tape. The shoebox was right on top and I accidentally cut into it just enough to leave a small, open wound. I set down the knife, lifted out the box, put it in my lap, and flipped it open—it was the hinged kind you can open and close with one hand. I knew there were photos inside, pictures of my dad and my mom and me, a few of some aunts and uncles, one or two of my father's parents.

They lived in Nevada, but I met them several times when they came to visit. My mother's family, about whom I know little except that they were "Bible-thumpers" from Ohio, had excommunicated her at age sixteen, when she married my father, a man with no job, a dishonorable discharge from the Army, and a six-month stretch in prison for selling drugs behind him. Not even his death brought them back into our lives.

What I'd forgotten were the three VHS tapes from when I was a little kid. Right after I had emptied out my mother's apartment, I borrowed a friend's VCR player and played the tape labeled "LIZ SECOND BIRTHDAY." Started to play it, at least. Seeing my parents alive and together, all three of us alive—seeing again how my dad walked, hearing his voice, his laugh, watching him scoop me up, lift me into the air—it was all too much for me. It was one thing to deal with my memories of them, these ghosts in my head who might jump out and yell "Boo!" or wrap me in their arms, or grab me and hit me, but whom I could contain, assess, label, organize. Having them come to life on a screen was another thing altogether. Almost immediately, I stopped the tape and pushed the button that spat it out of the machine, then sat sobbing and shaking for a very long time.

I doubted I would ever want to look at any of the videos again, but that night at the Windrush, I did sift through the photographs—one of me and Petra both wearing tiaras and waving plastic scepters made me laugh—and some of the little mementos I'd saved of my mother: the dangly silver-mesh earrings she wore that fascinated me when I was a kid, the little pink pocketbook the police had given me after the accident that killed her. There was a small change purse inside it, a rolled-up ten-dollar bill inside of that, and shards of a mirror she probably used to snort coke.

Also in the box was her Social Security card, a Mother's Day card I must have made for her in kindergarten, and the lease on the mother-in-law apartment, her signature childish and shaky on the "Tenant" line. I spent a half hour crying before putting them away.

When I'd collected myself sufficiently, I put the shoebox back into its carton, returned it to the coat closet, washed the steak knife, and slipped it back into the silverware drawer. Then I sat on my bed for a while, trying to meditate—I'm very, very bad at meditating— and trying not to think about the past. Around ten o'clock, I tiptoed into the living room just in case Anne was sitting there. But she wasn't. Just as well; I was pretty wrung out by then. Early though it was, I went to bed, reading Hilary Mantel's *Beyond Black* until I fell asleep. I was almost finished with it and already worried about what I was going to read next. My addiction is novels, stories, fiction. Fiction is the escape, the substance I can't live without.

———

My second morning at the Windrush began much like the first. Again I slept deeply, dreamlessly, as far as I could remember. I opened my curtains with a sense of happy anticipation and was not disappointed: The sky was blue and the river glittered bluely back at it. Along the sidewalks, rows of small, bare trees stood neatly at attention. Anne was in the kitchen when I got there just after eight o'clock. Fresh coffee in the pot, a mug for her at the table. I poured myself a cup and took it to my room. No conversation except hello.

At 9:15, she knocked on my door to say she would see me at 10:00 as planned. At 9:45, I returned to the kitchen, got an apple and some yogurt, and ate them at the dining table. Then, into the living room for our rendezvous.

Anne was again already sitting at her desk when I entered. She had taken out the notebook I'd read from yesterday and sat with her hands folded on top of it. The fatigue of the day before had left her face. She looked fresh, composed, ready. She smiled but made no small talk, no inquiry as to how I was or how I liked my room, no little civilities. She was too eager to continue the reading.

As I took my own chair, she nudged the notebook over to me. I picked it up.

"I'll look for Greg again and start there?" I asked, paging through to where we'd left off.

"Yes." After a pause, with that dry tone of hers, she added, "You begin to see the shape of this story."

I thought it best to answer only with a very small, noncommittal smile. Greg's name wasn't in the entry I'd opened to, nor did it occur in the subsequent one. In fact, I had to sweep through nearly two weeks before he reappeared—two weeks in which Anne got a haircut that was much too short, planned and hosted a cocktail party for a dozen lawyers and their wives, and took Steve on a dinner date with an old friend of hers from Boston and the friend's lecherous husband, who lunged at Anne, mouth open, as she emerged from the ladies' room after dessert. They also went to hear Van Cliburn perform with the New York Philharmonic. He was very good.

Finally, at nearly the end of the notebook, came a reference to Greg, now shortened to "G." for the first time. I reported this change and Anne said, "Interesting."

Saturday March 2, 9 p.m.

Yesterday ran into Greg yet again, the man from Len and Amy's. (And from the mailroom, and the subway.) He happened to come into the lobby while I was down at the door picking up galleys of the debut novel by Cynthia Someone I'm to review for Prairie Schooner. This time, after saying hello, he unmistakably sought out my company. In fact, he followed me into the elevator, ostensibly to ask whether, and how much, he should tip Rodrigo for coming to 6C to clear a clogged drain. We went up alone. Standing just a bit closer to me than such an exchange would warrant (the image in my head was of a sparrow's cautious approach toward a crumb at someone's feet), he put to me his ostensible question. There was no doubt but that his real question was something quite other. A tentative question, I would say, speculative but also quite forward. Given the pre-text, there was a certain absurdity about it that made me laugh later on, but at the time, I absolutely backed away, again resorting to the civil tone of the respectable married woman.

I told him how much Steve and I tip for what services, but in honesty (and if I can't be honest here, where can I?), my answer had no more to do with tips than his question, and for all my wifely modesty, I know that my gaze told him that I saw him as he was, heard his real meaning. When we stopped on ten, I almost expected him to come out with me. But he didn't, only looked at me steadily as the doors closed. I found myself watching the floor numbers drop on the dial till he reached the lobby.

Here a line had been left blank. I mentioned this to Anne and went on.

Made beef stew for dinner, and just as well, since Steve was very late getting home. This seems to happen often since he took on the Covington case—we've had an unfinished game sitting on the chessboard for over a week. His long hours are an inconvenience vis-à-vis knowing when to make dinner, but not wholly unwelcome, as they've allowed me to get through a draft of my review for the Sunday Times. *I've always liked Muriel Spark and although this one's certainly not "The Prime of Miss Jean Brodie," it's quite well done. A relief—so much more cheerful to recommend a book than to have to tear one down. It does have its longueurs, but—*

"Never mind all that," Anne said. "Just look for Greg again."

I scanned ahead but came to the last page of the notebook without finding him. Anne gave an impatient "pff," took the notebook from me, withdrew the desk key from her pocket, opened the drawer, put it in, and removed the other journals. The fact that she'd locked these back up before I arrived, even though we'd be sitting there together while I read, gave me an idea about keys. I filed it away for later consideration.

"Which one is next?" she asked, fanning the books across the desk.

"This one, right on top."

I pushed the others back toward her and again she locked them into the drawer.

"Very well. Go to it. Look for Greg again."

I skimmed until I found his name, some ten days later. In the interim, I saw as my eyes skibbled over the entries, Anne called her father, went with "Pauline" to see a show of Gauguin paintings at the Museum of Modern Art, ate some fish that upset her stomach, and, unaccountably, found a missing ring in the pocket of her new wool jacket. It was all painfully routine and, to my disappointment, contained nothing of any interest to me about her life. But there might be something, somewhere, sometime. I looked up and told her I was afraid of flipping through too fast in case I missed Greg and was pleased when she replied that she appreciated my concern and that I should go at whatever pace I thought best.

Searching again, I found a night when she'd forgotten a leg of lamb in the oven and burned it. There was another phone call with Ginny, wretched in consequence of having had to sign her divorce papers that day. Finally, there was Greg.

"Okay," I said. I cleared my throat.

Monday March 11, 8 p.m.

Greg and I nearly collided today on the sidewalk at 57th and Lex. I was heading home after lunch with Adrienne.

Adrienne Hedges, I knew, was Anne's then-agent, not a heavy-weight dealmaker, but widely respected.

Avoided talking about And Sometimes Y with her—it's always better with her to keep quiet until she sees the whole manuscript—and was waiting to cross to the westbound M57 stop when I saw him. He had just gotten off an eastbound bus, on his way, he told me, to see the dentist. It's uncanny how often we meet.

I said, "What a coincidence," smiled and turned to cross 57ᵗʰ—I could see my bus leaving Third—but he put a hand on my arm to stop me. A gentle hand, light but immobilizing.

"Kismet, I'd call it," he said.

In another context—from another mouth—I would have thought the term ridiculous. Instead—well, in short, this struck me as "instead."

He went on, "I think you're a novelist?"

I was surprised that he knew this but only said yes.

"Susan, my wife, and Amy Reeves belong to the same reading group," *he reminded me. "Amy mentioned to her that you write."*

"Ah."

Our conversation was more shouted than spoken over the grinding screech of an arriving train under our feet, the rumble of passing trucks, my bus across the street and, of course, the gabble of voices usual among the pushing mob. Is it absurd of me to write that all of this "fell away," as in pulp romances? Whether or not, it did.

"I stopped in at a library to look up what you've written," he told me.

Somehow I found this a bit creepy as well as flattering.

"And did you take out one of my books?"

He smiled. "I borrowed them all. They're waiting in my studio, where I have some privacy. Which would you recommend I start with?"

I was momentarily distracted from his question by two of my own: Why would he need a private place to read a book? And what kind of "studio"?

Then I replied, "Whichever strikes you. There are only three."

"Then I'll start with, 'Linda and the Swan.' I like the title. It's witty but also suggestive."

Well, now my heart was won. What writer could resist such a pithy, and accurate, formulation of her intention?

"Once I've read it, I hope you'll have lunch with me so we can talk about it," he went on. His bland delivery of the words softened their meaning. "Novelists have always fascinated me, and I've never known one. There's a little restaurant I like uptown. Maybe we could meet there."

Curiouser and curiouser. I said something about how busy I am and went on, "In fact, I've got to fly or I won't be in time to—" Here my mind went blank. Take a chicken out of the freezer? See my own dentist? Meet a friend? I was unable to think of a suitable lie and left the sentence unfinished. Greg gave a slight bow to signify that he understood me and said he had to get going himself. I ran across the street, the matter of lunch unsettled. When I'd reached the stop, I saw he was still standing at the corner where we'd met, looking at me.

Irritatingly, I found my thoughts returning to him all afternoon.

People are always saying they want to read my books when we meet, but so few really do. I would have been annoyed that he'd chosen to borrow rather than buy them if they weren't so damn hard to find. Distracted by these thoughts, I went to Jefferson Market and mechanically tested avocados for ripeness, wandered among the cheeses, lined up at the fish counter. Sole for dinner, with mashed potatoes and a salad.

I looked up to let Anne know we'd reached the end of the entry. She nodded, not yet tired—if anything, revivified—and said to keep going, looking for the all-important initial. It didn't take long.

"He comes up the next day," I said.

She nodded.

Tuesday March 12, 8:30 p.m.

Woke at 4 in the morning from a sort of wonderful nightmare featuring the ubiquitous Greg. We were lying out in the open somewhere on a little rug spread over the grass, so entwined, and kissing with such abandon, that we barely noticed a hubbub around us. This was a theater troupe setting up a stage for a play that night, an outdoor, one-night performance of the sort that roving players once took from town to town. After a few moments more in our rapt, public clinch, I broke away with the classic declaration, "I am a married woman." This was no secret to him, but my saying it aloud broke the spell and I scrambled to my feet. What he did then I don't know, only that I turned my back on him and, weak with passion, fairly limped away.

That was the end of the dream, which had the quality of a nightmare only because of the shame I felt after waking up. A remnant of erotic languor still clinging to me, I thought of the real-life Greg and the few interactions we've had. The theater troupe, the stage, I can only imagine were the cast and stage of my daily life—friends, colleagues, dinner parties, publishing, Steve, the deli counter at Balducci's. As for Greg, I presume he is Sex personified. I went back to sleep after reading for half an hour (V. S. Pritchett, extraordinary), but the spell of the dream has hung over me all day, so much so that I singed the rice I made for dinner and could hardly follow Steve's recounting of the latest twist in the Covington case. Not that I'm riveted by it, but it's very absorbing to him, and if I lose track, I know he'll be hurt. Such is marriage.

"Is that the last of it?" Anne asked as I paused.

"For that day, yes."

"Well—look for him again, but this time I'd like to hear a little of the context. The 'stage' in my dream, you might say. Read whatever comes next."

By now it was clear that "him" meant Greg.

The next entry proved to be only two long paragraphs, the first about a cold she'd thought she had caught but luckily didn't, the second quoting part of a letter she'd written to the *Times Literary Supplement* to protest a crushing review of Christine Geer's latest novel.

I read these to her.

"Should I go on to whatever comes next, or look for Greg? That's not a lot of context."

"Hmm." She smiled at me—really smiled, and really at me. "Yes, no, yes, no?" Playfully, almost girlishly, she tilted her head left and right with each word. "What do you think we should do?"

SIX

What did I think we should do? My class didn't start till 3:00. I thought we should keep our noses down and follow Greg, baying like hounds; I had indeed begun "to see the shape of this story." Never mind Anne's occasional references to her troubles with *And Sometimes Y*, or the scattering of names from the literary world. Compared to the "episode," their interest for me was minor. As for the rest, I doubted that even Anne could have been interested in the shopping, the dinners, not to mention the case of Covington v. whomever he was suing.

"Look for Greg again?" I suggested, trying to keep my voice light.

"Very well. Flip through till you find him."

Gratified, I flipped, but it was a long time before our quarry returned. My eyes were starting to sting—from "skimming through" the alphabetic briar patches—but this, of course, I kept to myself. Finally, some dozen pages before the end of the notebook, he reappeared. The entry in which he popped up was even less legible than the others, I saw to my dismay. It had clearly been written in a hurry, the letters sloping forward as they sprinted toward the edge of the page.

Monday March 13, 11 p.m.

Good grief! Greg is a pianist, and not only that, a famous one. I can't think how I failed to recognize him—I must have seen his picture more than once, when the Times *reviewed his concerts or recordings. We even have an album he did of Haydn's piano sonatas, with a photo of him on the back. I hadn't caught his last name at the Reeves's dinner and never asked later. What did it matter, after all? But not to know his face? How ridiculous of me.*

He told me who he is over lunch today, without any fanfare or self-consciousness. He'd caught me again in the mailroom on Saturday (does he lurk there, waiting?) and said he had finished Linda and the Swan *and was eager to talk with me about it. Giving me the name and address of the café he'd mentioned when we bumped into each other in midtown (La Bouchée, not only all the way east on York Avenue, but north of 86th Street), he suggested we meet there at one o'clock this afternoon.*

The revelation of his profession was only one of several during our time together. As I had guessed from its address, La Bouchée proved to be a very obscure and indifferent café distinguished only by its considerable distance from the Windrush. Greg was already seated when I arrived, even though I was a few minutes early myself. The place was almost empty, yet he'd taken a table near the back. He stood to pull out my chair, then scrape it in.

The waitress brought us a pair of large, greasy menus that offered all the dishes you'd expect to find in such a place. She left, returned to pour us some water, went away with the pitcher and came back at once, notepad in hand, to take our orders. Salade Niçoise for me, a croque monsieur for Greg. In a thick Italian accent, she asked what we'd like to drink. I took a glass of the house white; Greg took the red. Mine was nearly impotable, as his also seemed to be.

Left alone, we avoided looking into each other's eyes, afflicted by a new shyness. Our conversation was halting at first, the kind of awkward chat people have who scarcely know each other. As advertised, he had read Linda and the Swan. *He told me nice things about it and asked quite insightful, almost writerly questions, but also the usual sort (where do you get your ideas, do you do you type or write longhand etc.).*

Then, naturally, I asked about his work and finally learned who he was. He trained at Juilliard, where he'd met his wife. She was studying violin. They often performed together when they were in their twenties, but she'd had to stop in 1954, when she developed something called focal dystonia in her left hand. I had never heard of this. Evidently, it's a rare condition musicians sometimes develop. A hand freezes up, or a finger or two can't be controlled, or—I didn't quite follow what he said, but whatever it is, the musician can't play anymore. If I understood him correctly, it's pretty much irreversible.

I couldn't quite think what to say to this and only murmured, "How awful for her. For both of you! I'm so sorry." Then I turned clumsily to the standard questions people ask concert musicians—how much do you practice (a lot), where (at the studio he referred to the other day), were your parents musical (mother yes, father no). Both were Jews, he went on without my asking, but after emigrating from Russia, they anglicized their surname and turned five-year-old Grigori into Gregory. His father had a tailor's shop on the Lower East Side.

With a guilty feeling that, in view of his fame, I ought to have known the answer, I asked if there were composers he particularly played. (Yes. Haydn, Mozart, Beethoven, though of course he also plays many others.) In fact, he added casually, he'll be playing a concert of solo works by all three at Carnegie Hall this Saturday night, including Beethoven's Appassionata. This is what he's been rehearsing for recently and would work on at his studio later this afternoon.

Before he got to this astonishing announcement, I had been studying his appearance. (Afterward, I was too startled by his fame to see him except through its veil.) He is not merely short but decidedly short, hardly taller than I am. But his face is alive in a way few are and this is what chiefly strikes the eye. He is intense almost to the point of giving off heat, but he can also be playful. I saw several details about his person I'd missed till then. For one, how much the two different colors of his eyes suit him, suit his asymmetrical features. He has dark, thick, rather unkempt hair—just what one imagines a classical pianist's hair should be.

I also had a chance to observe his hands, not notably large—rather the opposite—but with a fluid gesture. One wants to say his fingers are "strong and sensitive," but of course it's impossible to see this when a man is wielding no more than a knife and fork. We hadn't so much as shaken hands when I came in. In this first arranged meeting, taking place without a word to Steve, I felt awkward about touching him, even so formally as that. Perhaps because he sensed this, he held himself more in reserve than heretofore, with none of the boldness he'd shown before.

After I'd asked all my boring questions about his profession (and I hope one or two less dull), he steered me away from this line of talk. He asked how long I'd lived in the Windrush and I told him, explaining that Steve and his ex-wife had lived there before their divorce. This was the first and only mention of Steve, just as his wife's former musical career was all that was said of her. I was quite aware of these notable lacunae, but helped by the wine (which I drank in spite of itself), I felt a little thrilled by them—thrilled by the whole thing, in fact: the steady scrutiny we eventually gave each other, the out-of-the-way meeting place, the increasingly obvious, if unspoken, understanding that something drew us together ("Something!" How demure!), as well as the tacit knowledge that neither of us was going to mention this meeting to our respective spouses.

Our food arrived and went largely uneaten, a bite of canned tuna and some olives from my salad, a couple of corners of his sandwich for Greg. Given its quality, this was no great loss. We each ordered a second glass of wine, however. Later this afternoon, I remembered why I seldom do this, and certainly not on an empty stomach. By the time the dessert menu arrived and was turned away, the café au lait I ordered was far too little and too late to straighten me out. When he offered to take me to his studio sometime and play something for me there, I instantly agreed.

He grabbed the check and I let him. When he came around the table to pull my chair out, I felt his breath on my neck. I can still feel it now. Outside on the sidewalk, we walked together to the subway entrance at 86th Street. He walked close to me and I let him. He came near enough so our shoulders touched and I let him. When we said goodbye—he was heading across town to give a guest lecture at Mannes—I put out my hand to forestall the cheek-to-cheek kiss I imagined was coming. This was my only, flailing attempt to maintain propriety. He deferred to the gesture, politely holding up his end of our gloved handshake, but he said nothing before he turned and left me, and this said everything.

I paused, then told Anne she had left a line blank here before writing a bit more, late that night. I realized now that I'd been so caught up in what I was reading that I'd forgotten to monitor my delivery of it. I wondered how I had sounded to her—whether I'd seen the periods coming and read "for meaning" in the way she wished. I wondered all the more because, of course, I kept thinking of Tim, imagining his first lunch, or drink, or dinner, or breakfast, alone with his "other woman." All she said, though, was, "Go on."

11:30 p.m. In my study.

Holy mother. Steve came in just as I was writing the sentence above and almost scared me out of my wits. I clapped this notebook shut like a teenager caught reading "Lady Chatterley's Lover" and nearly dropped it on the floor. I'd been writing in bed in our bedroom as usual while he took care of some work at the dining-room table. I now see the bedroom was a ridiculous choice for making notes like these. After tonight, I'll write in my journals only in here and always keep them locked in my glass-fronted bookcase. I'll put the keys somewhere else—maybe inside a shoe? Not that he's ever gone near it. Even if he were curious about what I write in my journals, I know he's too honorable to look. I can't say I like having something to hide from him.

As for tonight's scare, I was sure at first that he'd noticed my panicked attempt to ditch the pen and notebook. However, and most fortunately, he wasn't even looking in my direction. Steaming toward the bathroom, he only distractedly answered my choked "Hi" with a quick one of his own. He went in, closed the door, and as soon as I heard the water running, I bolted in here, dropped the notebook at random behind a shelf of poetry books, and ran back to the bedroom to do my impression of a novelist quietly absorbed in Ivy Compton-Burnett's "The Mighty and Their Fall" (which in calmer moments I have in fact found quite absorbing). Then I waited for him to get in bed and turn the lights out so I could pretend to go to sleep. My heart was still pounding so hard, I'm surprised it didn't wake him. And now I've crept out and recorded this little coda to today's escapade, and so good night.

I fell silent—there was no need to announce that we'd reached the end of this entry—but my brain was ticking, ticking. "Next Saturday night," she had written on Monday, March 18th. I counted forward to Saturday. "March 23," I said to myself over and over. 3/23/1963. I itched to write it down. I willed Anne to decide we'd read enough for the day, even though we were well short of the one-hour mark.

My wish was granted. Anne, who seemed to be in some kind of trance, dismissed me, barely remembering to take the notebook and lock it in the drawer. She still had an otherworldly look when, several hours later, I passed through the dining room on my way to teach. She sat before an untouched bowl of soup, hands in her lap. She appeared not to ignore me but genuinely not to see me.

I had been busy since the reading that morning. As soon as I got back to my room, I opened my laptop and started searching the *New York Times* archives. In a matter of seconds, I had the name of the pianist who played at Carnegie Hall on March 23, 1963: Gregory Morris.

Gregory Morris! I literally gasped when the name appeared on the screen. I like classical music well enough; as a freshman, I took a music class that gave me some fundamentals, and a few years later I had a longish romance with a music major that left me with a taste for chamber music in particular. But I wouldn't have needed any of that to know that Gregory Morris was—or had been—a very famous pianist. He was a child prodigy, went to Juilliard on a scholarship, performed with the New York Philharmonic at the age of twenty-three. He had toured the world, played at the White House, recorded Mozart's most famous piano concertos, all as a very young man. Somewhat like Leonard Bernstein, or Yo-Yo Ma today, he became known not only for his playing but for his infectious passion for music and his desire to make it accessible to people who thought it a closed, elitist world.

Searching Google, I learned that as he entered his thirties, he began to present master classes at conservatories and routinely spend summers at Tanglewood. Students spoke of him with both affection and awe, as various articles about him stressed, giving instances of the way he mixed his erudition (he was a keen musicologist in addition to everything else) with warmth and humor. As for his occasional performances with his wife, Susan Morris, these had drawn little attention from the press: a passing mention in a profile, short reviews here and there.

Then, when he was in his forties, Susan Morris suddenly died. No cause of death was given in the brief obituary of her in the *Times*. Within months, Morris began to cancel concerts, refuse interviews. He stopped recording. At first, his publicist said it was because he was in mourning, but as a year passed, then two, then three, it became clear that he had simply withdrawn from the public. Eventually, he began to teach, not at Juilliard but at the less celebrated Manhattan School of Music. Except for this and his continuing ties with a few friends from his old life, he became a virtual recluse. It was said that he had a broken heart.

This was the man who, at the zenith of his career, had pursued Anne Taussig Weil with the sureness, swiftness, and (I had no doubt by now) practiced skill of a serial philanderer.

I searched for images of him, then for clips on YouTube. Anne had described his face well. The pictures, all black and white, showed a man attractive almost in spite of his features. When he was caught at the keyboard, you got a sense of his size, just shy of "diminutive," yet enlarged by his connection to the piano itself, his visible engagement with the music he was playing. Quite a few of his recordings had been posted on YouTube, but almost all with only a still picture of the album cover or of Morris himself. I listened to several of these, using earbuds just in case. I was not—am not—sufficiently expert to speak to the quality of his performances, but the quality of the recordings, though it improved as the years went on, never reached anything like what you'd hear today. I was disappointed to find only two brief clips of footage showing him in action at the keyboard. Both were in grainy black and white and had very poor sound.

Only after all this did I look for him on Wikipedia. **Gregory Alexander Morris,** the entry began, **June 12, 1919 – December 14, 2010.**

December 2010. Two months before Anne offered her room for rent.

S EVEN

Having spent an hour researching Morris on the internet, I erased my search history. Maybe I had read too many spy thrillers, maybe it was yet another echo of my self-protective childhood habit of hiding, but I told myself it couldn't hurt. I turned off my laptop and slipped into the empty kitchen, where I stood at the counter and wolfed down a peanut butter sandwich. I shoved my teaching materials into my backpack, put on my winter armor (cardigan over pullover sweater, coat, hat, gloves, scarf, dauntless spirit), and opened the door just as Marta came out of the elevator, on her way up from the basement with a basket of dry laundry in her arms. I held the apartment door open for her and we exchanged a brief, friendly hello as I grabbed the elevator.

I had intended to take a walk in the Village before going uptown, to try to think through the revelations of the morning, but the cold was so bitter that I soon fled into a coffee shop on 14th Street. My head churning with questions about how the "episode" would continue, I ordered a cup of mint tea and let it steep till it got cold while I daydreamed about the future. If Weil's affair went far enough, it would make a story sufficiently sensational to have Professor Probst and her colleagues on my review committee sitting up in their beds to read all night. Of course, there was the non-disclosure agreement, but as I finally remembered the tea, it occurred to me that even that document had a bright silver lining: If the liaison had been known to the public, there would have been no need for such a precaution. Whatever Weil and Morris's story was, it was mine.

I paid my check, re-bundled up, and went down into the subway. Thankfully, my thoughts turned to the less complicated subject of the class I was about to teach. Today we would be discussing the start of second-wave feminism. I had assigned selections from *The Second Sex* and the whole of *The Feminine Mystique*. This was my favorite unit in the course and, naturally, a topic I enjoyed talking about. The whole course was one I enjoyed. But I was always glad to teach any class sent my way when I was a doctoral candidate. Not only did I love the job and need the money, teaching kept me inside the university. I knew too many doctoral students who had drifted out of orbit and eventually let their dissertations float away like children's lost balloons.

Class was good that day, yeasty with the subject matter and full of sparks even though all but two of the male students said nothing, wary of putting a foot wrong. I handed back papers from the week before and reminded them to read Tim O'Brien's *The Things They Carried* for Friday; I had put it on the syllabus to help frame their understanding of the anti-war movement.

Then I visited the music library. Two biographies of Gregory Morris had been published, one in 1961, the second in 1980. The library had both and, feeling lucky to get my hands on them with so little trouble, I checked them out and went to my office to start reading them.

Though I had already been to my office on several occasions since the breakup with Tim, this time, for some reason, a tidal wave of homesickness inundated me as soon as I opened the door. If I had still been living with him, I'd have spurned the office and gone to my desk in our nice, warmly lit bedroom. But I wasn't. I was sleeping at Anne's. This small, dreary, crowded, institutional room, with its stingy window and tiny desks, was now the closest thing I had to a home.

I stood just inside the door, let my backpack and coat slide together off my shoulders, and collapsed cross-legged on the floor. There I burst into sobs—racking, heaving sobs, like a child's, the kind where you can't catch your breath between outbursts. I had cried more than once since Tim ditched me, but nothing like this. This was a volcanic, cheek-drenching, nose-streaming, chin-wetting, shuddering explosion.

After a minute or so, I had the presence of mind to reach up and lock the door behind me. Seemingly unable to move, I used my scarf to soak up the muck and muffle the noise, then let myself go again. My thoughts were not mostly of Tim but of how little sense of "home" I had, how few safe havens I'd ever had in this world. My childhood home was a place of fear, anger, and sorrow—sorrow was the nicest part—and my various college digs were mostly temporary and peopled with unwanted roommates. The dark, cockroach-infested studio on Broadway I'd given up to move in with Tim was the nearest thing I'd ever had to a home of my own. I felt very sorry for myself. It was an exhausting cry, a long one, and obviously much needed.

Finally spent, I took a few deep breaths and slipped across the hall to the bathroom to blow my nose, wash my face, gulp down some cold water. Then back to the office and, by degrees, to normal, or what passed for normal with me in those days. I had taken the biographies to my office rather than to my room in the Windrush because (surprise!) I feared that Anne might somehow find them if I kept them there and throw me out.

Again, I understood that my anxiety about such things verged on paranoia—Anne could hardly walk, let alone putter around in my room out of curiosity—but at the time, I was dominated by the conviction that a single misstep could prevent my ever earning my Ph.D. I look back at those days and envision myself playing an imaginary, human-sized game of pick-up sticks, in which everything, and everyone, leaned on everything else—a game in which one false move, one careless word, one too-broad smile might keep me from achieving the life I'd worked so long to create.

All that said, I want to mention that, paradoxically perhaps, it's also true that I wasn't fully conscious of what I was doing at that time. From the moment I recognized that Anne was the one who'd placed the ad on Craigslist, I moved through my days on a kind of autopilot, methodically taking the next action, then the next, toward my goal, hardly allowing myself to think—hardly even thinking of thinking—about the nature of those actions.

When I did think about what I was doing, I told myself that the end (memorializing and celebrating the importance of Anne Weil's work—and, incidentally, earning my doctorate) justified the means (deceiving an infirm, half-blind, very elderly woman, day after day, in her own home). I was honoring her, not preying upon her. But mostly I did not think. Mostly, I just moved forward, no more reflective than a fish.

All this was very far from my usual *thinkety-thinkety-overthinkety* state of mind. The only other period in my life I can compare it to is when I applied for college. Miss Hart, God bless her, encouraged me to aim high, go for the best education I could. But I told her that I had to go to school somewhere close to Fleissport, that I couldn't leave my mother on her own, that she might start using again, or hook up with an abusive guy like my father, or OD, or even purposely kill herself.

"You'd be surprised what you can do when you have to," said Miss Hart. She also reminded me of a central tenet of Alateen and its allied twelve-step programs—that we cannot control the actions of others, only our own. (Miss Hart had confided in me by now that she, too, grew up in an alcoholic household.) So, like a person sleepwalking, I filled out application after application to schools across the country, knowing that I could not leave my mother but knowing also that I would have to leave my mother so I myself could flourish. Even when I wrote back to Columbia to accept their offer, the cognitive dissonance continued. Not until late July did the numbness wear off—the numbness that had allowed me to approach half a dozen schools located hundreds, or thousands, of miles from home.

My mom was an intelligent woman, but not an educated one. She had dropped out of high school after her sophomore year, and her youthful drinking and drug use had no doubt undermined her intellect. Not to mention the years she spent being smacked around by her husband. When I finally told her my plans, her feelings were mixed, to say the least. We were sitting at our kitchen table on a Friday evening, a few slices of the pizza she'd brought home for dinner cooling in the box between us. At the words "admitted to Columbia," she jumped up and ran around the table to kiss me, tears of joy in her eyes. Then she said, "We have to celebrate!" and pulled a bottle of vodka out of the freezer. I declined a glass; she insisted. She drank; I pretended to drink. By bedtime, she was hammered and wretched, alternating between crying jags and shrieks of what sounded like physical pain, as if I were ripping myself bodily from her (as indeed I was), asking the Lord Jesus (usually no particular friend of hers) how she could survive this, and me why I was doing it to her. Nothing I said had any effect. In the end, I left her, still shrieking, and went next door to sleep at Petra's.

And then, four years later, a policewoman called to tell me she was dead.

I opened the older of the two biographies first. It had been written while Morris was at the peak of his performance career. The author had chosen his subject out of admiration, and he painted a decidedly rosy portrait of the man. Still, it included details of Morris's early life unmentioned in the articles I'd found online: the swiftness and ease with which he learned English and acclimated to America, the role he played in childhood as middleman between his parents and the family's new world.

Like Anne—like me—he was an only child. His gift for music, obvious to his mother and father even before they emigrated, was encouraged when he was in second grade by a teacher who heard him playing a piano in the school auditorium during lunchtime. (His Miss Hart!) And so on: sacrifices the family made to pay for his music lessons, a growing recognition of his potential by his teachers, the scholarship Juilliard awarded him, and, soon enough, his emergence onto the stage. All the same, Anne painted a much more vivid and particular picture of the man.

After a while, I got hungry and took my book down to Tom's Diner, on Broadway, where I sat at the counter and splurged on an omelet with rye toast, hash browns, and coffee. Around seven-thirty, the biography safely returned to my office, I took the train down to the Village, entering 10A just before eight o'clock.

Again, I had hoped Anne might be profiting by my absence to make use of her living room. But I found it dark and empty, the lights of New Jersey sparkling in the black night outside the windows. The dining room and kitchen were also dark. As I entered the corridor, though, I saw that Anne's bedroom door was open. Was she in there? Where else could she be? She had to be somewhere in 10A. From what Marta had told me, she made only brief, infrequent forays out of doors, and never alone or at night.

A small, hopeful flame licked up inside me. Maybe we'd run into each other as we rattled around the apartment later. But the flame was snuffed when I noticed the closed study door. From the bills and other mail there, I knew she sometimes used that room, but I had managed to forget this. Now I went to my own room to read and grade the two dozen papers my pupils had handed in that day. By the time I finished, the study door was open and Anne's bedroom door shut. Lost in the wonderland of student thought, it appeared, I hadn't even heard her thump by.

I climbed into bed early again and picked up *Beyond Black*. It was the last book Mantel published before *Wolf Hall*, and her powerful mind was in full sail when she wrote it. I was only thirty pages from the end, and it was a gift to me to be so deeply absorbed for a while in someone else's imagination, but my eyes tired before I finished it and I closed them, letting the book drop beside me on the bed.

Despite the heaviness of my eyelids, however, I did not drift off to sleep. Instead, I lay restlessly awake, my head buzzing with speculation about the possible course of Anne's liaison with Gregory Morris. I thought longingly of the glass-fronted cabinet just a few yards away. In my mind's eye, I saw myself tiptoeing into the study.

There I would pick up the nice, heavy, brass-handled magnifying glass, wrap it in my turtleneck sweater, and ever so quietly use it to shatter the bookcase panes.

I would toss all the journals into a garbage bag, grab my purse and coat, and disappear with them into the night. I even had a quick, Looney Tunes-style fantasy of sneaking up behind the dear old lady and conking her on the head with a giant wooden mallet. She would sink to the floor in a daze, flashing stars and tiny singing angels flying in a circle around her head, while I took the key to the Biedermeier desk from her pocket, unlocked the bookcase, then restored the key before she came around. At last, I drifted into a doze, only to wake up at 1:00 a.m.

I turned on my bedside light, finished *Beyond Black* (a great book; I would miss it), then turned the light off again, closed my eyes, and made myself count slowly to a hundred. I went through the alphabet naming towns that started with each letter (Eddystone, Flyspeck, Gettysburg . . .), repeated the exercise with women's names, then men's. I forced myself to listen again to my breathing. None of these tricks succeeding, I got up, pulled a sweatshirt over my pajamas, and headed to the kitchen to warm up a cup of milk.

A light was on in the living room, casting a yellow path through the archway into the dining room. I walked along it and found Anne, wrapped in her quilted robe, silver hair tousled, seated on one of the two velvet love seats. Her face was to the dark foyer, the back of her head to me. I cleared my throat so as not to startle her and softly said her name. I called her Anne, the first time I had called her by any name at all.

She turned to look over her shoulder. I had feared she would be displeased, would feel I was trespassing, but she smiled.

She took off her reading glasses and put on the now familiar tortoise-shell pair. "Can't sleep?" she asked in her low, rich voice. "Come sit down."

As I obeyed, taking a seat on the opposite sofa (whose springs, I was sorry to find, had sprung), she went on, "I wake up in the night quite often now, no matter when I go to bed. It's the pain in my hips and shoulders that does it. I've run out of comfortable sides to sleep on. I need a cushion of air, like a hovercraft. Anyway, I get out of bed and spend a few hours reading."

She lifted the Kindle in her lap. "My little friend," she said. "The motel of the book world, but a godsend to me all the same. Why are you up? Or haven't you gone to bed yet?"

I shrugged. "I don't know. I just can't seem to get to sleep tonight. I'm going to try some warm milk. Would you like some?"

"Thank you, but milk is one of the many foods I can't tolerate anymore." She smiled again, this time reminiscently. "My father once came home from a visit to a doctor and told me, 'Dear, don't get old.' At the time, I was a little scandalized—what kind of thing is that to tell your child?—but I've never forgotten it, and now I see his point. Go get your milk."

I hesitated before saying, "I could sit with you a while if you like.

If I'm not interrupting your reading."

"Not at all. Do join me—if you like," she said, emphasizing the word "you." She raised the Kindle again. "I'm reading a very long novel set in Ohio in the early 1900s, narrated by a young doctor who thinks he's losing his mind. It's one of those irritating books where the writer feels he must include every fact he learned while doing his research. I don't recommend it."

I took a deep, steadying breath before asking, "What kind of novels did you write? I mean, were they domestic stories? Family sagas? Topical, at all?"

She looked at me, cocked her head. "Don't you have a computer?"

I felt myself start to blush. "I just haven't—haven't—" I stammered.

"Looked me up? No? How very twentieth-century of you."

I thought she would feel insulted. Instead, she started to laugh. Laugh at me, is what it felt like.

"Honestly, I don't find it very interesting to talk about myself," she said, lightly but firmly enough to make my heart sink. All I wanted her to do was talk about herself. "Tell me a bit about you," she invited. "Not that you must, of course. Only for a little conversation."

With no choice but to oblige her, I said, "I'd be glad to. What would you like to know?"

I resettled myself, deliberately uncrossing my arms and legs to erase the defensive posture I'd reflexively taken. Had she somehow become suspicious of me? I told myself that only my guilty conscience would make me imagine that—and yet, why was she so definite about keeping the focus on me? What would make a person find it uninteresting to talk about herself? I wasn't sure I'd ever met such a person. Despite my awareness that these thoughts were unbalanced, paranoid, I nevertheless awaited her questions uneasily.

"Oh, where you grew up, what your parents did, do you have a boyfriend. Whatever occurs to you."

Like anyone over the age of ten, I have been asked questions about childhood many times. But unlike most people, I have put a good deal of thought into my answers. Sometimes, I've had a good solid upbringing in semi-rural Pennsylvania, my dad the local vet, my mom his childhood sweetheart. Sometimes, Dad owned a hair salon in our little town, where he was a barber and Mom a hairdresser. Or he was a grease monkey (reasonably accurate) and she a librarian (wildly inaccurate, though she did read popular "women's fiction" by the fistful).

As to how my childhood went, in some versions my family was still intact, still living in the house where I'd grown up. In another version, my dad had died of a heart attack when I was a kid. (Technically true: Cardiac arrest was the medical cause of his death.) Branching off from this account were two scenarios, one in which my mother had remarried and one in which she hadn't. No matter the story, I was always an only child, usually the kind who longs for a sibling, but occasionally one of the other sort—the kid who feels lucky to get all the attention. (Just writing that down made me laugh. You really, really do not want all the attention of a couple of addicts.)

Only to a very few people did I tell the truth—that both my parents used, and that both were children of alcoholics themselves. My dad had an eighth-grade education and worked, as I said, at an auto repair shop, when he worked at all. My mother worked as a dogsbody in a beauty shop, and from her paltry salary, she managed (usually) to buy us food, to pay our rent, utilities, and so on, and (always) drink.

I told Anne that my dad was a barber and that the part of Brookline where I grew up wasn't the fancy part. It was safe, it was okay, but it was the other part. I left my mother a homemaker, though it made my stomach hurt to say it, so comfortless a home was she able to make for us. I spoke of both my parents as if they were still alive and well. My intention was to portray a wholesome, stable, working-class background, and I felt I succeeded. By now I'd learned enough about possible causes of blindness to be able to explain why my mother couldn't read for herself: In her early thirties, a pituitary tumor had permanently damaged her vision. But the subject never came up.

Anne shifted this way and that as she listened to me, trying to get comfortable, or less uncomfortable, at least, and sometimes closed her eyes as if to listen better. When she asked how it had happened that I'd attended Columbia, I admitted to having done unusually well in high school. With becoming modesty, I added that

I'd been floored when they admitted me. I would never even have applied there if my high school guidance counselor hadn't told me to, and I had certainly never expected to be accepted. I'm not sure why I said it was a guidance counselor who had helped me instead of telling her the truth. Maybe some instinctive scruple about dragging Miss Hart into the moral murk of my current adventure.

"Smart girl," said Anne, with that curiously dry tone she sometimes had. "And good for that guidance counselor." A moment later, she added, "And do you have a boyfriend?"

For once I could answer sincerely.

"Not anymore," I blurted out, and my heart thumped as I said it. "That's why I was looking for a place to live."

"I'm sorry," Anne replied, though she didn't sound very sorry. "Well, it was very lucky indeed for me that you needed to move. You do read so very well."

As I thanked her for saying so, she yawned and reached for her cane.

"Forgive me for yawning, Beth. It's been a pleasure to learn a bit more about you, but I think I'd better try to go back to sleep. I'll see you in the morning. You go make yourself that hot milk," she added, as she took her first slow steps. "I hope it helps."

When we met to read the next day, I felt that my midnight chat with Anne had had a good effect. There was a friendlier feeling between us, less formal, more collegial. Still, I was careful to remain respectful, to keep my face neutral, an impassive helper with no particular interest in whatever she wanted me to read. Yesterday's journal was already on her desk. I picked it up and opened it, and she told me to start again with the entry after the one we'd finished the day before.

It proved disappointingly bland.

Tuesday March 19, 10 p.m.

Up early and at desk by nine, only to scrap new backstory for Laura. It just doesn't do what I need it to, so...back to reimagining. This ghastly, impossible book! Sometimes I think it will be the death of me.

Stuck at it till one, had lunch, and then out to get food for dinner. At Jefferson Market ran into Nick Spencer and talked about a couple of the people we have in common from Bread Loaf. Home again and back to the desk. Made myself sit for an hour in front of a blank page. When I stood up, it was still as virginal as when I had sat down. Started to cook at five and discovered the burners don't work again. Of course no handyman till tomorrow, so—

"Oh for pity's sake," Anne broke in. "The crap I bothered to write down! Go ahead and look for Greg."

I paged forward, glad myself to leave the useless stovetop behind. There was a good deal of other crap, as Anne had called it, and not even a morsel of literary gossip, during the two days before the sought-after initial reappeared. Anne waited patiently as I scanned through, but we were both relieved when I could resume reading aloud.

Thursday March 21, 10:00 p.m.

In my study, door locked. I am in a new world now. This afternoon, I went to Greg's studio "to hear him play." To "see his etchings" it might as well have been, although I doubt any etching ever so melted a woman.

The "studio" is a studio apartment, a single, soundproof room several floors above the public part of Carnegie Hall. I had heard that there were such places and on arrival had a pleasant sense of privilege at being admitted to one of them. Greg confirmed for me what I dimly recalled, that there are many musicians who practice or even live there (though I doubt many have the advantage of simply going downstairs to play a concert!). His place is so small that his baby grand takes up half the space, but there's still room for a daybed sufficiently long and wide for a man—a man of Greg's height and slimness, anyway—to sleep on. There's also a kitchenette, and he offered me coffee.

I didn't want any but said yes, a feint of sorts to disguise the nature of my visit, delay the inevitable, perhaps. To keep up the pretext of a tame, sociable rendezvous. That it was a rendezvous in the more significant sense of the word was overpoweringly clear to both of us, not just as the thing itself unfolded but from the moment he had first suggested it at lunch. The charge in the air both scared and excited me. I sat primly on the edge of the daybed, the only place to sit except the piano bench. His back to me, Greg began to busy himself in the kitchen.

In books, I've written scenes of "illicit" encounters, but "illicit" was then a word like any other. Now it flashed like a neon sign, fascinating, mesmerizing, terrible in the tawdry, blazing, blinking fact of it. And yet I didn't think of Steve, not once. My desire enveloped me, inhabited me completely.

Still we kept up the pretense of a civil, pleasant visit, generous on his part, politely curious on mine. The pretense multiplied the truth tenfold. I drank my coffee as if its taste were the very one I craved. We made conversation—and never has the expression "made" conversation been more apt, since neither of us had a genuine word to say. After an absurd ten minutes or so of this, Greg asked me whose music I would like to hear first. Liszt, Brahms, Rachmaninoff, anything crashing and romantic came to mind, but I said, "Bach?"

He gave me a knowing, amused look, went to the keyboard, opened and closed his hands, bowed his head, and threw himself into the first movement of the first French Suite. Such a tiny piece, not even two minutes, but the furious intensity with which he played it made an efficient end-run around my demure selection. He is indeed an extraordinary musician. When the last note had diffused into the quivering air, he stood up, crossed the room, and bent over me. With both hands, he lifted the hair from the back of my neck to kiss what he had exposed. The warmth of his breath there undid me and I surrendered.

His touch, his touch! We sank into each other. In the aftermath of lust—what discretion, this cinematic elision of what came in between, but I can't bring myself to translate it into words—after lust came tenderness, surely unearned after so short an acquaintance, but palpable all the same. We lay on the daybed entangled both by choice and the insufficient width for two, but entanglement of this sort is very uncomfortable, I've always found—the numb arm under the suddenly heavy body, the awkward angle of the neck as it tries to rest on a shoulder. This brought me back to my senses (or out of them, more accurately) and I sat up. A chill in the room I hadn't felt before, as well as the fact that he could now see my body in all its nakedness, made me stand and fetch my coat. I put it on, even buttoned it up, before sitting down on the daybed once more. What have we begun? Here there be dragons.

I stopped and was quiet for a few seconds, thinking Anne might like a minute to think all this over before we went on. But she asked if that was the end of the entry—it was—and told me to continue reading.

Friday March 22, 10 a.m.

Woke at five this morning in a state of high alert. As I was writing the above last night, Steve knocked on my study door and called through that he was going to bed. Quietly, I locked the journal away and joined him. To my surprise, I promptly managed to turn off my brain and collapse into sleep. But only till five. Lay awake hoping to sleep again but my mind continued its mad racket and I gave up at 6:00.

Now to finish writing yesterday's events—not that I expect ever to forget them. So.

Soon after I hid my nakedness under my coat, I asked Greg to check his watch and was astonished to learn I had been there less than an hour. All the same, I felt compelled to go away at once, to try to collect myself, I suppose, or maybe just relieve the intensity of the encounter. We kissed goodbye and made an appointment to meet again a week from Tuesday. He has many obligations between now and then, he said, most immediately the concert at Carnegie; but he also has another lecture to give, two days with a houseguest—a violinist he and Susan went to school with at Juilliard who now lives in Paris—and most of all, a great deal of preparation to be ready for another concert, this one in Philadelphia with the Berlin Philharmonic. I went downstairs alone while he sat down at the piano.

It was just as well I left when I did. We'd met rather late in the day and I had little time for any solitary interval. If I were to take a shower before seeing Steve—and that I certainly had to do—I needed to head straight home.

I cooked a hasty dinner. At the table, I could barely face Steve. It seemed incredible that I'd gone from that to this, from the frenzy in the daybed to broiled salmon and buttered red potatoes. I tried to appear my usual self, but when Steve asked his invariable nightly question, "How was your day?" my cheeks went hot. Thankfully, he was chasing a potato around his plate and didn't see me till the blush started to subside.

"How was my day?" In the few hours since I'd left Greg, my mind had been a movie house replaying and replaying our time together. What we did, how we had touched, even the awkward fifteen minutes after I got to the studio. The looks we had given each other. The way we parted. In the rare moments when my thoughts wandered from these

recollections, they wandered no farther than across the lobby. What was Greg's homecoming to Susan like? What were his thoughts about me? Was he as excited (and frightened) as I am about meeting again?

As Steve and I sat and ate and chatted, I couldn't help imagining that he somehow sensed that something noteworthy had happened during my day, something cloudy to him, but disturbing. Naturally, I felt compelled to erase any such suspicion, even going so far as to try to get him back into bed after he got up to go to work this morning. No dice, and in retrospect I wonder if this very stratagem only heightened any vague intuition he might really have that something is not quite right. He is a trial lawyer, after all. It's his business to read people—guilty people in particular.

After he left for the office, I sat down at my desk as usual but couldn't focus on my concerns about And Sometimes Y, in particular Laura's thinness as a character and my growing doubts about whether she even belongs in the story. Gave up after lunch and incautiously lay down on the living room sofa to read but fell asleep at once—a deep, dream-filled sleep that lasted almost two hours. The content of these rich, languorous dreams evaporated the moment I opened my eyes. All I remember is how sensuous they were.

Following this, decided I might as well devote the remaining hours before I had to cook dinner to taking care of the usual waiting list of annoying chores—paying bills, answering a few tedious letters, doing the laundry... Steve home at seven, the suggestion of a change in my demeanor still, I worried, in his manner. Surely I am imagining this.

And yet I'm afraid even to think of Greg when Steve is around. What if I say his name? I feel it might leap out of my mouth like the toad in the fairy tale.

EIGHT

R eading aloud Anne's account of her fevered visit to Morris's studio sent a queasy wave through my innards. Different as her infidelity to Stephen Pace was from Tim's to me (at least I hoped so!), it was infidelity all the same. So when she told me to give her the journal, that she wanted to end our session for today, I felt relief as well as disappointment. I could use a little time to myself. I handed her the journal, which she locked away with the others in her desk.

It didn't surprise me that she'd wish to pause here. Naturally, she would want to linger over this pungent, thrilling, rescued bit of her past. As her day went on, she would, perhaps, recall new details—the quality of the light in the room, the smell of the coffee she didn't want, the temperature of her lover's skin, the taste of his mouth, her own heightened heartbeat. She might even relive the tryst overnight in a dream.

As I began to stand up, though, she gestured to me to stay put.

I sat, confused. She held up a finger as if to say that she needed a moment to think. Then she folded her hands on the desk, inspected them, and looked up and smiled.

"My, my," she said at last. "What must you think of me?"

Her question and the tone in which she delivered it brought to mind what she'd said apropos of her wrecked vision: "You can imagine my vexation." Both sentences were *mille-feuilles* of rage, irony, and style. And for all the strange coyness of her delivery, both were passionately sincere. Were I to answer the question literally, my first reply would have been, "Wow, you skank! You cheated on your nice husband?"

I might also have said that I thought she'd been enviably sexual into her forties—and that she was a better writer than I'd taken her for. Some authors, I've observed, do write better when they write with their left hand, as it's sometimes called—when their goal is not to shape a work of art but simply to say what they mean.

However, her question wasn't really a question at all. It was a bitter acknowledgment of the fact that she'd been forced to share with a stranger this most intimate of scenes. Accordingly, I said nothing, only trying to telegraph with a fleeting smile some sympathy for her pain. And this was wholehearted. Weil's present-day predicament struck me as genuinely, profoundly mortifying, and entirely unfair. Later, I cursed myself for failing to use the moment as an occasion to say that she seemed to me to have been an unusually liberated woman and ask whether she saw herself that way. I needed to know to what extent *Vengeance* had been a political statement for her, if it had been at all. Yet I gave way to my own emotion.

"Well, whatever you think, there it is," she said after a short silence. She sighed. "What are your generation's norms of sexual behavior? I wonder. Are people unfaithful to their spouses? I mean,

I'm sure some are, but is it less shameful, more something to be expected and managed, lived with?"

"I don't know," I said. "I've never been married."

"I see." She was silent again, then continued, "Well, do you—hook up, I think is the term? I mean, not you particularly, but people you know, people your age?"

I hesitated, again wishing that I could be the one asking such questions. But I knew she was trying to get the spotlight off her own behavior, and yielded to her preference.

"I don't know what other people do, of course," I said after a moment, "but my friends... I think most of us, by the time we were sixteen or so, old enough to be out of the house without supervision, we did start hooking up. Having sex. Women—and men, obviously. And men and men, and women and women, and so on, for that matter. But lately the people I know seem to be more into finding something that will last, someone to have a real relationship with."

"But not necessarily to marry, I hope. You're only—twenty-four, I think you said?" And here she tilted her head and raised her eyebrows before continuing, "That seems very young to me."

"No, I mean—I think a lot of people go through at least one or two serious relationships before they get married. Committed relationships."

"And do they live together meanwhile?"

"Eventually. Most of them." As I said this, I felt a wave of sorry-for-myself. The subject of marriage had come up between me and

Tim occasionally, usually when friends of ours announced that they were getting married, but neither of us was very enthusiastic about the idea. My own parents' marriage had been such hell; and anyway, finishing my doctorate came first. Tim was no great fan of marriage either. His parents divorced when he was eight, an enduringly ugly rift that left him bouncing back and forth between them, doing his best to please first one, then the other, trying to keep them apart and himself together. If anything, he was even more skeptical about marriage than I.

"And what about children? Do your friends want them? Or have them already? Or are they too young?"

I thought of Petra, who could hardly wait to start a family and had taken to putting that fact right out there as soon as she started seeing someone new. And Carrie, with her wall-climbing son and spelling bee champion daughter. "I think most of the women I know want to have kids eventually," I said. "Most of the men, too. But I don't," I added truthfully.

"More focused for now on working for Planned Parenthood?" she suggested.

I had forgotten this lie and almost said, "What?" It came back to me just in time, and I nodded.

"Hmm. Well, this is all very interesting for an old lady like me," Anne said, in a summing-up way that indicated she was about to end the conversation. "Thank you for filling me in."

"Of course. But what was it like for you?" I quickly, finally asked.

"What was normal behavior when you were growing up? Did teenagers—well, not 'hook up,' I mean, but—"

"Oh," Anne interrupted me, voice airy, "you know. I was born into another world. In 1922, nice women were chaste, or claimed to be. Bad girls were fast and had babies 'out of wedlock,' as we called it. But then came the Roaring Twenties, and then the Depression. By the time I finished high school, Hitler was all over Europe. The London Blitz started the week I got to college. It felt like the world was about to end, and of course that makes you want to gather your rosebuds. My friends and I had a lot of fun, and no one thought any the worse of us. I wouldn't say we were promiscuous—now *there's* a word you don't hear much anymore—but we certainly weren't chaste."

I was about to seize on that word, "promiscuous," and use it to pole-vault the conversation into sexual politics, when she sighed, shifted in her chair, and reached for her cane.

"But that's all history now. You can read about it in books," she concluded. "Let's start again tomorrow. You really are doing an exceptional job of reading, by the way."

I thanked her for the compliment, waited a moment for her to steady herself on her cane, then went swiftly down the hall. I was annoyed by her useless, impersonal answer to my question, her obvious disinclination to trade information about her own experience for mine (not that I'd told her anything about mine), and seething at myself for failing to ask what I needed to know, no matter how uncomfortable it might have made her. It was all too true that what she'd said was history I could find in books. I had allowed my sympathy for her to prevail—an afflicted old lady, after all, reduced to listening to someone else read her sexual past out loud—and the consequence was that I'd let myself down. I was angry at myself, and this helped me as I set about my next task.

I had by now gone online and done a little research about keys. The lock on the drawer in Anne's lovely desk was quite a modern one, installed at least a century after the desk itself had been made, and I couldn't possibly unlock it without the matching key. The skeleton keys to the glass-fronted bookcase, however, were another matter. Thanks to the website of a British master locksmith, I had learned that the doors to such a piece of furniture were likely furnished with locks more for convenience than for security: The keys served as handles to pull the doors open, the locks as latches to keep them shut, and it was almost certainly the case that all the keys were the same. If this were so, those little numbered tags on Anne's key ring were either for show or because someone else had mistakenly tagged them and even she hadn't realized she needed only one.

A second online search informed me that the city offered dozens of locksmith shops that sold antique keys. Although there were two of these within walking distance of the Windrush, I gave in to my Spy vs. Spy compulsion to cover my tracks and called one in Yorkville, near Petra's place. The locksmith informed me I could buy a mix of twenty-five or so at a very modest cost. I didn't mention to Petra that

I'd be in her neighborhood because I didn't want to tell her why. I might have been morally sleepwalking through those days, but I wasn't deeply enough asleep to jump out a window.

And so, after a tuna sandwich hastily dispatched in the dining room of 10A (Marta was in the living room with the vacuum), I took the L across town and went up to East 91st Street and Zenith Locksmith and Key. The man at the counter had the look many locksmiths seem to have—a world-weary look, as if he had seen it all. Middle-aged, skinny, slouchy, with a dark, jaded, skeptical gaze. Despite the frigid weather, he wore only a thin, vintage Bruce Springsteen *Tunnel of Love Express Tour* t-shirt.

"How can I help you?"

I described to him my bookcase and its missing keys.

He tilted his head side to side a few times, as if to say this wasn't much of a challenge for a guy like him.

"So you buy a couple dozen that look like they might be right size and probably you're going to find one that works," he said. He disappeared into the back and returned with a large wooden box filled with hundreds of skeleton keys—tiny, huge, shiny, tarnished, iron, brass, silver, and gold all jumbled together.

"Enjoy yourself," he suggested before sauntering into the back room again.

I took out my phone, opened the photo I'd snapped of a keyhole on the cabinet, and sifted through the keys, comparing them with the picture. I had soon amassed a sizable collection. I called "Hello?"

into the back. The man emerged, looked at my haul, and charged me thirty dollars. I left with the keys rattling in my purse.

Then I took the bus across 96th Street and walked up Broadway to campus. As I passed my former building and went on to my office, I turned my face resolutely away.

This time, both my officemates were there. We had long ago come to an understanding that "hello" and "goodbye" would suffice when we ran into each other, so there was no need for any pretense of conversation. When one of us had official student office hours, the others stayed away. Otherwise, we came and went more or less in silence, using phones only in the hall and generally ignoring each other. It was a congenial, mutually respectful arrangement. We were all busy, and no one visited that stuffy little office just for fun.

So I nodded hello, divested myself of coat, hat, scarf *et alia*, and removed my laptop from my backpack. At my desk, I plugged in a pair of earphones and googled "Gregory Morris piano" on YouTube. I wanted to hear him play the Appassionata, the sonata he'd told Anne he was to play at Carnegie Hall. I was lucky. Two people had posted recordings of the whole piece. Thanks to my music-major boyfriend, I had already heard this aptly named sonata more than once and was among the hundreds of thousands who could readily hear the opening, at least, in my head. I'm not sure exactly what I hoped to learn from hearing Morris's interpretation, but I suppose that, as a doctoral candidate, I was simply in the habit of pursuing whatever research avenue I could. And I did find that listening to it gave me deeper insight into the man I'd been reading about in the journals. With my eyes closed, it conjured up a side of him that Anne's notes had not.

I moved on to clips of him playing three different Haydn minuets for keyboard. Here his touch was delicate, nimble, sweet, delightful. In their sunny charm, I heard the educator and mentor who had inspired so much affection in his students. Between the roiling, sometimes thunderous Beethoven and the Haydn, I felt I had had a look at two sides of his character.

I sat for a bit in silence, letting all this sink in, then checked the time. It was just after 4:00. In a vague, unexamined way, I'd had it in mind all day to go to an Al-Anon meeting if I could. I have mixed feelings about Al-Anon, mostly because I'm not very good at it. I just drop in and out of various meetings now and then, here and there, usually without saying anything. I've never tried to "work" the Twelve Steps ("work the steps" is the annoying term in general use, even though the far more obvious, sensible "take the steps" is available), never asked anyone to be my sponsor, never had a "home" meeting, and have trouble with the concept of a "higher power," not to mention "God." What kind of God lets so many children grow up at the mercy of addicts? What kind gives so many people the constitution that makes them addicts? Still, there was something centering about it; it was a way of checking in with myself. I looked at the New York City website and saw there was a meeting at a church in the Village at six o'clock. I packed up and jumped onto the train just in time to beat the rush hour, and was back at Anne's before five o'clock.

I found Marta in the kitchen, cooking and humming tunelessly to herself. She hadn't heard me come in and I startled her when I said hello.

"Oh my God!" The hand that wasn't stirring something with a wooden spoon flew to her chest. She smiled, shook her head, and laughed at herself. "You scared me!"

I apologized.

She apologized. She should pay more attention. How was I?

I was well, thanks. How was she?

Marta also was well.

Here the conversation lagged, but I hovered in the doorway. Whatever she was making, it smelled fantastic. I glanced down the hall toward Anne's bedroom door and Marta noticed.

"Mrs. Anne is sleeping, I think," she told me. "You need something?"

"No. Just wondered how she's doing."

Marta made a little "so-so" movement with her free hand. "Tired. Always tired," she said. "But she ate lunch. A scrambled egg. Sometimes she won't eat lunch. I am making a white bean stew for her dinner," she added, holding up the wooden spoon in her hand.

"It smells wonderful."

"Then you will also have some for dinner," Marta decided.

I smiled, demurred, told her I was going out soon, admitted I'd be coming back without having eaten, gave in. Marta said she'd leave some for me in the fridge.

The meeting was good for me. In fact, I can hardly think of an Al-Anon meeting that was ever anything but good for me. It was small, which I like, and there were both newcomers and old hands, which I also like. I recognized only one person, and I didn't know her more than to say hello, and that was okay with me too. I went in feeling tense and confused about my own motives and actions and left feeling calmer and clearer. In between, I had put my hand up and talked, when it was my turn, about my sense of being two people in the past few weeks: one who was willing to be deceitful to get what she needed, and a second person watching that deceitful one as if she were watching a play.

I heard myself talk about how familiar this sense of doubleness was for me, how much of my childhood I'd spent feeling afraid and how deceptive I'd had to be to keep myself safe, lying about my feelings and actions to escape my parents' wrath; the volatility and loss I'd grown up with, the damage it had done to me, and my determination to "better myself" in life through education and hard work. Many people in Al-Anon have similar stories, and many struggle even to know their own emotions after a childhood spent focused on the turbulent, dangerous feelings of the alcoholic grownup whose moods rule their lives. No one answers you when you talk at an Al-Anon meeting. You just speak while other people listen, and you hear yourself in a different way.

By the time the meeting ended, it had begun to sleet. The bare little trees of the Village already glistened with what would glaze over into a solid layer of ice by morning. I slowly walked the seven or eight blocks back to the Windrush, the faces of the people at the meeting and the things they'd said tumbling in my head like flakes in a snow globe. Each of us a different world, each of us a never-ending puzzle to ourselves. All different, all the same.

It was only 7:30 when I got back to 10A, but the place was as dark and silent as if it were dead of night. I went to my room to dump my backpack and purse—and the keys jingling inside it—and saw that Anne's door was closed. No music came through it, no sound at all. Her study door was open, the room empty. In the kitchen, I found a note from Marta taped to the fridge, telling me my dinner was in the Pyrex container with the blue top. I found it, reheated it in the small, elderly microwave oven, and ate it at the dining room table while rereading Philip Caputo's *A Rumor of War* for an upcoming class.

The stew was fabulous, as good as it had smelled, and the book even better than I remembered. Except for a short check-in call with Petra—she was in a hurry, on her way to meet her sort-of boyfriend Justin at the Paris Theater to see I can't remember which film—I spent the whole evening wrapped up in the book, the fresh, forceful, driving momentum of the prose mingling with the increasingly staccato tapping of the freezing rain against the window of my room.

I waited until eleven o'clock before venturing out to try my abundant keys. Anne's hours being what they were, I prepared carefully. For all I knew, she might have fallen asleep at seven and woken again by now. So I divided the noisy keys into two bunches and slid each into one of a pair of thick, noise-canceling athletic socks; these I buried inside the deep pockets of my terrycloth robe. I peeked out to make certain her door was still shut and no light shining elsewhere in the apartment—all clear—then closed my door behind me and slipped across the hall into the study.

I turned on the Tiffany lamp and, after a little hesitation, decided to leave the door as I'd found it, just slightly ajar, as it usually was. Then I searched among the hundreds of novels on the walls for Iris Murdoch's *The Bell*. I wasn't a hundred percent sure I hadn't read it already—I've read most of Murdoch, but they do sometimes run together in the mind—but I chose it because Anne had mentioned it in her journal. If she happened to discover me in here, I could hold it up and explain that I'd been intrigued by her mention of it.

I put *The Bell* in front of me atop the cabinet of wonders, then, heart in mouth, stomach knotted with fear, knelt and started trying the keys. Sure enough, after a dozen or so yielded no result, one turned a lock. I checked the other doors and found that this same key opened them all. For some reason, the discovery only ratcheted up my anxiety. I thought of my thesis, thought of the women whose neglected work I was trying to rescue, ordered myself to concentrate, and soon succeeded in my goal: to locate and abstract a notebook from the late fall of 1963, one that would record part of the period when I thought Weil must have written *The Vengeance of Catherine Clark*.

Then, a criminal in the night, I quietly locked the glass door behind which I'd found it, stuck my contraband under my pajama top and clutched *The Bell* over it, peeked out of the study, scurried back to my room, and quietly pulled the door shut.

Prize in hand, I flung myself onto the bed and hungrily began to read the journal. But what was it? At first, it seemed to be filled with nothing but reports of quotidian errands, meaningless (to me) phone calls from people I'd never heard of (and couldn't find on the internet when I searched them), lunches and dinners with the same, a cold that came and went.

Yet I'd chosen the period perfectly: It was clear she was writing *Vengeance*. Indeed, she was barreling through it. *"Eleven pages today,"* she scrawled on November 12th. A week later: *"Had an idea for Catherine's visit to M's ex-wife."* There were none of the false starts, failed characters, and roadblocks that littered her discouraged accounts of writing *And Sometimes Y*, no doubts about whether this or that worked, no mention of revisions at all.

As I read on, I noted with interest that Greg was never mentioned. What had happened between them? As for Steve, who I knew had died barely three months before the start date of the notebook, his name appeared only once, after a meeting with his estate lawyer.

"Took a taxi home so I could cry," she wrote that evening. *"It was wrong of me to marry him. I knew it even as I did it. I still remember so*

vividly the image that appeared in my mind the very first time we talked. It was a paperweight. A large, handsome, heavy, smooth glass paperweight. He was stable, substantial, a man who held things down, kept them together. A grown man, nothing like the moody beatnik boys I'd been with before. I believe he knew this, and in fairness to myself, I think that solidity was the very thing he hoped to give me.

"He wanted to protect me. And maybe even acquire me—this beautiful (as I was then), bohemian younger woman, with her tedious day job and unsafe apartment and arty literary aspirations—this woman so different from anyone he'd ever known. He could offer that untethered person a substantiality she would never achieve herself, and that pleased him. It was affectionate, a sort of largesse, but it also made him feel powerful. As did his money itself, of course, the ease of it. It flattered him to be able to shower it on me.

"I must try not to dwell on all this. His trust in me, his allowances for my alien 'creative' life, his awful death, my behavior toward him," she wrote at the close of this entry, *"it's all such agony to think about, and so completely useless."*

If the wellspring of rage that gave rise to *Vengeance* had been her marriage, you sure couldn't tell it from reading this.

It was almost one a.m. by the time I'd made my way through the whole, exasperating journal, and I had to force myself to stay awake long enough to photograph each of its pages. (Luckily, Tim had given me a digital point-and-shoot camera for Christmas the year I moved in with him. I hadn't used it much, but it came in very handy now.) Exhausted, disheartened, I looked around for a good place to hide the notebook before I went to bed. In the end, I stuck it under the sink, inside the case for my blow dryer. A little frisson of terror, lest it be found there despite these baroque precautions, shivered through me as I passed out minutes later.

––––––––––––––

In the morning, as before, Anne and I went about our separate kitchen rituals in silence—a more congenial silence since we'd had our late-night talk, it seemed to me. I withdrew to my room, Anne knocked twenty minutes later and put her head in to say she'd like to proceed at 10:00, and at 9:45, I emerged to eat my frugal yogurt. This done, we duly met in the living room.

The weather had changed again. Today, the sleet was gone, leaving the sky blue and the trees bright with ice. The wind was very high, screaming around the corners of the building and punching the windows like a soundtrack for *Wuthering Heights*. Anne gave me the notebook we'd been reading yesterday.

"Take up where you left off," she said, closing her eyes.

The next entry had been written later on the day of the previous one. I told her so and began.

10:30 p.m.

Through what twist of fate I have no idea, Amy Reeves called this afternoon to say that she and Len had tickets to hear Gregory Morris play at Carnegie Hall tomorrow night. The program includes Beethoven's Appassionata, she went on. Now it turned out Len had to run an errand of mercy just then. Did I want to use his ticket?

This was, of course, the concert Greg was practicing for yesterday. The offer so rattled me that I stalled, saying I'd have to call Steve and see if he was okay with it, even though I knew he'd be more than amenable, tomorrow being the last Saturday of the month, the sacrosanct night of his poker game at Joe Lister's house. Still, for plausibility, I waited ten minutes before calling her back to say yes. When Steve got home, I told him about it. He said he was happy I'd found something enjoyable to do while he was out. I think of my duplicity and cringe.

I looked up, the word "duplicity" ringing in my ears. Maybe Anne Weil and I weren't so very different after all—not fox and hen, but fox and fox. Or, more precisely, since we were female, vixen and vixen.

"That's all you wrote that night," I said.

"Yes," she agreed, her voice dreamy, distant. "Go on."

March 23, 11 p.m.

Home in a haze of pleasure and pride after hearing Greg play Carnegie Hall. (Although why "pride"? I had nothing to do with it.) Spent a ridiculous amount of time this afternoon washing my hair, letting it dry, brushing it, arranging it, putting on makeup, trying one outfit, then another. As if he were going to see me! But he might see me, I couldn't help thinking, we might somehow go backstage—Amy and Len know him, and they are Carnegie patrons. Ridiculous as it was, I couldn't help myself, and since I couldn't keep my mind on anything else anyway, it didn't matter. At least I felt properly dressed when I met Amy in the lobby.

She was full of chatter as always, in this case about how Beatrice Holloway has accidentally become pregnant at the age of forty-one. This surprising event provoked many reflections from Amy—on her own life as a parent, on how she would have felt if she had become pregnant at forty-one—and speculation on whether and how Beatrice might try to have it aborted. It also provoked a certain amount of reflection in me. My period has become so irregular and infrequent—I'm pretty sure I've even had a few hot flashes lately!—that Steve and I stopped worrying about birth control at least a year ago. Not sure if I wrote that down at the time. I haven't thought for a moment that I might get pregnant *by Greg. Now I am going to think twice, and hard.*

Anyway, I followed Amy into the auditorium praying to God she never learns a secret of my own. There's a kind of restfulness, though, in being with Amy. You don't have to say a word. She handles the whole conversation herself.

I was thrilled to find that our seats were in the eighth row of the orchestra, far enough left to see Greg's hands but close enough to the center to see his face. They were wonderful seats. I felt so grateful.

I studied the program as well as I could with Amy talking and talking beside me, but it wasn't easy, and all I learned was that, in addition to the Beethoven, Greg would play two Haydn sonatas and Mozart's in C major (K. 330, I took the program home). My attention snapped back to Amy when I realized she was talking about his wife: her irritating habit of taking contrarian views in their reading group, the way she always suggested obscure biographies when it was her turn to choose the book they would read, how curt she could be with someone she thought wasn't as smart as she was, what odd things she brought when she was the one to provide the refreshments they traditionally ate at the start of a meeting. Amy has known her for a long time, though, and she also described sympathetically and in grim detail the four miscarriages Susan had before she and Greg gave up hope. This interested me, of course. How sad for Greg to want children and be unable to have them! (Assuming he did want them, that is. I suppose it might only be Susan.) Though I kept trying to read the About the Performer page, in many ways, Amy was more informative. The miscarriages, of course, but also the fact that they'd married in the face of Susan's parents' furious objections. They had wanted their daughter to marry someone religious, someone steady, a man with a predictable future, which at the time was exactly what Gregory Morris did not have. They never spoke to her again.

Then the lights went down, a chorus of coughs went up, people wriggled out of their coats, opened their programs, unwrapped hard candies, in short, did all the usual idiotic things they should have done ten minutes before, and Greg appeared, tiny as he walked across the vast stage, then turned and smiled at the applauding audience—a genuine smile, as if he were thrilled by the prospect of performing for us. So winningly unlike other soloists at such moments, I think, who seem to feel their dignity demands only a brief, sober nod before they sit down. Then he took his seat at the gleaming Steinway and waited for the auditorium to quiet down, his head bowed, eyes closed, listening inwardly, I imagine, to the piece he was about to play.

Just as he lifted his hands to the keyboard, some imbecile right behind me copiously cleared his throat. Greg pretended not to hear this (or maybe his concentration was such that he really didn't). As soon as he began to play, his smallness relative to the stage vanished and his presence filled the hall. The first piece was the Mozart and he performed its lively first movement with a child's delight, smiling as he trained his eyes on his fingers, not to make sure they went where they were supposed to, but with wonder, as if they weren't his own but rather tiny, magical marionettes operated by some puppeteer above him.

It was a charming performance, and so modest. The Appassionata came after this, an entirely different animal, of course. He played it with as much authority, it seemed to me, as if he were Beethoven himself, as if the composer were breathing into him and making Greg's hands, his body, an instrument of his own expression. His body did become an instrument, no less than the piano, and somehow made the familiar chords and motifs new again.

I won't try to write it all down. It's enough to say that it was transporting.

After this he stood and bowed as a wave of bravos and loud clapping, even some stomping, swept through the hall. He left the stage—it was intermission—and the applause gradually subsided into the usual mur-mured critiques and the rustle of people getting up to head out to the lobby for a chat and a cigarette. I had a trying time during this because Amy, standing in front of our folded seats, immediately plunged into the story of why Len hadn't come tonight. Something to do with a nephew who might be charged with causing a multiple car crash on the New Jersey Turnpike. Her only remark about the concert was a quick, "He's good, isn't he?" Then straight back to Jersey and the nephew's mother, Len's sister, who since her divorce always turned to him whenever—etc. etc. On she went, uninterruptibly, until the warning bells sounded and I could finally sink back into the blissful spell of the music.

The Haydn sonatas comprised the second half of the concert. They made a nice contrast to each other, both lovely, the first in a minor key, with sections that wove in and out of sorrow, the second (D major, and familiar to me) brighter and more delicate. Both were humbly, perfectly played. Such pieces are not the kind to provoke shouts and bravos like those that had come after the Appassionata, but the applause as the program came to its end was enough to merit three curtain calls. After these, Greg finally came out once more and sat down to play a very short encore. He announced the composer and title before starting, an intelligent courtesy to the audience that I've heard many performers neglect.

"This is the third of Schumann's 'Scenes from Childhood,'" he said, before languorously, lovingly executing this simple and beautiful piece. It left me with tears in my eyes. He is a master.

Here a single line had been left blank. I said so, Anne nodded, and I went on.

Just reread the above. It sounds like the ravings of a fourteen-year-old recording her first kiss—breathless and, to anyone but herself, hilariously overwrought. Still, I think it's accurate. Maybe time—or the Times?—*will tell.*

This was the end of the entry. Below it came another blank line, and below this a new entry dated March 24. Anne told me to read it.

It started off unpromisingly with an account of brunch with Doris and Joe, whoever they might have been, at a place called Haffner's, then a quiet afternoon and her decision to cut Laura completely out of *And Sometimes Y*. ("God damn her," she added.)

The passage went on:

I don't think I've ever worked so hard on a book. I've certainly never kept at one so perverse for so long. Unless it's a genre novel, like a romance or maybe a mystery, there's simply no proportion between the work a novel requires and the reward it gets from the world. A national holiday with mandatory fireworks wouldn't match the effort with the result, nor do the half-dozen positive, prominent reviews even the luckiest authors receive (all over in a matter of weeks) and the paltry half-year (or less) most books are kept in stores before being returned. Given the hours you have to put in to write a book, you'd need a bestseller for the money earned to pay more than minimum wage. If I ruled the planet, every novel would be awarded a prize and every novelist a medal.

"Find Greg again," Anne broke in.

He was only a few paragraphs away.

I realize now that I didn't have time (or courage?) to include in my account of Greg's concert that Amy and I ran into his wife on our way out when it ended. We were trudging out with the rest of the crowd when

Amy spotted her, standing by the aisle some fifteen rows back from the stage, alone and waiting for a gap in the thick, slow stream of which we ourselves were a part. She stepped back so that we could edge in.

Having trapped her, Amy reminded us that we'd met before, then enthusiastically praised Greg's performance (as if she'd listened!) while I stood in silence. Like her husband, Susan is small. She has very short, curly, auburn hair and vivid features in a sharply chiseled face. There is some of Greg's intensity in her but none of his warmth or charm. Quite the contrary; she projects a forbidding toughness. Unlike the unflattering, conventional dress she had worn at the Reeveses' dinner party, her clothes tonight were pointedly informal: black boots, a black turtleneck, and black corduroy slacks, with a thickly quilted red leather jacket over her shoulders. She looked as if she were on her way to hear an evening of jazz at Birdland.

She received Amy's effusions with the unsmiling nods they deserved. When Amy reminded her that I lived in the Windrush, she gave me a vague, chilly smile. It occurred to me that this was the first time I'd seen her since the night we'd met, whereas Greg and I had bumped into each other four times by chance. I wonder how much she goes out. Rigid with guilt, I grinned at her uncontrollably as I said how very much I admired her husband's playing. It was a relief when Amy began to pour out the story of why Len hadn't come and how sorry he was to miss hearing the concert, a subject about which Susan plainly cared even less than I. By now, the aisle was empty enough for her to excuse herself to go backstage. Then Amy and I got our coats from the coat check, I thanked her again for taking me, and we went our separate ways.

"That's all for Sunday," I reported. "Should I go to the next entry?"

Anne nodded. Her gaze had turned to the windows, which rattled now and then as fierce gusts off the churning river shook them.

Tuesday April 1, 10:30 p.m.

After Steve left for the office, I took out Greg's recording of the Haydn sonatas and sat in the living room to listen. His technique and feeling are audible, but the intimate, reverent aura of the concert performance was lost. I was startled to find I could hear him take a breath before he began several of them. There is Glenn Gould's humming, of course, but I don't recall ever noticing a pianist's breath on a recording before. At each instance, a quiver of—I can only call it desire—ran through me, and I thought of that moment when he pulled out my chair at La Bouchée and I first felt his warm exhalation on my neck.

Yesterday, I considered leaving a note for him with the doorman to say how much I'd enjoyed the concert. But I felt he might not like that. Susan already knows I attended it, and why draw attention to any other connection I might have with him?

Naturally, my thoughts have teemed with the prospect of our next rendezvous. I worry that he will cancel at the last minute on some pretext or other to hide the fact that he feels too guilty to want to repeat our—our encounter. I can't quite believe he wouldn't genuinely wish to, but I can believe he might feel we shouldn't have done it in the first place, that he made an error in judgment he has now resolved not to repeat. While obsessing about this, I went about the usual business of the day, writing And Sometimes Y (or trying to), shopping for sirloin, cooking dinner, and reading Richard Yates's "Revolutionary Road" (very good) while eating lunch.

Oh, the Times! *How could I forget? The concert was reviewed this morning by Harold Schonberg. The review was drier than I would have liked, with a few of the show-off remarks that even excellent music critics seem to feel their superior knowledge demands, such as a quibble with Greg's "unorthodox rendition" of a passage in the Appassionata. Still, overall, generous, even glowing praise. I read it three times and examined the accompanying photo of him, which had been taken through that little round hole for photographers in the wall at the back of the stage. It caught him at a moment when his expression conveyed an almost exultant joy—a moment in the Mozart, if I had to guess—and I thought it said more than the review itself. What a cliché, the picture worth a thousand words, but like so many clichés, enduring because it is true. I cut it out—the review and the picture—and put it into my copy of "A Tree Grows in Brooklyn." That's one book Steve will never open.*

On the subject of books, having gobbled up "Revolutionary Road," I decided (Oh why? I wonder) to reread "Anna Karenina." I'm up to the part where Anna confesses her adultery to Karenin. (Which reminds me to say that I take the book out only when Steve is at work.) It reads very differently to me now from the way it did when I read it for 19th Century Russian Lit, of course, not only because so much time has gone by—I was twenty then—but for what I can only call the obvious reason. I do think publishers should print suggested ages on certain novels for grown-ups, as they do with children's books—"Ages 5-8," that kind of thing. "Anna K."

should not be read until the reader is at least thirty-five.

Again, I had reached the end of an entry and glanced up to say so. Anne was looking at me with unusual attention.

"I think we'll save the next bit of the story for tomorrow," she said, adding with her signature dryness, "There's a dilly of an entry coming up soon."

I nodded and handed the journal across the desk. I was about to stand when she added, "Stay a minute, if you don't mind."

"Of course." More than willingly, I resettled myself on the unyielding upholstery of my oval-backed chair.

"Have you read *Anna Karenina?*" Anne asked.

Reflecting that I had already admitted to a B.A. in English, I conceded that I had, in college.

"Do you think my opinion was right? Was it wasted on you?"

"Maybe. I'm not sure I have any way of knowing. I did like it a lot." Restraining myself from any scholarly dissection, I went on, "I definitely got swept up in the story."

"Did you? Well, do read it again in ten years or so. In the very unlikely event that I'm still alive, I'll be curious to hear how it strikes you then."

"I'm sure you'll still be alive," I said innocently, at the same time digesting this intimation, however light, that we would continue to be in touch after my stay here. Or at least occasionally get in touch. "Why wouldn't you be?"

I thought she might mention her heart condition, but she went in another direction.

"Because I would be ninety-nine. I certainly hope I'll be dead by then. Even now, there are many days when I feel like handing in my keys and moving on."

I laughed at the metaphor. Despite the solemnity of the woman in her author photos, her wry humor, her playfulness with language, show up in the voice of her novels—even in *Vengeance*, though only rarely, and in the bitterest way.

She laughed too.

"Life is a funny old thing," she said, but I don't think she meant it.

NINE

After three hours straight of grading my students' papers that night, I started *The Bell*—might as well, since I had it. I woke the next morning looking forward to reading the "dilly" Anne had mentioned, but when we met in the kitchen, I found her making tea instead of coffee. She turned to me and raised a warning hand.

"Get thee behind me," she said. "My throat is sore and my nose is...well, my nose is simply not itself, and neither is my energy. So I'm going to take this tea and get right back into bed for the day. You might as well go out if you like. We won't be able to do any reading till tomorrow, if then."

"Thanks. I do have to go to the office later, but I won't be there too long—maybe two or three hours." That would give me plenty of time to get uptown, teach, and return. "I'll be here till two-thirty and back by six at the latest. So if I can do anything for you, just let me know."

"What you can do for me is keep a distance away from me. The last thing we need is you losing your reading voice. You're a valuable commodity, Ms. Miller."

With that, she took herself and her mug off to her bedroom and shut the door. In spite of her suggestion, I remained indoors until I had to leave for school, in hopes that she might rally and want me to read after all, or even just do something useful for her. I wanted to help her, not only to bolster our relationship (I admit that crossed my mind) but out of ordinary human kindness. I locked myself into my bathroom, just in case Marta popped into my room, and sat on the toilet looking again through the journal I'd hidden under the sink. I'd been tired when I read the end of it and thought I might have missed something. But no.

Resigned, I uploaded the pictures I'd taken of the pages to my computer, then thought of nipping across the hall to replace this notebook with another. But I was too afraid; Anne—or Marta—might materialize at just the wrong moment. So, feeling uncomfortably like the frightened child I had once been, I returned it to its hiding place under the sink and turned my attention to finishing up what I needed for class. I ate a solitary lunch while continuing to read *The Bell*. As it turned out, I hadn't read it before. It was good, as always, to be in Murdoch's company, though I didn't think it one of her best.

Anne appeared around 1:30 and went into the kitchen to make herself some toast and more tea. Hearing her, I joined her and offered to help in any way I could—heat up some soup, or at least carry the mug and plate to her room. I had noticed that her steps seemed even less confident than usual today, and besides, at her best, she could carry only one thing at a time. I dearly wished to see her bedroom and was disappointed when she declined.

Then I went off to school and taught the first of a two-part class on student activism during the Vietnam War. I left the room with a backpack full of 500-word essays on first-wave feminism, my thoughts of Anne displaced by the prospect of having to grade so many papers. I lingered in the hallway in the students' wake, trying to decide whether to go to my office and power through them all at once or take the train back down to the Windrush, where I might learn if Anne was any better. Or worse.

I was still pondering this when I caught sight of Professor Probst. Most days, I would have ducked back into the empty classroom, hoping she wouldn't spot me and ask how things were going with my dissertation. Today, though, I was thrilled by the chance to talk with her. It had been less than two weeks since I'd moved into Anne Weil's apartment and I hadn't yet told her about it. I went straight over and stopped her with a big hello.

"Hello!" she replied, echoing the unusual, unexpected enthusiasm in my voice. She cocked her head. "What's up? How are you?"

Judging by the dates on the diplomas in her office, Professor Probst was then in her early fifties, but she looked a good ten years younger. She was fit and muscular, with the aggressive, almost menacing vim of an enthusiastic tennis player. Her blue eyes were bright and she wore her blond hair cut so crisply you'd swear she had it done every day. It would have been easy to mistake her for the sales rep of a vitamin company. But her wholesome, benign appearance was deceptive. In professional matters, she was brusque, shrewd, and challenging. As I had so recently been reminded, less mentor than interrogator.

"I had a stroke of luck," I began, and told her how I'd recently been looking for a part-time job to supplement my income when I happened upon an ad seeking a reader for a woman with impaired vision. Not without some pride, I explained how I'd managed to figure out the identity of that woman. I went on to say that I'd gone for an interview at once and learned I would be reading something of great importance: unpublished journals that Weil had kept in the 1960s.

I skipped over the fact that I'd presented myself to her as no more than a former English major. I also thought it best to omit the content of what we'd read thus far, saying only that, in a very dramatic—in fact, a sensational—manner, it threw unprecedented light on the inner workings of her mind, especially with regard to *Vengeance*, as well as previously unrevealed aspects of her personal history. I have read enough novels to know it's best to arouse the reader's curiosity first and deliver the goods later.

Professor Probst listened attentively, ignoring the constant flow of students around us, but said nothing until I finished—no exclamation of surprise, no congratulations on my good fortune.

"Extraordinary," was all she said. Then she checked her watch and hurried off. It wasn't until I was on the train downtown, reflecting on how subdued her reaction had been, that I remembered the non-disclosure agreement.

Disappointed by Probst's subdued reception of my earthshaking news, I wandered down to the Windrush to eat an uninspiring dinner of Progresso tomato soup and baked beans. Then I went to D'Agostino's and bought some fresh vegetables, fruit, yogurt, and so on, put them away in 10A's dingy kitchen, answered a few emails, washed out a pair of woolen socks, and finally, deflated after a day during which Anne and I had made no progress, got into bed at ten o'clock. I returned to *The Bell*—thank God Murdoch wrote not just a lot of books, but a lot of long books—and turned out the light after a couple of chapters.

As I drifted off, a little vision appeared in my mind's eye of two foxes racing side by side through a snowstorm, their red fur frosted by the fast-falling flakes, their bodies all muscle, their black noses twitching, nostrils flaring, legs a blur. Two vixens intent on getting their needs met. Anne—Anne as she had been in 1963—and me.

At 12:30, I woke from a nightmare in which Tim and Professor Probst—a very unlikely combination—almost came to blows outside Columbia's campus gates. I immediately forgot every aspect of the dream except those details. Hoping to shake it out of my head—for all its weirdness, it revived in me a piercing desire to be near Tim, to hold his hand—I turned on the light and again picked up *The Bell*.

Then another idea came to me, so obvious I couldn't believe it hadn't been my first. This was an hour when, despite her fear of a cold, Anne might be awake and out in the living room for one of her frequent midnight intermissions—and ready, perhaps, to talk. It occurred to me that I ought to set my alarm for one a.m. every night just to check, though I never did.

I put on my robe and slippers and looked down the corridor. Sure enough, through the dining-room archway, I could see a light on in the living room. I hesitated, uncertain whether to go first to the kitchen and put a cup of milk into the antique microwave or simply walk into the living room. I decided the former would give her some warning that I was up and around. A few minutes later, the warm cup in my hand, I stuck my head through the archway, as if to peek discreetly in.

This time she was seated on the love seat facing me. I had a prompt sense-memory of sitting on its broken springs and wondered how they suited her achy bones. I could see that my plan had worked, that she'd heard the beeps of the microwave and hadn't been startled by my arrival.

"Hot milk?" I offered, holding out the mug.

"Not for me, thank you."

"Oh, yes, I'm sorry. I forgot you said milk doesn't agree with you." I dared to walk a few steps into the room, even though she hadn't invited me. Then, as her silence continued, I asked, "Are you all right?"

A look of uncertainty passed briefly over her face.

"Yes. I think so. Yes. I do think I'm feeling better." And finally, "Would you care to sit down?"

"Sure. If I'm not disturbing you," I added demurely.

"Not at all."

As I settled onto the love seat across from her, the mug cradled in my hands, she lifted a Kindle from her lap. "I've given up on that annoying historical novel. Now I'm rereading *The Aspern Papers*. Do you know it?"

For a long moment, I sat mute. Struck dumb, horrified; I wished I were back in bed with my nightmare. *The Aspern Papers*! It couldn't be a coincidence. She was onto me, if only subliminally. She had sensed my intention. Unless—the consoling thought flashed into my mind—unless it was simply the fact of her being an elderly woman with papers she didn't want anyone to see. That could have made her think of Henry James's novel, inspired her to reread it. Couldn't it?

She smiled into my silence, the pleased smile I'd come to know. Smiling always made her look much younger than she usually did. The tails of her eyebrows lifted; the skin over her cheekbones tautened, bringing them out; her mouth curved in a way that made her drooping neck seem somehow irrelevant.

"Maybe not?" she suggested in the light, dry voice she sometimes used.

"I know the title," I managed at last.

"Well then, if you like Henry James at all, you might want to read it. It's short."

"I'll try it," I said.

"I'm glad to put it down for a while now and talk, though," she went on. "It's very tiresome to have to magnify the print so much. By the time I've made the letters large enough for me to read, only thirty-odd words fit on each page. Not that there are really pages on a Kindle, of course," she added after a pause.

I shook my head, hoping to convey outraged sympathy. "So maddening," I said. "So *mean*."

"Oh, I suppose I'm better off than your mother," she said. Even this second time, it took me a moment to remember why she would say this. Luckily, she hadn't paused for me to agree. Instead, "I'm sure she's been very grateful to have you to read aloud to her," she went on. "I know I feel most fortunate to have you reading to me."

Like Wordsworth's, my heart leapt up.

"Tell me your ambitions, Beth," she continued, leaning forward. "You said once that you'd like to do copywriting for a good cause, but is that really the extent of your goals? You're very smart. You have a degree in English, an interest in literature, and some knowledge of it. Wouldn't you like to build on that, go into the publishing world, perhaps, be more than merely a casual reader of books?"

I started to sweat.

"There aren't many jobs in publishing these days," I said. "Not conventional book publishing, anyway. And the entry-level pay is dismal."

"Writing, then?" she offered, her low voice even lower than usual. "I understand that e-books have made even self-publishing a perfectly respectable option."

"But not a lucrative one," I rebutted. "Except in a very few cases." The words "Writing, then?" had sounded sly in her mouth. I wondered if she could see the perspiration now filming my forehead and comforted myself with the knowledge that she almost certainly could not.

"Besides, I'm not sure I'm a very good writer," I continued. "I mean, I'm not like you." (It had occurred to me after moving in that I might do well to tell her I'd decided to try reading one of her books, but I wasn't entirely sure I would have the sangfroid to carry off such gross, blatant misdirection.) "I've never been able to write fiction. I don't even understand how novelists come up with their ideas."

She persisted.

"There are other kinds of writing. Critical, historical, biographical." She paused and drew out the next word. "Scholarly."

Now I was almost ready to jump up and shout, "Stop torturing me! Just spit it out!" But how could she know? I had been so careful!

"Does that interest you at all, non-fiction? Maybe you'd go back to school and get an advanced degree. You're certainly sharp enough for it. Intellectually, I mean."

Her voice had dropped yet lower on the word "sharp" and my anxiety tightened another notch. Sharp like Becky Sharp. Shrewd. Selfish. My breath started to quicken. The truth was that ever since I'd read *Vanity Fair* in Miss Hart's English class, Becky Sharp had been something of a role model for me. Not morally, of course, but reading about her made me realize that, even though I was a girl, I did not have to be sweet, weak, puling Amelia Sedley. Nor did I have to carry forever my fear of my parents' volatile moods. I had a choice in life. *Vanity Fair* had given me a transformative jolt—and now here I was, all these years later, writing a dissertation about how novels can empower women.

"I'd encourage you to consider it," Anne was continuing. "I've done some teaching—graduate seminars and so on. I think you might do very well as a graduate student."

"I'm not sure a higher degree in literature is a ticket to employment," I ventured.

"Maybe not. Still, you never know. And—well, you're doubtless too young to have heard it, but there was once an ad campaign with the slogan 'A mind is a terrible thing to waste.' I believe that."

At last, some friendly god had smiled upon me and given me words to turn the conversation.

"What was the ad for?" I asked, and she told me about the United Negro College Fund. Because I already knew this, by the time she finished explaining, I was ready with an observation about the changing terms for minorities—how the word "Negro," once respectful, had become offensive; how the NAACP, important as it was, still had the words "colored people" embedded in its name, words that so chillingly conjured Jim Crow and apartheid, and—and yet, I went on only slightly incoherently, "people of color" was now emerging as a favored locution . . .

And so on.

As I clung to this topic, she joined me—murmured assent, mildly demurred, added her mite. But when at last I ran out of ideas, she returned to her earlier theme.

"You see? The way you dissected all that, the history, the language, the shifting culture behind it—that's the kind of work you should be doing, don't you think?" Again I felt a chill—could she possibly have guessed that that was exactly what I was doing? Then she yawned and said, "I think I'm ready to go back to bed."

She had set her cane by the side of the love seat and now turned to take hold of it. She gave me a last look before pushing herself to her feet. In her face was something I'd not seen before: approval, it seemed to me, as if I were a house that she had decided, after some hesitation, to buy. Then she stood and made her halting, three-footed way to bed.

TEN

I woke the next day with a tight chest. It had taken me over an hour to fall asleep following my talk with Anne. My mind was seething, obsessed with the fear that I'd aroused suspicion in her, wondering what she might have meant by bringing up *The Aspern Papers*, even what her use of the word "sharp" might signify. Checking my phone, I noticed the calendar icon and realized that a week had passed since I'd moved in. I wrote her a check for forty dollars.

I found her already in the kitchen and asked if she was still feeling better.

"Yes," she said, but her manner invited no further conversation. This was entirely typical of her behavior in the morning, I knew that, yet it seemed to me her tone had been unusually abrupt, cold. She didn't say whether she felt able to listen while I read to her today and I didn't ask, lest I receive another brusque reply. Despite what she'd told me last night about my value as a reader, I wondered if she might have changed her mind about having me live here, if she would ask me to move out. I took my coffee into my bedroom and worried nonstop until, finally, she knocked on my door and told me she'd meet me in the living room at ten. Then I had breakfast and made my way to her.

Check in hand, I crept in, dreading that I might find an empty chair after all. To my relief, though, she was at her desk as usual, the journal we'd been reading before her. She said good morning, which she had neglected to do earlier, and added that she believed she'd decisively beaten her incipient cold. I sat down and handed over the check I'd prepared. She glanced at it, smiled a little smile, and put it into the locking drawer. She had taken it without saying it would be my last; my whole body relaxed. Calmer, I opened the journal and found the place where we'd stopped on Friday.

The next few pages were filled with afterthoughts about her assignation with Greg. These veered from wild yearnings to be at his studio again to regrets about having gone there in the first place. She wrestled with the idea that she ought to end this "madness" now. She had been unfaithful only once; it was still an isolated incident. It would fade into the past, be absorbed into her marriage without Steve ever knowing about it. These passages, however, were always followed within a few days, if not hours, by others that described her desperate, gut-deep longing to surrender to the gravitational pull of desire—desire in its purest form—and taste again its exquisite fulfillment.

I read these parts to Anne but only briefly summarized many paragraphs between them, paragraphs that recorded reflections and events of a much more mundane variety. There were further struggles with the recalcitrant *And Sometimes Y*, two nights when she was awakened by leg cramps, yet more meals she cooked, hurried preparation when she was asked at the last minute to pinch-hit for an ailing Violet Prentice (a name I'd never heard and was later unable to track down) by moderating a panel called "Where Do Characters Come From?" at the Society Library. On the day following this panel ("I think I did well in the circumstances," she noted) there was at last a chance meeting with Greg, though not of the kind she hoped.

Thursday April 4, 11 p.m.

Beware of wishes; you may get what you want. That was today's lesson.

Last night, on our way out to see "Whatever Happened to Baby Jane?," Steve and I ran into Greg in the lobby. Steve recognized him from the Reeveses' party, said hello, and paused to make polite chit-chat. Had he seen Len and Amy lately? How had he met them in the first place? Did he and his wife like their new apartment? Had they gotten to know any other Windrush residents?

His taking the time to talk was unlike him and I worried again that I had said Greg's name in a dream or otherwise, somehow, given myself away. His last question particularly disconcerted me. Steve is so cool, so much in command of himself, his manner, his behavior!

Greg handled the encounter better than I did. I barely kept myself from letting go of Steve's arm to move toward him. I tried to look at him just as I would any new neighbor I'd met once or twice, but I felt my pulses quickening and had to drop my eyes. Thank God some woman on her way to a party in the building interrupted us to ask Greg if he could possibly be the famous pianist Gregory Morris. We left them together.

Steve, who had carried on the entire conversation himself—I never said a word except hi and bye—commented as we went up the block, "Nice guy, but a strange guy, don't you think? Uncomfortable. Anxious. If I were deposing him, I'd think he was hiding something."

"Hiding something!" My heart seemed to freeze, but I tried to hear the words objectively, to recognize that what struck my ear so alarmingly was no more than the product of my own guilty fantasy that he has guessed something.

In a steadier voice than I'd expected to be able to muster, I agreed, then joked, "Maybe they really, really don't like their apartment" and turned the conversation to the movie, saying I'd had to stop Peggy Bockhauser from giving away the plot when I saw her a few days ago. Steve said Tom Land had done the same thing at the office, and from there it wasn't hard to pass on to other innocent topics. I hardly followed what we said, speaking mechanically as my mind careered between whether Steve has found me out and what Greg thought of how I'd behaved. Surely I must, must stop this thing in its tracks. My whole life is here—and it occurs to me as I write this that Greg and Susan Morris may be our neighbors for decades. What am I thinking?

"God, that day. I'd forgotten about it," Anne said, as I finished her account of this chance meeting. "I hope we're getting close to— to when I did continue to see him."

And in fact this proved to be not far away, just a few pages later. I read aloud:

Monday April 8, 8:30 p.m.

This afternoon, after so much anticipation, so much eagerness and fear and tormenting ambivalence, I went to Greg's studio for our second rendezvous. For all that hand-wringing, I went as if I'd never had a second thought. I flew there like an arrow, like a homing pigeon—and what's more, with my diaphragm in.

As for Greg, he seemed really to have had no second thoughts at all. I arrived to find the curtains already closed against the day. Even before we said a word, he began to take off my clothes. He did it slowly, in silence, turning me to unhook my bra, observing every inch he uncovered until I stood naked before him. It was unspeakably arousing. That he was also aroused became plain as soon as he removed his own clothes. I had wondered if I should take them off for him, as he had for me, but he went to it so quickly that I had no chance.

Still without a word or a kiss, he took my hand and led me to the daybed. The studio was cold again, but he didn't pull up the covers. Instead, he sat and scrutinized me as I lay full-length before him. Finally, I reached up and brought him to me. He stretched himself against my body, still for a moment, looking into my eyes, then slithered down until his head was between my legs. He hardly needed to do more than kiss me there before I came. Came rather loudly, but what did it matter? The studios are soundproof.

Then he wriggled back up to put his face to mine, rose on his arms and came down, more or less falling on me. He entered me a moment later and stayed there, moving with more and more force, till I felt well and truly fucked.

After he'd come (with quite a lot of noise himself), he lay against me for a whole minute, catching his breath before saying, "Hello."

It was so funny just then, the funniest "Hello" I ever heard. We exploded with laughter, rocked with it, so much so that I almost fell off the bed. When he caught me and pulled me back to him, I was astonished to feel him already hard again. He slid his hand down my body and felt to make sure I was ready for him. In he came, this time moving slowly and looking directly into my eyes.

Then we were quiet for a long while, just listening to our own breathing. How odd to think that all this time, nothing had been said but that single "Hello." Eventually, I began to wonder how long it had been since I arrived. I got up and walked over to look at my watch, which he had left near the pile of clothes on the piano bench. Today, I walked brazenly, naked though I was. It was three o'clock; I had been there almost an hour.

"I need to take a shower," I said, "and then I'll go. It was awful the other day, leaving here with no time to recover, and your smell all over me."

He grinned like an animal reveling in having marked his turf. I went into the bathroom. It is very small and purely utilitarian, with the pink and black tiles fashionable thirty years ago. They've lost their shine, and the grout between them is yellow and crumbling. The shower is tiny, a triangle in a corner with a cloudy glass door. No shampoo, a dry, cracked, and not especially clean bar of soap. I turned on the water (a paltry, lukewarm spray), put my face up into it and was startled to feel a cold rush of air. Greg had crept in behind me. He crammed himself into the stall, how I don't know; it's so very small.

Then, from out of nowhere, it came to me to wonder if he's done this before. Until now, absurdly, it had never even occurred to me he might have had other women up to his studio. What a fool, when he's so widely known, so gifted, such a celebrity. And his charm, his easy seductiveness. Now I asked myself about that very ease. He has made me feel as if his need to be with me were an unprecedented compulsion, something entirely unexpected, irresistible to him, uniquely provoked by my qualities, as if I were the great exception in his life. But after all, has he really shown any of the shock I feel, the surprise at my own behavior? On the contrary, he came straight to me, sure of himself.

I froze. How could I have failed to think of all this? I wondered. A man who travels constantly without his wife. Who is in the public eye all the time, admired, applauded, adored on stages all over the world. He is a star. Women must swarm over him.

I shoved these images out of my mind as soon as they came into it. At the least, I told myself, even if he's slept with many women, his feelings for me are different—a real bolt from the blue, a true coup de foudre. *That he feels out of control of his desire, as shaken by it as I am. And before I left, I was sure I was right.*

There were a few lines left blank here. I looked up to tell Anne and found her faded eyes were tearing up. She said nothing. After a pause, I went on.

Cut off five minutes ago as Steve came down the hall and knocked on my door. All he wanted was to be reminded what night we're going to the Halyards' for cocktails. Thankfully, he only poked his head in, too briefly to see my agitation. My heart has settled down now, and so—and so, back to the shower.

Greg reached around me and took the soap out of my hand. Then he slid it over my shoulder blades (there was no washcloth), rubbing in gentle circles before moving on to another spot. The nape of my neck. My spine, the small of my back and—and on all over me to my feet. Then he turned me around—the gap between us was so slight that even looking down we couldn't see each other's bodies—and repeated his downward transit. Even at my most sensitive points, his touch was exploratory and tender more than erotic. Tender. He was very tender.

I didn't try to return the favor, just said, "I have to go."

He slipped out of the stall and handed me the single towel in the room, a bath towel on the small side and not very fresh.

"Dry off in there," he said. "I'll get your coat so you don't freeze when you come out." Still dripping himself, he returned with it and wrapped it tight around me. I suddenly remembered the delicious, luxurious sensation of being wrapped in a sun-warmed towel by my father after I'd climbed, teeth chattering, out of a hotel swimming pool. How old was I? I must have been very little, because the towel seemed as large as a blanket.

When I'd gotten back into my clothes, Greg offered me a cup of coffee. But I didn't want to stay too long. That is, I did want to stay, but I knew I'd regret it later, so I told him no.

"Anyway, I should let you practice," I said.

"Unfortunately true. I leave for Philadelphia tomorrow afternoon, for a rehearsal Friday morning."

"*Then I'm off.*"

He helped me into my coat, kissing my earlobe, then my cheek, my nose, my mouth. How exactly I remember all this! By now we were facing each other, of course, and I'd started to button up to go into the cold—I always forget how cold it is at this time of year—when he put a tentative hand on mine to stop me. He looked at the floor and said in a low voice, "Forgive me. Maybe I'm asking too much, but is there a chance you would meet me there, so we could spend a whole night together?" He sounded like a schoolboy, shy and afraid I would take offense. "Would you like that?"

"I would like it very much."

Suddenly, he began to cry. Real tears, copious enough that three rolled down his cheek.

"Thank God," he said. "Thank you."

I smiled and brushed the tears away. It was at that moment that my sudden, mad suspicion that he is some sort of callow playboy disappeared. Perhaps it was the hesitancy with which he suggested the idea, confessed to his desire, as if he really feared his request might offend me. Perhaps it was the tears. Whatever it was, it was a huge relief.

"But can you think of a way to get out of town so suddenly? A discreet way?" he went on.

A plan had already come into my mind, as readymade and detailed as if I'd been keeping it in my back pocket for just such an occasion.

"As it happens, I have a close friend in Philadelphia, an old friend, a childhood friend. She's single, just divorced, no kids, and Steve knows she's been very low lately. If she needed someone to spend a day or two with her,

be there for her as she dealt with—oh, a medical emergency, say—he would never question my going to help her. I think she'd agree to cover for me," I added.

I didn't like the clarity of my own last words. They made it all too plain that I would be betraying Steve. I would have to lie to him, not by omission but outright, something I haven't needed to do so far. Still, I said them.

And yet, the moment they were out, a hot flame of resentment rose in my chest. What right did Steve have to imprison me, to commandeer my time? Why should I be accountable to him for my every movement? This was no more than a sort of defensive self-justification, I realize, to excuse myself from blame. Steve is not a bad man—he is a good man, if a somewhat unimaginative one—and I doubt he would ever be unfaithful to me. As for "imprisoning me," he's never done anything remotely like it. Never said a word to discourage, let alone forbid, my stays at Yaddo or Bread Loaf, never objected to my frequent (and innocent) dinners with Matt Bianchi, never tried to prevent me from writing when he had a day off from work, or even when we were in Paris on vacation.

As I read this paragraph, I thought of the early scene in *Vengeance* when Howard Clark explodes with fury at Catherine for refusing to quit her job. "You do this and people think my wife has to work!" he shouts, stalking around and around her as she sits on their living-room couch. "Is that why you do it? On purpose to humiliate me? Just stay at home, for Chrissake! Just stay home, Cathy. How hard is that to do?"

Later, he blames her miscarriage on the stress of the office job she'd insisted on keeping and, still later, finally persuades her to quit when she is—very briefly—pregnant after the previous miscarriage.

In this passage of her journal, I saw that Anne was capable of conjuring anger at Stephen Pace when it suited her. But could pure imagination have sustained the torrent of rage in her book? Questions flew back and forth through my head as I continued reading.

Happy as a child, Greg threw his arms around me. He squeezed me almost painfully, then loosened his grip and kissed me on the mouth before whispering, "Just to let you know, I'll be there three nights—Thursday night, Friday night, and Saturday, of course. Sunday afternoon I have a date for coffee with an old teacher of mine and then I come back to New York. So you can pick the night that works best for you. Or—" the whisper dropped till I could hardly hear him—"you could come for all three."

"Three," I echoed. "Three nights." It was unnecessary to say more.

"Of course you'd be alone a lot," he went on. "You couldn't come to the rehearsal, and that afternoon, I'm scheduled to eat lunch and play a little music for fun with some friends in the Berlin Phil. You couldn't visit me after the concert. We couldn't be seen together anywhere." Almost apologetically, he added, "People recognize me."

I should have realized, at once, this would be a problem but I hadn't. A lurch of disappointment ran through me. I said nothing about it, however. Instead, "I'll find plenty to keep me busy on my own," I told him. "I go there to see my friend now and then, but I haven't been to the Barnes in years. Or the Academy of Fine Arts. For that matter, I can really go and visit my friend, or just take a bus tour of the city; I've never even seen the Liberty Bell. But what about Susan? Won't she go with you?"

"Susan leaves tonight for a week in Taos with an old friend from Juilliard," he said. He had stepped back and let go of me, but our faces were almost touching and his voice was still low. "She often uses my absences to get out of town herself. It's not that my career doesn't interest her. It's just painful for her to see me in the spotlight since she's had to stop performing."

I found that I didn't give a damn about Susan. I was almost happy about her affliction if it kept her out of my way. What is happening to me? I've known myself to be ambitious, competitive, even ruthless, but not, I think, cruel.

"So we'll have time to ourselves—plenty of time," he went on. "Every night, and most of Saturday besides."

I nodded, smiled. Looking back, it astonishes me that all these plans were thrown together in a matter of minutes, as if we were a pair of practiced thieves interrupted mid-crime agreeing to flee in different directions and meet up later. And aren't we thieves? Thieves and con artists, swindling the people who trust us most.

ELEVEN

After the paragraph in which Anne branded herself and her lover criminals, she left a few lines blank. When I looked up to say so, she raised a hand to stop me from resuming. I was grateful for the breather. For several reasons, I found the morning's passages difficult to read aloud. One reason is obvious: they were so extremely explicit, so completely intimate, and there sat its author, not two yards away from me. But the scene also provoked insidious thoughts in me—thoughts about what Tim may or may not have done with his "other woman" before he ended our relationship.

With the journal resting open in my lap, I waited for her to say something, unsure whether she wanted only a pause or was ready to end the reading for the day. She took off her glasses and a long minute went by while she sat very still, head bowed as if she were inspecting the surface of her pretty desk. I took advantage of that minute to reread what she'd written apropos of her own deception. "Thieves and con artists." The phrase reverberated uncomfortably inside me.

As for "What is happening to me?" that was, more or less, my own recent question about myself. Was I ambitious? *Check.* Competitive? *Check.* Ruthless? Not until lately. It interested me that Weil would write that she had occasionally been ruthless. For me, this was the first time. But as to being cruel—no, I insisted to myself. No, I did not feel cruel. I felt I was on a mission, and like people on a mission, I felt righteous.

When at last she looked up again, all the animation had gone out of her face. Her eyes were dull, cheeks drawn, shoulders slumped. Even her martial spine was curved, touching the back of her chair. Clearly, the passion of the tryst she'd just revisited had been superseded in her mind by the final self-accusation.

"Go ahead and read the rest of the entry," she said, voice flat, listless, as if she were an admitted murderess in the dock.

I complied.

Midnight

At nine, phoned Ginny from my study, with the door closed and in the hushed voice of a conspirator. Which I am, and am now making her as well. She was reluctant but agreed to have a sudden attack of appendicitis Wednesday morning, to have called an ambulance for herself and been taken to the hospital. They operated within hours but it turned out it had ruptured, complicating matters and making her recovery precarious. (I know about all this because it happened to Pauline Cornish, of course.) Now, she would "tell" me, she was just out of the recovery room and calling to beg me to come and help her. She needed someone to deal with the doctors, to make sure they followed her case with attention, see that the nurses took good care of her, and help her figure out whatever decisions might have to be made farther down the road.

I imagine it was easier for her to join me in my deception because she hasn't seen Steve in a very long time. I always go to see her, somehow; she never comes here. Steve is almost theoretical to her, a character I sometimes mention. Moreover (and this is a relief to us both), she's very unlikely to be put to the test. I'll say I'm staying at her apartment and call Steve daily. I'll tell him she has no phone in her hospital room. I suppose he might someday come to suspect the whole story and ask her to confirm it, but she can do even that in a pinch. She's not a bad liar. After all, she lied to me about the state of her marriage for years.

Still, it's a nasty thing to ask of her and I feel especially bad because I don't, in fact, plan to get together with her at all while I'm there. This is partly because I think it would be even harder to lie to Steve if I do see her, healthy and whole as she is, but more because I want to keep every possible minute free for Greg. I'm ashamed of myself, but the truth is I'm too eager to be with him to care.

I've mentioned a man named "Greg" to Ginny before, but have been careful not to tell her who he is, and she hasn't asked.

There was another blank line here but I didn't bother to mention it.

I've just read over the above. I should have written it in invisible ink. I should lock it in a vault. If Steve were to see it, he would know without thinking who "G." is. Then God help us.

Again a blank line.

On the subject of Steve, he wanted to have sex tonight and I went along as (almost) always in order to behave normally, even though it made me feel like a whore. (Now there's a sentence.) Much worse than that, I have a chilling feeling that I really did murmur Greg's name as I fell asleep. Did I? If so, did Steve hear me? With another man, I would think surely not, or he would have reacted. But Steve can be so controlled. He stores up information until he's had a chance to analyze it, a lawyer's habit.

God I miss Greg. Already, even though I saw him this afternoon. I want to hear his voice. I long for the smell of his hair, its singular, tangy scent, to feel his hands on my wrists as he reared up over me. The power of his mismatched eyes on mine, on my body. I keep saying to myself that I'll see him soon, and not for hours but for days. Yet it isn't soon enough.

"That's all for that entry," I told her.

Anne's eyes turned to me from her apparent scrutiny of the delicate desk. Her face had regained its expressiveness and she put her glasses on again. She was smiling the small, nostalgic smile I had noticed in the past, and I saw once again the hauntingly beautiful film star she might have been. After a moment, she announced that she wished to end today's reading here.

The next morning, to my alarm, I did not find her when I went to the kitchen. Though it was a Sunday, Marta appeared at ten and reported that Mrs. Anne was once more feeling unwell, that she had asked her to come in and help her as she spent the day in bed.

I offered to go out and get chicken soup, cold remedies, a humidifier, anything that might be of use. In part, I was still curious to see her room. In part, I was eager to ingratiate myself further. But most of all, I am glad to be able to say, I was genuinely concerned about her as a fellow human. I was sorry she was suffering, and anxious lest this cold or flu or infection or whatever it was carry her off forever—and not only because I would then lose access to the journals.

In the last few days, I had come a long way from my fantasy of conking her on the head. If I had once thought of her as mere prey to be devoured, I saw her now as a truly remarkable woman. Half-blind, shut in, constantly in pain, she was still curious and engaged with life. She endured with grace and even humor the mortification of revealing her most intimate doings to a stranger. I did still see her, in a sense, as my quarry, but I also thought she was gallant. Should I live to such a great age, I hope I have even half her strength of mind.

The next morning, Marta came in early, at eight o'clock. She hovered noiselessly around the house, peeking often into Anne's bedroom to make sure she didn't need anything, offering tea, soup, a heating pad, cough syrup, fetching whatever she asked for. I went up to campus for the afternoon to prepare for class the next day and returned to 10A that evening to find her still there. Anne had been awake for only a few very brief intervals during the day, she told me; all the same, she stayed until ten p.m. and returned at eight the next morning.

During the night, in her absence, I heard nothing from Anne. But I dared to open her door slightly and left mine open as well. I slept uneasily, waking often to listen for her. I missed Tim. I felt worried and alone and at some point woke from a nightmare I have now and then in which my father slams his arm across my mother's face. That's all there is to the dream. I'll never know for sure, but I suspect it's something that really happened, and that it ends so quickly because I don't want to remember what happened afterward.

After three days in bed, three days during which Marta came early and left late—and I, even later, shuttled various journals to and from the magic glass-fronted cabinet and photographed their contents in my room—Anne finally reappeared in the kitchen, shaky but determined to resume her morning rituals. She dismissed Marta's offer to make her coffee and insisted on making her own and, as before, some for me as well. She sat at the dining-room table with a mug and a piece of cinnamon toast, reading something on her Kindle. At nine, she walked slowly to my room, looked in, and said we'd continue our readings again at the usual hour. Today, however, if I had no objections, we would meet in her bedroom. She was better—and sure she had nothing contagious, she added—but still weak and inclined to stay in bed.

I had no objections.

"Very good. I'll see you in an hour. If I happen to be asleep, just leave me be and we'll aim for later, if you're available. Or tomorrow if not."

"Of course."

I was glad to find her awake and composed when I went to her at ten. I entered her bedroom with a feeling almost of triumph. Finally, I was in! The room was large and very warm. In a queen-size bed covered with a white comforter, Anne sat propped against three pillows. Peach-colored velvet curtains had been partly drawn back to admit the light. A pair of armchairs covered in peach-and-yellow brocade flanked the double doors of her closet. Facing her stood a tall bureau and a heavy wall unit that held a phonograph and hundreds of record albums. Wall-to-wall carpet, white and plush around the edges but a depressing gray in the middle, spread across the floor like dirty snow.

Anne asked me to go to the dining room and fetch a chair for myself; the armchairs in here were too far away and too heavy to drag to her bedside. I went and returned with my awkward burden, making sure to look around no more than was normal for someone orienting herself in an unfamiliar room.

"Put it here, close to me," Anne said, waving a hand in the direction of the walnut nightstand beside her, one of a pair on either side of the bed. On its shining surface were a lamp, a clock, a phone with comically huge push-buttons and a backlit dial, yet another magnifying glass, Nyquil, nasal spray, a box of Kleenex, a bottle of Advil, a thermometer, her reading glasses, several prescription bottles whose labels I longed to inspect, and a glass of water with a little matching carafe to refill it. Beneath all this was a shallow drawer fitted with a lock.

I set the chair next to the nightstand and sat down while Anne produced a key from under the pillows beside her. It was a real key, I noticed, small, but with teeth. She unlocked the drawer and withdrew the journal we'd been reading before she got sick. I wondered with annoyance why she needed so many locked drawers. I certainly didn't have any. Neither had Tim, nor the Smolnikovs, nor even my parents, who habitually kept a number of things (drugs, needles, booze) that really should have been locked up.

Today, for the first time, she took off the glasses she usually wore and put on the ones she used for reading. She opened the notebook herself and glanced in.

"Can't make out a damned word." She shut it, handed it to me, and switched glasses again. "Go ahead and look for Greg. No, wait. First close the door."

I did so—no doubt she didn't want Marta to overhear us—and returned to her bedside. I'd begun to page through the journal when she spoke again.

"If I should happen to close my eyes and drift off, just make a note of where we are and tiptoe out," she said. And then, as fast as it had been born, a new hope died in me as she patted the pillow beside her and added, "Leave the notebook under here."

"Sure."

I skimmed ahead. The journal recommenced on Wednesday, the day after she and Greg made their hasty plans. Anne had written a lengthy entry at 5:30 that afternoon. I read aloud a passage about her growing anticipation, the tone alternating between an almost childish elation and stern reminders to herself that the unaccustomed, luxurious time and freedom she and Greg would have in Philadelphia might just possibly dilute the concentrated passion they'd felt before (or rather, that he had felt before, since she was sure her own would only increase).

She also reminded herself that, as he'd warned her, she'd be alone a lot. She had called the Barnes and made an appointment for a visit early Thursday afternoon, after her arrival and before Greg's. She had toyed with the idea of seeing Ginny on Friday after all, while Greg would be rehearsing at the concert hall, but discarded it. She would just go to the Academy of Fine Arts. No matter how well she filled her time, she reflected, it would be humiliating to have to keep away from him, to have to hide herself from his colleagues, especially at the concert itself.

Next came an account of a second call to Ginny, to rehearse with her the details of the story Anne was going to tell Steve—the elaborate, brazen falsehood she was going to tell him—which Ginny must remember as well, just in case. Then more notes on mundane matters—Steve's laundry, a wine stain found on a tablecloth—which I read to myself.

Soon, though, came a new entry, written that night. I read it aloud.

Wednesday April 3, 10:30 p.m.

The moment Steve got home from work today, I went into the foyer and told him something urgent had come up, something I needed to discuss with him. He asked if it could wait a few minutes, took off his coat and hat, loosened his tie, put away his briefcase, went into the dining room, and poured himself his usual Scotch before coming to find me in the kitchen, where I stood slicing mushrooms and onions. I put the knife down and we went to the living room together.

"Listen, Ginny called an hour ago. She's at the Pennsylvania Hospital," I began. "Her appendix burst yesterday. She had no idea what was wrong with her when it started—who thinks they have appendicitis in their forties? But the pain was so bad that she finally called an ambulance. They took out everything they could, but the rupture caused a very bad infection. She'll have to be in the hospital for weeks, but the first days are the most dangerous and she may need emergency care again.

"So anyway, she was calling to ask me—to beg me—to come to Philly and watch over her. Keep her company, you know. Make sure the doctors are monitoring her and doing what they should, go to the nursing station if they ignore a call from her, get her a private nurse if she needs one. All that—you know what hospitals are like. She has friends there, of course, but no one she feels comfortable asking to do all this. I can sleep at her house, so that's no problem."

By now I'd begun to worry I was saying too much, explaining what was obvious in an abnormal and noticeable way. I throttled back.

"So I have to go there as soon as I can. I couldn't say no. I'm sorry to leave you alone for I don't know how long. Till she stabilizes, at least."

Even as I said it, I was amazed at how easily it all tumbled out. It was a good lie, a well-chosen lie. Steve knows that Ginny has been my closest friend since kindergarten, and it's natural I'd want to fly to her aid in this emergency, natural she would want me there. And he knows how alone she's felt since her divorce. He agreed right away, even offering to reserve a train ticket for me (hurriedly, I said I'd done this already) and accompany me to Penn Station (no need, I'd be fine). I told him there was a meatloaf in the freezer and a container of leftover lamb stew to keep him going while I was gone. He said not to worry, that he'll manage. He can easily go out to eat after work, and there was always Chinese takeout if he felt like eating at home. Why even finish making dinner tonight? he added. Why not order in right now, so I can use the evening to get ready? His kindness killed me, just as Shakespeare says.

I did make dinner, of course, and tried to keep the conversation on him and his day rather than risk having to lie in even more detail. When we'd finished eating, he spread his work out on the dining room table—he is thoroughly swept up in this Covington case—but not before asking if there was anything at all he could do to help. Everything he said reminded me why I married him, how solid he is, how good, how solicitous he can be, why I agreed to share my life with him even though I knew—and I think he knew—that I was never fully, romantically "in love" with him. He has always loved me more. Writing this makes me think of the line in Middlemarch where Eliot says that for a husband, the certainty that his wife will never love him much is easier to bear than the fear that he will fall out of love with her. I believe there's some truth there, but—oh, I doubt Eliot had in mind a wife who flat-out betrays her husband! I've never felt lower than I did this evening, meaner, more despicable, not when I went to bed with Greg, not when I made love with Steve that same night.

Here Anne made a sound that I first took for a grunt of

discomfort, the grunt of a sick person starting to feel worse. I paused but soon saw my mistake. Her eyes were narrowed, her jaw set, her face unusually fierce, but she wasn't in the kind of pain I'd imagined. Her gaze was fixed on nothing of significance—a random spot in the air, it seemed. Or perhaps something of great significance: the past.

TWELVE

Anne dismissed me after I'd read the account of her lying to Steve. Five days passed before we resumed.

The night of that reading, the illness that had seemed to be waning returned in force, and Anne went back to spending all her time in her bed, where Marta obsessively waited on her. Only once did Anne emerge from her bedroom. It was the second day after our session. I was feeling restless and had decided to go out for a cup of coffee, but when I went into the foyer to get my coat, I found her standing, leaning as always on her cane, bundled up in her own coat, a fur hat, gloves, and an enormous scarf. Marta was holding her arm. I retreated at once into the living room and listened while the front door opened and closed.

I returned to my room and waited several hours for them to come back, finishing up some notes I'd been keeping on our reading sessions and also photographing a journal I'd taken from her study the night before. (I also, I admit, made a quick foray into Anne's bedroom to see if her nightstand was unlocked, or the key lying somewhere, forgotten—but no.) I was in my room, still snapping pictures, when the front door opened and they made their slow way inside. Anne went back to bed right away; I hid my camera and the notebook and wandered out of my room, hoping to run into Marta and learn where they'd been. It was soon clear that she had been looking for me.

"Dr. Braudy told her to come and see him today," she said, or rather, erupted, bursting with the need to share with someone else what was happening to Mrs. Anne. "Her fever is higher than I realized. Maybe the thermometer here doesn't work, I don't know, but he's afraid she'll get pneumonia. He took some blood from her and told her that she will be fine, but when he left her alone to get dressed, he waved to me to come into his office. He said her heart is weaker. It's always been weak, I think I told you that before, but now it's much worse. He's not sure yet what is making her so sick, but she must not get pneumonia. That's the main thing. Pneumonia could kill her. She has to rest. Rest and drink fluids and eat to keep her strength up. He said she is much too thin. She weighs like a feather, hardly anything."

I had realized almost from day one that, having cleaned and shopped and cooked and "done" everything for her for almost twenty years (she had told me she started in 1992), Marta regarded Anne as much more than her employer. Over all that time, a deep attachment—on Marta's side at least—had taken root. As she spoke, her eyes began to swim with tears.

"Oh, I'm so sorry to hear that!" I said. And I was sorry, but even more than sorry, I regret to say, I was alarmed, almost panicked. If she should die now, die before we came to the denouement of her affair! For a denouement there must be, and not a happy one. Like the journalists who had interviewed her at the height of her fame, I was certain that *The Vengeance of Catherine Clark*, with its raging anger, had to have grown out of something deeply personal in her life. But what? What? The truth behind the plot of that socially transformative book went to the heart of my dissertation. If I never learned the whole story, if she died now, Apartment 10A would become part of her estate and I would have to move out. She must survive. Not only survive: recover, live. A foxhole atheist, I shoved my shame aside and prayed to the all-powerful God I didn't believe in to spare her.

Meanwhile, Marta put a hand on my arm and looked up at me, her tearful eyes pleading. "She has always been so good to me. She pays me for eight hours a day, even though it's only six. She helped me become U.S. citizen. Now I don't know what to do for her," she said. "Will you help me? Will you be gentle with her? Don't let her make you read too long. She can't afford to get worn out."

"Of course not. I'll be very careful."

At this, she gave me a hug. "You are a good person," she said.

"*You* are a good person," I corrected, and slunk away.

I lived on a knife's edge during those days. As usual, Petra and I talked or texted daily, if only to say hello. We met one night for dinner at an East Side sushi place we liked and she asked me how I was managing without Tim. I was managing, I said tightly, and asked about Justin to change the subject. I was managing, but it wasn't always easy.

As for Justin, Petra was still seeing him and still unsure if she should go on doing so. He was a nice guy, really funny, he liked her a lot, and he wanted kids. But somehow he just wasn't the kind of person she could imagine spending the rest of her life with. Did that matter? Maybe it was a failure of imagination? Maybe she should hang in and see what happened . . .?

I listened, tried to ask intelligent questions and sort through her feelings with her, but my thoughts were elsewhere, and (to my shame) I suspect she knew it. Would Anne get well, well enough to continue the readings? That was the only thing on my mind. Would she even want to revisit the journals anymore? Marta continued to come early and leave late; she went in and out of Anne's room, eyes frightened, mouth set. When I stumbled on her heating up broth in the kitchen one afternoon, she told me she'd been trying to persuade Anne to hire a night nurse. Trying in vain: Mrs. Anne only muttered that she didn't want to wake up at three in the morning and find some stranger dozing in her armchair. Afraid of tiring her, Marta had dropped the subject.

My fear that I might suddenly be ejected from the apartment prompted me to profit by the certainty that Anne would not be hobbling around the place in the wee hours, a silver lining if ever there was one. Every night, I went into her study to take, then return, two or three journals. These I photographed, usually without reading any of the contents. There were so many notebooks, and each held so many pages to turn, focus the camera on, and capture, that after a while my fingers would start to cramp from the repetitive motion of clicking the shutter.

From time to time, the storage chip in the camera would fill to capacity and I would have to remove and replace it with another. Though I also uploaded the photos to my computer periodically, I kept the tiny chips as backups, storing them in an empty Altoid tin at the bottom of my backpack.

I could have made better time if I'd dared to photograph the journals during the day, but I still worried this could result in disaster. When Marta was in the apartment—and she was now there fourteen hours daily, every day of the week—she might at any moment come into my room to change my towels or put fresh sheets on my bed. She always knocked before she entered, but it was a mere courtesy, to let me know she was about to open the door. I'd have locked it if it had a lock, but it didn't.

I was also afraid to take the notebooks out of the Windrush to a copy shop, where the work could be done for me. I had an almost superstitious terror I might lose one. If, after we'd finished the "episode," Anne happened to ask me to read from a journal and I'd lost it, I'd be sunk. And what if she were to die? Might not someone— someone she'd appointed to inherit them—or destroy them, perhaps—discover that one of the journals, numbered so prominently, was missing?

Who that someone might be I had wondered more than once. What plans had Anne made for her journals after she died? Maybe, as I'd once imagined, she had found some institution willing to house, catalog, and archive them. Maybe she'd chosen a literary executor—a long-ago student or younger friend who would do with them what she or he thought best. Anne had told me she'd written them with the expectation that they would never be read. But did she mean never during her lifetime, or never at all? If the latter, it was as I'd feared from the day we met. She either meant to get rid of them herself—soon, no doubt, maybe as soon as we came to the end of our readings—or had instructed her executor to destroy them on her death. More than one writer has sentenced their unpublished papers to such a fate.

And so, one night when my fingers had tired of clicking, I ventured out to search for her will. For thoroughness, I went first to try the drawer in the delicate desk in the living room where she'd always locked up the journals, but of course it was locked.

Then I riffled through the two unlocked drawers on either side of the kneehole. These turned out to contain only ordinary papers: paid bills, insurance policies, co-op rules and notices (the Windrush was one of the earliest rental buildings in New York to convert from rental to co-op, I'd learned), a well-worn personal phone book with many names crossed out, presumably as their owners died.

Her study was the only other logical place she might keep a copy of her will. The only one accessible to me, that is, since her bedroom was off limits, and the likeliest of all was a safety deposit box at a bank. There were two filing cabinets under the long desk in the study, and I spent several hours thumbing through their drawers. They turned out to contain some papers of interest to me, but nothing like a will. Mostly I found the predictable, minimally useful detritus of a literary life: contracts for books, royalty statements, publisher releases of copyright, an option agreement and contract for the movie version of *Vengeance*, and so on.

But there were also several partial manuscripts of novels eventually abandoned and, most significantly, an entire unpublished book called *The American Tour*—along with the many rejection letters that doomed it to the drawer. This would make very useful material for my dissertation, as would, to a lesser extent, the manuscripts she never finished. I stole a bundle of them one night and had them photocopied at Staples before returning them the next day.

On the sixth morning after her relapse, Anne rallied enough to send for me to come to her bedroom and read again.

Thirteen

After our long hiatus, I had a hard time hiding my surprise at how changed Anne was when I went to her bedroom to continue reading. She had looked a bit pale and piteous the first time I'd sat at her bedside, but this recent bout of illness had ravaged her. Now she had none of the ruined beauty of that imaginary film star. Now she was a sick old lady. Her skin was drained of color, her eyelids drooped; she had lost so much weight you could see her skull under her skin. It was an effort for her not to let her head loll against the pillows, and when she said "good morning," it came out as a weak croak. She had been through a terrible siege.

"I'm afraid I must look much worse than the last time we met," she said, while I hovered in the doorway. I had carried a chair from the dining room into the corridor but left it there till she told me to bring it in. "I'm sorry if it shocks you. I've been to hell and back, and this, evidently, is what they do in hell. Well, not all the way back," she amended. "As you observe."

"It's good to see you again," I said, hoping to dodge any more discussion of her distressing appearance, which I could not dispute. "I'm glad you feel up to a reading."

She beckoned me in and I moved the dining room chair to its place near the night table.

"That was adept," she commented while I settled myself. I knew she was referring not to my furniture-moving skills but the way I'd evaded either agreeing or disagreeing with her remarks about the change in her appearance. "What politicians call 'pivoting,' I believe."

I saw now that she was as mentally sharp as ever, and as sensitive to language. Exposed, I felt my cheeks heat up. Though I wanted very much to know the state of her health—more exactly, whether she was still in mortal danger—I could think of no delicate way to elicit the information. "How are you?" seemed ridiculous, a question that answered itself. Instead I offered her the check for my rent. It had been due two days before but, given the circumstances, I had left it unpaid until she recovered.

She took it, smiling as she had at my previous check. Her smile contained no trace of satisfaction at receiving it but, on the contrary, suggested that she'd just as soon have handed it back. All the same, she put it under the bottle of Nyquil on her nightstand.

"Do you still have the journal we were reading?" I asked. "Should I fetch it from somewhere?"

"It's here."

From under the pillow beside her, she produced one of the spiral notebooks whose size, weight, and feel were now so familiar to me.

"What do you think of my journals, by the way?" she asked as she handed it over. "I don't mean the contents, but do you find them well written?"

I was startled into telling the truth. "Yes! Very much so."

"I do too," she replied. Her tone was meditative and her voice had begun to regain some of its usual depth and timbre. "Surprisingly so. I've very seldom read any part of them at length. I've mostly used them for recordkeeping, so I could look up when I started having headaches, or finished a novel, or figure out who introduced me to someone else. That sort of thing. Now that I hear you reading them, though, I must say I find them extremely vivid. At least the interesting parts. Astonishingly vivid, considering that they were jotted down almost without thought."

"I agree."

She turned her head on the pillow to look at my face. "And what is it like for you to read them aloud?" she asked. "It must be embarrassing, all that sex and obsession and detail, and me such an old lady."

It was useless to deny that she was old, and almost as useless to pretend I hadn't frequently felt embarrassed.

"It's fascinating," I said. "Really. It isn't often you get to see someone's lived experience exactly as they saw it themselves."

"Nicely put," she replied.

"I mean it."

"Well, you've done an excellent job," she said. "Even at the most...the most torrid points, let's say, you've kept a steady voice. No melodrama, no swelling intonation, and no shrinking into whispers, either. I thank you. I doubt anyone could have done better."

"My pleasure. My honor," I amended, my first answer having hit too near the truth.

Her eyes still on me, she gave what I would call a musing smile. I don't believe I've ever used the word "musing" as an adjective before.

"Yes, I think so," she murmured. "I don't mean that it's an honor, of course," she added, with the wryness so characteristic of her, "only that I imagine that for you—well, never mind, let's get started reading. I think we're coming to some very intense bits and I don't want to tire myself out before we've begun."

Wondering with considerable anxiety what she meant by the unfinished phrase "I imagine that for you," I bent my head and found the page where we'd left off. Anne was right. The very next entry started "April 4, 9:45 a.m. On the train."

The hand was shaky. I saw her sitting in the train car, pen in hand, notebook on a foldout tray in front of her, joggled side to side by the motion. I had to work even harder than usual to make out the words.

"Took an early train, although Greg won't be in Philly till 6:00 or later. I had to leave home early to make it appear I was rushing to Ginny's bedside and figured I might as well get out of town right away. I'll go straight to the Barnes, then the hotel, to stay in the room—our room—in case he calls.

How sensible and well considered this plan looks! Yet I feel frenzied, divided between guilt after saying goodbye to Steve as if mercy were my errand—he praised me for my commendable devotion to Ginny—and an almost unhinged excitement at the prospect of three full nights with Greg. Dozens of pictures of how it might be, what we may do, are revolving uncontrollably in my brain. They are lascivious images, but also roman- tic—as romantic as a teenager's fantasies of how deeply her boyfriend will kiss her next time, a girl who sits in class writing over and over in the margins of her notebooks her hoped-for married name: "Dorothy Cooper, Dorothy Livingston Cooper, Mrs. Harold Cooper." Anne Morris, Anne Morris—I haven't quite come to that.

But the yearning to be with him is no less strong than that young girl's. Where is the line between lust and love? I think of his tenderness and my own crazed need to be with him again and—

I must stop myself, anything more really would be adolescent.

Here there was a gap.

"That's it for what you wrote on the train. The next entry is that afternoon," I said.

"I see. Go on."

Four-thirty p.m., Philadelphia

In our room at the Lantern Inn, which is more a bed-and-breakfast than the hotel I'd expected. It is decidedly far away from the Academy of Music, where Greg will play. Of course this makes sense—a tiny, out-of- the-way place where no one connected with the concert could possibly want to stay—I wonder how he even found it—but its obscurity reminds me of La Bouchée, home of the inedible lunch and undrinkable wine, and thus is rather depressing. (He also has a room he won't use at the Warwick, booked for him by his agent.)

After visiting the Barnes (amazing, as always), I checked in here under my own name. This is how Greg had reserved the room, since I'd be arriving before him. Our hostess is a large, excessively chatty woman named Mabel Baker, who asked when Mr. Weil would be arriving. She then insisted on carrying my little suitcase upstairs and into a spacious, light-filled room with a double bed covered with a thin white tufted spread. She explained that the inn had once been a private country house.

Now, as I could see, Philadelphia had grown over it, surrounding it with little homes and businesses. She showed me the en suite bathroom (including a suggestive claw-footed tub as well as a shower stall), the closet, a plastic electric kettle with a supply of instant coffee and Sanka. She showed me how to control the heat, how to open the windows, how to dial out on the telephone, everything except how to sit in the chairs, then stood chattering at me until I broke in to say I needed to use the bathroom.

This finally sent her to the door, where she paused and turned around to inform me that we were welcome to use the kitchen downstairs whenever we liked, and that the inn was locked up at ten but the key with the red ribbon on it that she'd given me would open it, and that we could reach her at any hour by calling the number of the inn.

Only then did she go away. A few minutes later, I phoned downstairs to make sure a caller could dial the inn and be put through to our room. No one answered.

So here I will sit, waiting for Greg to turn up. In a moment, I'll put down my pen and pick up Welty's "The Ponder Heart," but I think I'm more likely to stare at the pages than actually read the words. I am in such a state of desire that it's all I can do not to lie down and get myself off.

"Oh my God!" Anne broke out, before I could tell her that this was the last of the day's entries. Galvanized by embarrassment, she had come alive again. "Oh, Beth! Oh, for pity's sake, how I wish I could one day read your diaries to you! If there is a God in heaven, that day will come." She gave a rich, whooping laugh, started coughing, and buried her face in her hands.

I wished I could have told her how important it was to me, as a student of second-wave feminism in the United States, to know just such details as these: how a woman of her time behaved sexually; how much, and what, she thought about her own sexuality; how she acted on her desires; how freely she articulated her thoughts and actions; what terms she would use. Naturally, I was also embarrassed, reading these words in the presence of their author, but any embarrassment was well worth the knowledge gained.

"I don't keep a journal," was all the answer I came up with.

"Very wise," she said. She took another minute to calm down before asking, "Did I write more that day?"

I told her she hadn't. The next entry was dated April 5, 10 a.m.

"Then let's keep going."

No time, no wish to write in here since Greg arrived at 7:30 yesterday. After rushing at each other like magnets, we fell into bed, clothes still on but quickly off. The sex—lovemaking?—was as passionate as last time—more so, since we came simultaneously. After a few minutes of recovery, he mentioned that he was hungry, and since I was too, we showered—together—and dressed again to go out.

By then it was 8:30 and the only place we could find that seemed still to be serving was a pizza parlor. So we shared a pizza and returned to the room too full to jump into bed again. Instead, we talked about his schedule for the remainder of our stay and what I would do when not with him. He apologized but stressed again how crucial it was that I stay out of sight, give no sign of our connection at the concert. Of course I knew this already, but it was humiliating to hear.

After this, to bed again, and sex again. (Forgot to say I'd put my diaphragm in soon after writing the entry above.) For a man in his forties, he is astonishingly able to get hard twice in a row. After that, no less deliciously to me, it was lights-out and time to sleep. This morning it was a tender pleasure to waken to him stroking my back and whispering that it was time to get up. We made love quickly—he had to be at rehearsal at the hall at 9:30—then bathed together too hurriedly to take full advantage of the capacious tub. Then we went out for breakfast at a coffee shop Mabel had suggested when we came downstairs. (We'd politely declined her invitation to join the other guests in the dining room, where scrambled eggs and sticky buns were on offer.) When she addressed Greg as Mr. Weil, we exchanged a private smile.

Then breakfast and his departure and my return here to write the above.

Ah. I forgot to note that I called Steve yesterday afternoon. How shamefully far he is from my thoughts. I reported Ginny's perilous condition, her pain, the concern of the doctors treating her, their careful watch to make sure the antibiotics—I.V. antibiotics—were successfully fighting the infection. They had already told her she'd have to be hospitalized for weeks, maybe more than a month. Not that I'd stay all that time, of course, just a few days to make sure she was on the mend. I felt vile. I am vile.

"Should I go on? The next entry was written that afternoon." I thought of my promise to Marta and the advisability of suggesting that Anne take a nap, but she seemed energized by what we'd already read and instructed me to continue.

3 p.m.

Went to the Academy of Fine Arts, took a break to eat a solitary lunch, then strolled around the galleries for another hour. So many extraordinary paintings, especially the Eakinses, naturally, but I've seen them before and was ready to go home.

The last two words were crossed out, a rare sight in the journals. I said so, she nodded, and told me to continue. She had altered the sentence to end, "to return to this now enchanted room to wait for him."

Called Steve again when I got here and told him Ginny's condition was much better. The antibiotics were working and she was over the worst of the pain. Her admitting doctor, an experienced man in practice for a good twenty years, had been exceptionally attentive. Moreover, the nursing staff had proved responsive, competent, and even kind. Providing nothing changed, I expected to be able to come home the day after tomorrow.

How easily all this comes to me. Maybe being a writer of fiction has its practical uses after all.

There was a line left blank after this and I paused before going on.

It won't be long now before Greg gets back. Six at the latest, he said.

"The end?" Anne asked.

"Yes, until the next afternoon."

"There's nothing about the rest of the day?"

"No."

"I wonder why."

"Keep going?"

"Please."

Saturday April 6, 5 p.m.

A very frustrating day, I am sorry to say. It turns out that Greg's habit is to "take it easy" on the day of a performance. I wish he had told me this in advance, but apparently he never thought to till after he woke (late) this morning. I had been up since seven. I tried to rouse him with a kiss on his neck, but he only turned over, away from me.

Once he was awake, he put his arms around me and kissed me. However, although I could feel he was hard, and although I was certainly ready, there was no lovemaking. Instead, we went out to breakfast at the same coffee shop as yesterday. I'm afraid I was unable to hide my disappointment.

He saw it and explained that playing piano is a kind of athletic activity for him, and that just like many athletes, he rests up before a game (a performance, of course, in his case), including refraining from sex, since for him there is a vital connection between his libido and his musicality. This did help me not to take it personally but didn't lessen my frustration.

Keeping near the Lantern, where he could be quite, quite sure no musician from the Berlin orchestra (or any orchestra, for that matter) would happen to turn up, we took a couple of short walks—the weather was mild today and the trees were starting to leaf out—along unremarkable streets. In between, we returned here and read (!) in a common room downstairs(!!). We found little to say to each other. He asked how I'd been since our last meeting at his studio and I asked the same about him. Neither of us had much we cared to report. In the circumstances, I didn't feel like describing my intense longing to see him, my success in recruiting Ginny, my trickery with Steve—Steve, so innocent and so easily hoodwinked. Greg did share with me his own excitement as this weekend approached and how difficult it had been to do without me till then. He said nothing about Susan, though, and this omission made me wonder— again—if this kind of affair could possibly be routine for him. I almost asked but was too afraid of the answer.

Finally, he showered and dressed for the concert. I didn't join or even watch him in the shower, and he stripped to his underwear and put on his concert finery in self-absorbed silence. Just before his departure, he asked me to leave the room so he could call Susan. I did, but sullenly, resentfully. Who am I? I must be out of my mind! Of course he must call her, just as I must keep in touch with Steve. I exiled myself to the common room, where

Mabel set upon me with questions about what we'd done with our day, whether we'd seen or planned to see the Liberty Bell or the Benjamin Franklin Museum, as she had suggested, and so on. I fended her off with anodyne lies.

After some ten minutes of this, Greg appeared downstairs in his overcoat. Mabel was still with me and asked where he was going and why I wasn't going with him. He answered easily that he was on his way to a dinner to celebrate the retirement of a beloved U. Penn. professor.

"That's where I went to school," he added. "That's why we're in Philly." I wondered instantly if he was always so ready with a lie, then remembered I've already proven myself equally quick to deceive, if not more so.

As our hostess watched, he gave me a perfunctory kiss and said he'd probably be late. Then he was gone.

FOURTEEN

Anne finally stopped me after I'd read her account of Greg's departure for the concert, saying she needed to rest for a while. Her previous energy was gone, her face gray; she had slumped back into the pillows, exhausted. I returned the journal to her, stood, and began to remove my chair.

"No, leave it there," she said. "Maybe you'll come back later today if I feel better. And if you have time."

"I have time."

Her voice sharp with rue, "I don't," she replied. "Which is why I've been trying to get us to the end of this story as fast as possible. Beth, I have a weak heart," she went on.

I tried to look surprised and concerned to learn this "news."

"It's been weak ever since I was eleven, after a bout of rheumatic fever. Strep throat, you'd call it now, but back then, before penicillin, it was very dangerous. I've always known I might have a stroke or a heart attack and die early—that I might very likely do so, in fact. Well, that didn't happen," she added with a weak smile. By now she looked even worse. I wanted to urge her to rest, for my own sake if not hers, and resolved to keep this conversation brief if I could.

"Now, though, the end is near. How melodramatic that sounds! 'The end is near,'" she repeated scornfully—*scornfully*, even though she was so obviously spent! "Like a soap opera. Would it be better to say, 'There's no doubt I'll die soon'?"

It was a rhetorical question, the question of a writer asking herself how best to put something, and I kept quiet.

"Yes, I think so. 'I'll die soon' is dramatic, but not quite so clichéd." With no trace of self-pity, "I'm quite reconciled to this fate," she went on. "In fact, I'm happy about it. The last ten years or so have been a snowballing accumulation of bodily breakdowns, increasing pain, loss of friends, humiliating disabilities, my vision above all. But the soul outwears the sheath, as Byron wrote, and I do want to hear the whole of this story before I go."

Despite her assertion that she was ready for death, despite the fact that Marta had already told me her situation was dire, I felt torn between sadness for her and bitter disappointment for myself. I had learned so little about her sense of herself as a writer! I needed more time to gain her confidence, become a familiar face—and so, somehow, get her to tell me the answers to my original questions: what she thought the impact of her work had been, why *Vengeance* had had such a strong effect on women when it appeared, which books or teachers or public figures she saw as her influences, what the biographical roots of Catherine Clark's story had been, the extent to which she'd considered herself part of a women's "movement."

The journals were a superlative record of her inner life, and now and then, in essays and magazine features, she'd expressed her views on the position of women in society, but after Professor Probst's warning, I feared I would need a direct, prolonged interview—or a series of short ones—to produce the kind of material I needed to succeed in my dissertation. I noticed my jaw was clenched and tried to relax it.

"I'm very sorry to hear that," I said. "I've enjoyed our readings. I've enjoyed getting to know you." I doubt I've ever uttered greater understatements.

"And I you. Our conversations have been a nice distraction from my health, or rather my deterioration. And I've come to like you," she went on. Her smile seemed genuine, but not especially warm. It was a secret smile, I would have said, a knowing smile, and a little sad. The smile of someone who thinks she knows more about you than you do. "Which is very fortunate."

After this, she let her eyes close and sent me away.

I stayed in all evening, hoping against hope that she would rally and ask for me to read again. I ate another can of baked beans for dinner instead of going out. But she remained quiet, doubtless asleep. Even Marta went in to check on her only a couple of times.

Then, shortly before she went home for the night, Marta knocked and came into my room. She had offered to stay with Mrs. Anne, she said, even sleep on the floor beside her bed, but Mrs. Anne wouldn't allow it. Now she asked for my cell number and wrote it down on an index card, making gigantic numerals with a thick black Sharpie.

"I am going to leave it with the magnifying glass on her night table, next to her lamp and phone," she said, "in case she needs help in the night. I hope she will be able to read it. At least I got her to leave her door open. Could you please leave yours open too, so you can hear if she calls out for you?"

I said of course I would and told her I'd already taken to doing so. I slept uneasily that night, gnawed by the fear that Anne might die before morning, afraid to fall too deeply asleep in case she did call out for help, and worried that, if she did, I wouldn't know what to do. In the morning, Marta returned. She went in to see Anne and came out to make tea and some Cream of Wheat for her. I hovered around the apartment—ate breakfast in the empty dining room, read and answered emails, graded some papers. The hours went by and still Anne issued no summons for me. At last, I resorted to reading *The Bell* in the living room.

And so it happened that at two o'clock, when the intercom buzzed, I was curled up on one of the red velvet love seats there. Marta was in the bedroom with Anne, so I answered. "Patrick Quigley is here," said the doorman.

I recognized the name, of course. Telling the doorman—it was Peter; I knew them all by now—to ask Mr. Quigley to wait there just a minute, I hung up and went down the corridor to make sure he was expected. I found Marta already on her way to answer the buzzer, which she too had heard. Reseating myself in the living room, I tried to look absorbed in my book while she called down to Peter and said to send the visitor up.

When she opened the front door, I glanced toward the foyer—casually, I hoped—to see Quigley, still cheerful, still red-cheeked, unbuttoning his coat. A short, solid young woman in a pencil skirt and a cable-knit sweater was giving Marta her coat. She trailed after Quigley as they came into the living room.

"Beth," Quigley said, shaking my hand before I had a chance to stand. "This is Amber Waring, my assistant."

We nodded to each other and I started to get up.

"No, don't trouble yourself. We'll be on our way in a moment," Quigley said. "I'm glad to see you here. I'm sure you've been welcome company for Anne. Marta tells me she's in her bedroom?"

He looked around, plainly wondering where this room might be. Then Marta appeared and took them through the dining room to the hallway, leaving me to speculate on what errand could have brought them to the Windrush. After what Anne had told me about her health the day before, I could only think that she was changing her will. People did such things on their deathbeds (if such hers was to be), at least in books and movies. It might have been a long time since she'd written it. Maybe a legatee had died since, or she'd decided to leave some money to the Authors Guild instead of PEN. Or maybe, I could not help but think, she wanted to leave some little souvenir to me. Copies of her own books, perhaps, or even her whole library. Who knew?

On the other hand, it might be that, having arranged to hear what she wanted of the journals, she'd decided to direct now that they be burned on her death.

I noticed that in my own mind I had used the word "burned" and saw it for what it was: a relic of a vanished time. No doubt they'd be shredded in the impersonal jaws of a machine in Quigley's office. The image of Patrick Quigley sitting at his desk and dropping one flaming notebook after another into a metal wastebasket made me laugh out loud, in spite of my renewed horror at the idea that this intimate record of their author's life might be destroyed.

A minute or so after Marta escorted the visitors to Anne's bedroom, I heard her washing dishes in the kitchen. After a long time—almost an hour and a half—Quigley finally came out and called for her. She went, and I heard Anne's door close behind her. Soon afterward, all three emerged. Then they made a detour into the kitchen. Through its open door, I heard them murmuring, sharing their concern about Anne's worsening health, I imagined, Marta perhaps filling Quigley in on the recent, grim visit to Dr. Braudy. His cheerfulness was gone when, on his way to the front door, he silently nodded goodbye to me.

At six o'clock, Marta put her head into my room to say that Anne would like me to read to her. After her lengthy conference with her lawyer, I had stopped expecting this and gone out to get a breath of air and buy some groceries. Now I was thankful my absence had been short.

I went straight in. Anne was sitting up against the pillows, looking weak but serene. Whatever was wrong with her will, she must have fixed it. The journal was in her lap. She gave it to me and thanked me for coming.

"Of course. I'm glad to," said I, ever the willing handmaiden. I found the place where we'd left off.

"I'm tired," she admitted, "but I've had a little nap, and somehow I feel more aware than ever of how short my time may be. So, whenever you're ready." She pulled the quilt up and slid her hands under it despite the warmth of the room.

"We're still on the day of the concert, but a bit later on."

She nodded. I began to read.

6:30 p.m., the Lantern Inn.

Dressed and ready to leave for the Academy of Music after eating the world's quickest and most depressing dinner at the coffee shop around the corner. The Copper Kettle, it's called.

I phoned Steve right after Greg left, to report on Ginny. After two days of I.V. antibiotics, her condition is much better. Of course she'll be in the hospital for a long time, but if nothing changes, I'll come home tomorrow afternoon. As for me, I'm fine, just a little worn out.

Steve caught me up on his own day—lunch at Keen's Steakhouse with Victor Moore, an afternoon spent reading up on best practices in treating a brain hemorrhage, and his plan to stay home and thaw the meatloaf I'd left for dinner. It was unusually warm in New York. Was it warm in Philadelphia? I didn't know; I had been in a taxi, then at the hospital all day. Then we hung up.

Off to dress and make myself up for the concert, not that Greg will see me.

"There's a blank line after this, before another entry you wrote that night."

"Thank you."

10 p.m., the Lantern.

A beautiful evening, one I will not forget. I arrived at the Academy of Music half an hour early, but since it turned out to be a gorgeous theater, in the opulent style of the era when it was built, I was happy enough to wander around for a while before taking my seat.

Greg had given me the ticket. It was in the orchestra, on the left side but more than twenty rows back from the stage. A precaution, he explained, though I can't imagine what purpose it served. Surely all the women in the first nineteen rows can't be having affairs with him. And how would friends of his, if some were in attendance, have any idea of my connection to him?

Still, there I sat, reading the program. It had the same biography and photo as the program at Carnegie. I continued to feel just a little of the irritation his standoffishness (if that's the word) had provoked in me during the day. But I was also anxious to see him in his glory—indeed, bursting with pride and longing to tell my neighbor he was my lover. (Perhaps this was why he put me so far back in the auditorium.)

Then the lights went down, the orchestra came in and tuned up, the audience quieted, von Karajan appeared and was greeted with applause, which swelled as, last of all, Greg walked onstage. He nodded, smiling, to acknowledge the welcome, then sat down at the piano. Now all of my resentment vanished. How I loved him in that moment—I will call it love.

Von Karajan waited for silence in the hall, then looked to Greg to be sure he was ready before raising his baton. As it came down, I realized that such a performance is indeed a kind of athletic event, with a starting gun, a team, an obligation to keep up, to do one's part (quite literally) without a moment of let-up—particularly for any soloist at the center of the racing wheel. Then the music engulfed me, sublime, transporting. Beethoven's "Emperor." As at Carnegie, Greg's bows after the last notes died were met with wild applause. Waves of audience members leapt up, one after the other, until the whole auditorium was on its feet. Whatever motivated that ovation, it wasn't merely the ignorant tribute a celebrated musician so often receives after even a lackluster performance. He had richly earned it.

Someone handed him a bouquet, he shook hands with Von Karajan, then with the concertmaster. He stepped back to gesture to the orchestra, to share the acclaim with them. He was on and off the stage four times before the applause let up. Then, in a buzzing crescendo of chatter, the audience began to filter up the aisles and out to the lobby for intermission.

I went with them, taking my coat and hat. Greg had warned me he wouldn't appear in the second part of the concert—a soloist in this type of program doesn't, he explained—and I had made up my mind not to stay. He, of course, will wait till the concert ends, after which he'll go out for a drink with his colleagues—and without me.

Still, soon enough, I'll have him all to myself.

I paused here and looked up to find Anne lost in a haze of reminiscence.

"I remember that concert," she said dreamily. "I remember it even more clearly than the sex we had. Reliving all that," she went on, "our desire for each other, and the details of the particular things we did together in bed—listening to you read those passages brings back the texture of the time for me, the strange sort of...sort of waking dream we were in together. But the way Greg played that concerto—that, I've never forgotten."

I asked if I should go on to the next entry.

"In a minute. I want to savor what you just read."

Smiling, she closed her eyes. In that smile was certainly pleasure at the memory, but also a certain ruefulness, it seemed to me, a recognition of how very deep in the vanished past all this sweetness was now. I thought it tactful to look away and trained my gaze on the nightstand. On it now, along with the phone and the carafe of water and so on was the index card with my cell number on it.

It was quite a while before she opened her eyes and told me to continue. The jagged handwriting made it clear she had written the next entry on her way back to New York.

Sunday April 7, 3:30 p.m. Just past Trenton on the train.

Greg and I agreed to meet at his studio again this coming Friday. Now I feel as if my stomach might explode. Everything inside me is churning and clawing, the way it did when I was a little girl and told Mother a lie. How will I manage to keep from Steve where I've really been, all I've done since I left him behind? My mind is full of the weekend, especially last night. Though our lovemaking was far less vigorous—Greg was tired after the concert—it was sweet, lingering, emotionally connected in a new way. I'm sure he felt this too.

In fact, I'm quite, quite sure, because while he was still inside me, he said, "I don't know how I lived before I met you." That's a lot to say—and I have to confess that, so soon after seeing him in the spotlight at the concert hall, I heard it not only as a grown woman would but also with the thrill of a girl with a crush. Actually, I think I do have a crush on him. It feels just like that—although also, of course, a thoroughly adult attachment to him, one I've already allowed myself to identify as love. Whatever love is. I've always disliked the word love, especially the way "I love you" is used to signify some ultimate, permanent surrender—as if "love" never changes, as if it means the same thing to every person at every stage of life. A precise, concrete word, like "chipmunk" or "shoe." How silly, how false.

But all that is about language. The truth, the physical, literally gut-wrenching truth, is that I don't see how I can go on living with Steve.

FIFTEEN

After Anne's complaints about the indiscriminate use of the word "love," she left a gap of two lines before resuming the entry.

"Did I?" she asked absently, when I'd informed her of this, her thoughts clearly somewhere else. I let her think in silence a moment or two before starting to read again.

I didn't answer Greg in words, only buried my mouth in his neck, then drew back to hold his face in my hands. I held it a long time as we looked at each other without speaking—he into my unremarkable brown eyes, I into his intense, mismatched ones.

Lucky me.

Oh! I think I forgot to write down that when I packed for Philadelphia, I brought the Instamatic camera Steve gave me for my birthday. Yesterday, I told Greg I had it and that I wanted a photo of us together. I could see right away that the idea made him uneasy. All the same, at the handy but now rather tiresome Copper Kettle, where we had lunch before parting today, he suddenly suggested it himself. We'd left the inn by then, taking our suitcases with us. He told me to get the camera from mine and I did so, awkwardly, opening it in on the floor in the gap between our table and the next, kneeling to fumble my way through it. Then I zipped it up again and sat down with the camera. When the waitress returned with our order, Greg asked her to snap a picture of us. I hadn't noticed this waitress at the Kettle before. She was very young, pleasant, a little mystified, maybe, at why two people in what she must see as middle age would want a photograph of themselves, but glad enough to oblige.

Greg pulled his chair around next to mine—behind us was a large poster of the Liberty Bell—and put his left arm around my shoulders and his right under my skirt. Then, while I tried not to burst out laughing, he kissed my cheekbone, holding his lips against it until the flash bulb erupted. And now, somewhere inside my valise, is an undeveloped piece of disastrous evidence.

Or maybe not? Maybe it's blessed evidence whose discovery could free both Greg and me to spend the rest of our lives together. But it's too soon to think of that, or so I tell myself. At all events, once I've had the film developed (at a place far from the Windrush—even far from Carnegie Hall, for good measure) I will hide it, and well. Maybe I'll bury it in the pages of "Persuasion," another book Steve will never take from the shelf.

"That's all you wrote that day," I said, glancing up. At the sight of her, the words "You look tired" popped out of my mouth. Crazed as I was to keep reading, to hurry to the end, I justified this to myself by thinking of a selfish motive: concern that, if she got too worn out, she might collapse for keeps. My real reason, however—I think I can say it with honesty—was genuine dismay at her appearance, concern that listening was taxing her too much. Continuing would be unkind. "Should we wait till tomorrow for the next part? I can be here whenever you're ready."

"I suppose so," she said, reluctant as a child told to go to bed. She sighed. "Can we make an appointment to meet at 10:00 tomorrow, as we used to do? Here, of course, not in the living room. I doubt I'll ever see the living room again."

"Of course you will," I said—said "stoutly," as Victorian authors used to write of a worried character reassuring a dying friend. I stood and handed her the notebook even though I suspected that, in her exhausted state, she might for once forget to take it away from me. As I left, I asked whether she wanted Marta to come. She did.

"Don't forget, you can call me if you need anything in the night," I blurted out.

She smiled at me, holding my eyes with hers for a long moment before saying good night.

I stayed up late, reading *The Bell* in bed—by now, finally, I was nearing the end—and waiting and waiting for sleep to come. I drifted off around one o'clock. When I awoke, alert at seven, I knew I had not slept deeply. I put on my robe, splashed my face in the bathroom, then went to peer in through Anne's open door. Inside, what looked like a waxen doll lay on her back beneath the covers. For a moment, I thought she was dead. Then she gave a gentle little snort and I went to the kitchen to make myself some tea.

When Marta arrived at eight, I gave her a quick account of how the night had gone, like a nurse handing over a patient: how quiet she'd been through the night (very quiet, at least as far as I knew), how she'd asked me to return at ten today to continue reading. By the time I went in to do so, Marta had given her coffee—the mug was still on the nightstand—opened the heavy curtains, tidied the bed, poured water into a clean glass, and refilled the carafe on the nightstand. Anne was again sitting up against the pillows, hair brushed, lipstick applied, looking altogether much better than when I'd left her.

"Good morning. How are you?" she asked, contrary to her habit.

"Well, thank you. How did you sleep?"

"Like the dead." She gave a crooked smile. "That's one advantage of this new decline in my health: I don't wake up in the night anymore. And sleep feels delicious."

"Would you like another cup of coffee?"

"No. Just the next installment of *The Thrilling Adventures of Anne Weil*, please."

She took the notebook from under the pillow beside her and gave it to me. Turning to the place where we'd left off, I began to read.

The next entry had been written the day after her return from Philadelphia. It started with an account of her uneasy reunion with Steve when she got home—how she struggled to answer his kiss in kind, how much more difficult it was to describe her time with Ginny in person than it had been on the phone. *My cheeks flushed and I could barely get the words out of my mouth,* she had written.

For dinner, they ordered Chinese food; Steve hadn't resorted to this during her absence. To evade him afterward, she said that while she'd been in Philadelphia, she'd had some new ideas for *And Sometimes*

Y (although in fact, as I knew from my swift skimming of the journal passages not pertinent to the "episode," she had already, finally, given up on the book). So she was able to excuse herself and go into her study alone. Later, she pretended to call Ginny from the extension there, then reported to Steve that she sounded relatively strong, that she'd been transferred to a private room, and that she was grateful to Anne for getting her through the worst part. They'd agreed to check in with each other daily. In actuality, Anne did plan to call her the next day, to thank her and let her know she was safely home.

Then came bedtime.

Steve wanted to make love. (Have sex? I don't know what to call it.) I excused myself on the grounds that I was exhausted after my time with Ginny. He said "Of course" and I felt guiltier than ever. In fact, I wonder how I will ever have sex with him again. I see now that not only will I feel like a whore, as I have before: I will in fact be a whore, taking his money, living off him, accepting his kindness as if he were the only man in my life, when he is not.

"Hmph. There's a pleasant memory," Anne interrupted.

I didn't know what to say to this and kept quiet until she told me to continue.

Now I'll take the film to be developed. I long to see our photo, to hold that moment in my hands.

I looked up.

"That's all there is that day. The next entry was written the day after."

I hesitated.

"Well, don't stop there."

Tuesday April 9, 4 p.m.

Picked up the pictures this morning at a place in the photo district that offers overnight developing. Unable to wait till I got home, I found a bank where I could stand in a corner and open the packet. There were two other pictures on top of it—a shot of me on the slopes at Sugarbush from when Steve and I were there the first week in December, and another of us in the hotel lobby with the couple we met there.

And then Greg and me together. Greg in profile, lips against my cheek, me absolutely grinning with happiness. I stared and stared at it until the security guard began to stare at me. It's a wonderful shot, but I wish we had taken two, so I could see his whole face. Still, this half will do. I can hardly wait to show it to him, in fact, can hardly wait to see him at all. Friday seems so far away.

Hurried home to feast on it in private before Steve returns from work. Sitting curled in my office armchair, lost in the captured moment. I must have been there half an hour before I glanced at the clock, roused myself, and stuck the photo into "Little Women."

Here Anne interrupted me again. "I still have that picture," she said. "Would you like to see it?"

"Yes. Very much." This, of course, was God's honest truth.

I stood up to get it, but she stopped me.

"It's right here."

She opened the drawer in the night table beside her and drew out a photo in a simple silver frame. She put on her reading glasses, picked up the magnifying glass, and looked at it. Immediately, tears began to spill from her eyes. She turned her head away from me, trying but failing to suppress a series of racking sobs.

"I can't see his face," she whispered, dropping the picture on the bed.

I hadn't thought of this, though I should have, since this was the very affliction that had caused her to look for a reader in the first place. The pain of being unable even to see such a cherished image must have been crushing. I said what was in my heart.

"I'm so very sorry, Anne. I'm so very, very sorry."

"He died recently. As you probably know," she said. She blew her nose, collected herself. Meanwhile, my antenna went up: Why would she think I'd know the date of Gregory Morris's death? It was true that the *Times* had run a sizable obituary, but what reason would I have had for paying attention to it?

"He was ninety-one," she continued, having recovered some of her composure. "You'd think I'd have expected it, and I did, I suppose. But I've always found that it doesn't matter how obvious it is that someone's death is approaching, or even if it would come as a merciful release from suffering. Loss is loss. You can't escape grief.

"His death is what made me want to revisit the journals," she went on. "I wanted to remember how it was. I still want to, and I'm happy I found you to help me—more than you might imagine—even though hearing it hasn't always been easy, to say the least. I'm sure you've noticed the effect some of the passages have had on me. But I was more alive during that time than I've ever been since."

I tilted my head and nodded, hoping she could see the sympathy I truly felt. She was old, and grieving, and bereft. I almost cried myself.

After a long moment, she sniffled mightily, blew her nose again, and pulled herself together. Brightening, "Anyway, here it is," she said, handing me the picture.

This was the first time I'd seen a candid shot of Gregory Morris. He was a different man from the one in his formal, public photos. The picture was black and white and had faded a little over the years but, profile or not, he was alight with vigor, vitality, masculinity, and desire. As for Anne, she looked as if she might jump out of her skin. Clearly, the joy of being with her lover, of feeling his kiss—not to mention his hand up her skirt—had electrified her. I gazed at it for a long time.

I think she was gratified by my interest; she certainly gave no sign of impatience. It occurred to me that she might never have shown it to anyone but Morris himself. And somehow, my first thought was not what a stupendous ornament it would be for my dissertation, if I could just get hold of it. That struck me only later, as I fell asleep.

SIXTEEN

After Anne showed me the long-ago snapshot from
Philadelphia, she carefully returned it to the nightstand
drawer, put out her hand to receive the journal I'd been
reading from and slipped that in as well, locked the drawer, slid the
key back under the pillows next to the ones she was leaning on, and
said she needed to rest for a while. Could I come back when she
woke up?

I told her I'd be glad to. We agreed she'd send Marta to me when
she was ready.

As it turned out, I had to wait all afternoon. At three o'clock, I
started to get stir-crazy and thought of going out for a walk in the
neighborhood. The weather had warmed a bit since I moved into
the Windrush and Marta could call my cell whenever Anne was
ready for me to read again.

Just realizing I could escape, though, calmed my restlessness. I
stayed indoors, thinking about how it must feel for Anne to be shut
into 10A day after day, too frail to venture into the winter cold,
whether she wished to or not, and never outside these walls except
for some urgent medical reason. How long had she lived imprisoned
like this? And her remark that she might never see her living room
again—the poignance of it!

When Marta finally knocked on my door, I went in to find

Anne looking terrible despite her long rest, her eyes still pink from the morning's tears. I hovered in the doorway, not certain if I should sit down.

"Are you sure you're up to this now? I can come back a little later."

"No, please stay." She smiled. Her voice had lately lost all trace of its cultivated, thrilling depth, but her mind was as sharp as ever. "*'But at my back I always hear Time's wingèd chariot hurrying near,'*" she quoted. "Not that any coy lover is teasing me. Go ahead, pick up where we left off."

She gave me the notebook and closed her eyes while I glanced at the next entry. It had been written the same day as the last one, but hours later.

12:30 a.m.

Sex with Steve tonight. He suggested it with affection—and lust— and I felt I couldn't say no without running the risk of provoking suspicion, especially after our time apart. Anyway, I couldn't put it off forever.

For me, it was as guilt-ridden and unnatural and bizarre as I had feared. A distorted kind of sex, as if in a funhouse mirror, only no fun. I faked an orgasm, something I've never ever done before. I suppose I acquitted myself adequately. He hugged me in the friendly way we've developed, then dropped off to sleep, and here I sit almost wishing someone would force me to wear a scarlet A.

I wonder how Greg is dealing with this. Is it different for a man? Do he and Susan even have sex? I don't like to think about it.

"That's it for that day," I told Anne, whose eyes were still shut.

Without opening them, "Skim ahead and find the next mention of Greg," she instructed.

"Let me see..."

I did as she wished, searching for anything of note. The following day was almost entirely taken up with routine events: phone calls with friends, including one from Ginny; a stopped drain in the bathroom sink; what Anne made for dinner (brisket); worry about whether she'd ever think of a new book to write, now that she'd dropped *And Sometimes Y*. I turned the pages loudly enough for her to hear that I was still looking and finally came to a passage that mentioned Greg. Anne had run into two different friends in the lobby that day, "but not Greg, alas. (And fortunately, not Susan.)"

This I did read aloud, as well as an entry written the next day reporting that, to her relief, she got her period that morning. Not only did this confirm she wasn't pregnant, she would also be able to plead off from having sex with Steve that night on the grounds of bleeding and cramps. This worked, not only that night but the following one, as she later recorded. "For once I'm happy that such messy, bloody lovemaking puts him off."

Interspersed here and there in the days before Friday were more remarks describing how guilty she felt about her secret liaison with Greg. Just as frequent were sighing descriptions of how she yearned for their next rendezvous, how often she took out his picture and gazed at it. She wondered if he felt the same. To be frank, reading these parts aloud, I felt a bit embarrassed for her, almost as much so, albeit in a different way, as I'd been embarrassed by the explicit sex. As she had said herself, a teenager with a big date coming up could have written the same.

Then came Friday.

April 12, 9 p.m.

My heart is thumping as if it will burst out of my chest. From the moment I walked into Greg's studio today, it was clear that our weekend together changed something that cannot be changed back. As if we'd agreed to it in advance, we came together without a word, went to bed, made love. It was fierce and urgent, the kind of lovemaking with no room for lingering caresses, and over in no more than five minutes.

As soon as we'd finished, we threw on some clothes and sat down across the room from each other as if to do business. Greg spoke first.

"Look," he said, "I'm going to leave Susan." He paused, then went on, "Does that frighten you? I should tell you it's something I've thought of before, it's not just because of us. But it is true that I want to be free to be with you. I need to be with you, even if you don't feel the same."

"I wouldn't say it frightens me," I said slowly, almost dreamily. "It's your decision, after all, your life. I can't say I don't feel guilty about whatever part I've had in it. But I understand, because—well, this is a little different, maybe, but I've realized that, no matter what happens between us, I can't go on living with Steve. It's not fair to him. He trusts me. He's good to me. Pretending to be the woman he thinks I am when I will never be that woman again—that's a lie I can't live with. I dread telling him,"

I added, "but I have to. I really have no choice. At the same time . . ." I paused. "At the same time, I wonder if we've both gone crazy, you and me. A folie à deux. How long have we even known each other? And now to turn both of our worlds upside down! What do you think? Have we lost our minds?"

Greg crossed the room to sit beside me on the piano bench. He took my hand.

"Not lost, found," he said. "For me, at least. I love Susan, I always will. We've been together since we were teenagers. But our marriage . . ." He left the sentence unfinished. "Life is short. Continuing as things are truly would make me crazy."

A moment later, he dropped his head against my shoulder. When he lifted it and spoke again, I saw that he'd already given considerable thought to how to do what we needed to do. Tomorrow we must break the news, he said, he to Susan and me to Steve. He'd have done it tonight, but he has a master class to teach.

There were two blank lines after this. I said so and went on.

Just reread the above. Seeing the words on the page, I can't help but wonder again if I've taken leave of my senses. "Staying with Steve is a lie"? What insane sentence is this? How did this happen? But there it is. And I don't think I've taken leave of my senses. I've come to them—literally, to my senses. I have found a new person inside of myself. She is hungry, and willful, and I can't unfind her.

So. Next steps.

Greg will reserve a room at the Waldorf for tomorrow night. We'll meet there as soon as we've said what we have to say at home, then stay on for a few days. Greg wanted to stay until we find a suitable place to rent, but I insisted we move to his studio and camp out there. Weeks at the Waldorf would be a ridiculous expense, it seems to me, no matter how much money his success has brought him. (Hearing myself say this, I realized that the financial pluses or minuses of life with Greg have never crossed my mind. So different than with Steve, whose wealth—as he and I both knew, however tacitly—was a factor in my decision to marry him.)

Greg was reluctant to give in and we compromised by agreeing to spend four or five days in luxurious comfort. We settled a few other practical details as well. Then, with nothing more than a long, fierce hug at parting, I left for home.

So I'll tell Steve tomorrow and leave here at once.

"There's another blank line after that. The next entry was written that night," I said.

"Read it."

9 p.m.

Bedtime soon. I'd expected this last night of sleeping with Steve would be terribly upsetting, nearly too poignant to bear, but I find that I'm almost looking forward to it. I do still have affection for him, after all, and love him in my way. In fact, he hasn't changed at all, and so nothing has changed in my feelings toward him—nothing except my own shame and guilt because of my duplicity. When I married him, I did it with a whole heart and full intentions of keeping my wedding vows. Tonight feels like a welcome chance to say goodbye to all that, however covertly. For dinner, I made the chicken pot pie he likes so much and listened with real attention as he explained the settlement he's brokered between the Presbyterian Hospital and the family of his client whose brain hemorrhaged.

All the same, even though I won't lie beside him unwillingly, I would greatly prefer not to have sex.

Here she'd left another blank line. I said so and continued.

I'm thinking now of what I said to Greg about not being able to stay with Steve. "No matter what happens between us," I told him, and I did mean it, I do mean it. How could I stay and go on lying? I surely can't stay and tell the truth.

I hope I remember that certainty if it turns out to be true that (as some little part of me still suspects) Greg may sometimes have been unfaithful to Susan, may have slept casually with an admirer on the road or even, as I've imagined before, at his studio. Men are men! If it is true, isn't it likely that one day he'll be unfaithful to me in my turn? I know he loves me. I know that. *And for my own part, I know that I must "leap into the boundless." There's nowhere else for me to go. Still, he loved Susan too, and that little voice whispers in my head, What if? What if?*

This last sentence brought the writing to the bottom of the page. I turned it.

"There's nothing else for that day," I said. I didn't mention that the next passage had obviously been written while she was overwhelmed with emotion. The handwriting zigzagged above and below the lines, less legible than ever.

"Then just go to the day after."

Saturday April 13, 5 p.m. Room 428 at the Waldorf.

Here alone, waiting for Greg, still shuddering two hours after telling Steve. I had thought very carefully about exactly what I'd say, but I can't write it down here. It's too sickening. With every sentence, I felt as if I were hacking him with an axe.

I knew it would be awful, but not like it was. He hardly said a word. Didn't ask who it was, didn't argue, didn't yell, didn't reproach me, didn't cry, just sat there. If I hadn't seen his hands clench, his body grow rigid, I'd have thought he couldn't hear me. God, if only he'd screamed at me, kicked a chair over, slammed his hand against a wall, anything but sit in silence!

The moment I was done, he said he'd take a few things and find somewhere else to stay. Today, immediately. I objected—I would go. Why should he leave his own home? But he replied that the idea of staying there nauseated him. He didn't say that this was because our home was where I'd lied to him while we shared what he thought was a happy marriage, but he didn't have to. He took a few minutes to pack up some papers and clothes and left the apartment.

"It skips after that to 1:30 in the morning," I reported.

I hadn't looked at Anne since starting the previous entry and saw now that she'd begun to cry again.

"I think you'd better continue," she said, her voice unsteady. "I'd rather take what's coming now than put it off."

"You're sure? I can read tomorrow morning. We've already read so much today."

"Quite sure."

I gave in.

1:30 a.m.

Home again, and shaken to the core. Greg never turned up tonight. Why should I even record this? It's not as if I'll ever forget it.

Writing this through a rain of tears.

From the blotches where the ink had run, blurring her words, I knew already that she'd been crying then.

I waited for hours—seven hours—without hearing anything. Waited in an agony of suspense, frantic with speculation about what could be delaying him. Maybe Susan had detained him with weeping or a furious screed or threats or God knew what and he didn't want to leave her that way. If the two of them were embroiled in some sort of climactic emotional drama, I told myself, it was natural he'd stay, and moreover, be reluctant to make a call that would only inflame her more. But beneath all this—oh God, hadn't I known, somewhere in my heart, that he might betray me? Why did I let myself imagine that a man would break up a marriage of more than twenty years—a marriage to a woman he admits he will always love!—for an affair of barely a month? The thought kept pushing itself into my mind and I kept pushing it out. He was the one who raised the idea! Surely it couldn't be. A man would be the devil himself to suggest such a plan and not follow through.

By eight-thirty, I was hungry. I called down to room service and asked for a grilled cheese sandwich, the blandest thing on the menu. I couldn't eat even half of it. I doubt I will ever eat a grilled cheese sandwich again.

I had a couple of books with me, but it would have taken Scheherazade to hold my attention. I paced the room, washed my face, and made it up again for when he arrived, turned on the radio for a minute, then the television. Again and again, with increasingly violent shivers of terror, I wondered if he could indeed have changed his mind. But if that were so, why wouldn't he call to tell me? He isn't a cruel man, and for Susan, a call with such a purpose would be a welcome victory. I sat with my head in my hands, telling myself that he would not, could not fail me.

Finally, the phone rang. I said hello. Greg answered in a voice I hardly recognized. Flat, dead.

"Go home. I won't be coming. You should leave."

That was all he said. He hung up before I could ask why, what had happened, if he meant he wouldn't be coming tonight or would never come. Might Susan possibly have been out all day and all evening, so that he'd had no chance to tell her until late at night? I know this is wishful thinking; his tone wasn't that of a man apologetically warning of a brief delay—far from it. It was the tone of someone announcing doom.

And he'd hung up on me. Unless Susan had a gun to his head (he spoke exactly as you'd expect in such a case, come to think of it), he has no intention of ever following through with what he said he would do just yesterday. He has changed his mind. He has changed his mind.

How will I survive this?

"There's another gap here, a few lines." Anne was still crying, but not as copiously. Her voice broke as she told me to continue.

I wanted to call him back but even then didn't dare phone him at home. Whatever he's done to me, I don't want to avenge myself on him. I love him. God help me, I doubt I will ever stop.

Besides, he might simply have meant that he wouldn't be coming tonight; if so, a call from me would only ratchet up whatever drama was going on between him and Susan. And what if she answered?

I waited another two hours, hoping he'd call again. Eventually, I got angry. How does he even know I still have a home to go to? How could he abandon me this way? At twelve-thirty, I packed up and left. As I passed the front desk, the clerk saw my suitcase and asked if my husband was in the room or if we were checking out. My husband.

"Checking out," I muttered.

"Then I'll prepare the bill."

I had no choice but to pay it. I was lucky to have enough cash for this—I'd taken a lot with me, since I was running away—but the ridiculous price left me without money to take a taxi here. Stricken, humiliated, unable to control my tears, I waited in Grand Central for the shuttle, trudged to the No. 1 platform, and waited again alongside a drunken, raving woman. Then I walked home from 14th Street in the dark middle of the night, alone, my now vainglorious suitcase in my hand.

Coming into the building, I made myself say goodnight to Andrew as I normally would, then fled to the elevator—the elevator where Greg stood too close to me two months ago, asking how much to tip the handyman. The day he launched what I now see was his seduction.

Upstairs, I turned the key I'd turned with such different feelings this afternoon and came into an empty apartment, as empty as if all the furniture were gone. For a while, face down on the sofa, I sobbed like a child. I could not lie on our bed. My bed. Then I came in here, to my study, to write this, closing the door behind me as if it mattered.

"Maybe we should stop here for the night," I said, looking up to find her dry-eyed but with hands clutched to her temples.

"Maybe so. Yes. I'm very tired. I need to rest." Her voice was muffled, almost inaudible, the mumble of a person too weary to speak. She had stopped listening to her own story and begun to relive it.

I stood up to give her the notebook again but she'd already sunk back against the pillows, eyes closed, almost asleep. Quietly, gently, I slipped it under the pillow beside her and left.

S E V E N T E E N

The morning after Greg Morris jilted Anne—for I had begun to think of the events in the journals as if they were happening as we read them—I found an email in my inbox from a man named Pierce MacAuley. We'd been friends in our undergraduate days—Pierce was on financial aid too, and we met working side by side at the salad bar—but there was always some undercurrent between us, something unexplored, and I was unreasonably happy to read that he was moving back to the city. A theater major, he'd become a casting agent in L.A. soon after graduation. Now, he wrote, he had an offer from an agency in New York that was too good to turn down. He'd love to get together sometime and catch up; he hoped I'd be up for that soon. Meanwhile, though, he needed to find a place to live, and he wondered if I knew of anything...

I laughed out loud.

A few hours later, Marta let me know that Anne wanted me to read to her again. I found her in bed as before, but the look on her face was fearful, as if she were scheduled to go into an operating room for serious surgery. She said hello in a tone that didn't invite an answer and, without speaking, I sat down in the wooden chair at her bedside and took the journal she silently handed to me.

April 14

Disaster.

That was all the entry said. After this, a page had been left blank. On the next, she had written at length.

9 p.m.

Shattered. How to write down what's happened? I feel like a character in a horror story. It's a way to distance myself, I know, disassociate, protect myself. But do I deserve protection?

There was a gap of two lines before she went on.

Last night I slept in the guest bedroom. I woke abruptly after four hours and sat up, briefly disoriented. Then I remembered in ghastly detail all the events of yesterday.

I sat thinking that I must find Greg. If he'd tried to reach me at the hotel again, if he'd shown up there after all, I'd have been gone. He wouldn't dare try calling me here: What if Steve picked up? But I could try the Waldorf. And if he wasn't there, I could go to his studio.

In another part of my brain, I knew he would never come back to me. Will never come back to me.

Still, I tried the hotel. No, there was no Mr. Morris there, and no Mr. Weil either. Stomach clenched, I made myself eat a piece of toast, drank some coffee, and dressed to go to the studio.

I closed the door of 10A with a sense of relief. It's already haunted by my brutal scene with Steve. How I bludgeoned him, crushed his contentment, how, for him, my announcement had come out of a clear blue sky. Where might he have gone? How might he be doing? Guilt, guilt...Yet no regret. What I told him yesterday was true. I could never stay with him after all I've done.

I went down in the elevator but never left the building. Two police-men and three firemen were in the lobby. The policemen were talking to Vincent, the doorman on duty. They stood close to him, keeping their voices low. A moment later, another policeman came in from the street. Two medics followed him, armed with a stretcher and bulky cases of medical gear. Then our new super—I can't think of his name—appeared and led them through the door to the service elevator. The policemen who'd been talking to Vincent went out to the sidewalk and I took their place to ask what was going on. I've never seen police and firemen in the lobby at the same time. One or the other, but not both. The scene was so unexpected that, for a moment, I forgot my own catastrophe.

From Vincent's vantage point, I could see the ambulance and fire engine outside the building. I asked what had happened.

"Was there a fire? Is anyone hurt?"

Before he could answer, Rodrigo came out of the C/D elevator, paper-pale and visibly trembling, a policeman on either side of him. They sat him down in one of the wing chairs by the fake fireplace. One stayed with him; the other went into our elevator.

Now Vincent turned to me, leaned over, and said softly into my ear, "It's Mrs. Morris. Mrs. Morris jumped out of the window."

I've read in poorly written novels of a "cold hand" seizing the protago-nist's heart. Now I know what it meant. I felt the blood drain from my face. I thought I might be about to faint.

"Mrs. Morris?" I echoed, my voice barely audible even to myself.

"Yeah, I don't know if you know her. Knew her. Mrs. Anhalt called me right after—I guess you'd know Mrs. Anhalt. She's in your elevator line, in 6A. So 6A being right across the courtyard from 6C, she actually saw it. She saw Mrs. Morris pull the window wide open and jump. Well, not jump, I guess. You can't really stand up inside a window here and jump, but open it and climb out and, you know, let herself fall into the courtyard. Mrs. Anhalt was at the sink in her kitchen, washing dishes, and she said the movement caught her eye.

"So I hung up and told Rodrigo—he was right here, he just happened to be looking through the repair requests—and he went straight down to the courtyard to see if he could help, and there she was. Or there someone was. I guess a person that falls six stories doesn't look much like a person anymore. Rodrigo said it was nothing like what you see in a movie. He said she kind of exploded. The poor kid. He'll never get that out of his head." He shook his own head, then went on.

"Anyway, I called the cops and they sent the ambulance and, you know, the firemen came. Maybe the cops called them? Anyway, a couple of them are talking to Mrs. Anhalt now. The police, I mean."

I must have gone into a state of shock, because I could hardly take in what he was saying. I heard the words, but they were almost unintelligible. All the same, I understood enough to ask, "And this happened half an hour ago?"

"About that, yeah. You might of heard her when she hit the pavement. Joe did. He was in the basement mopping the floor."

With a clutch of horror, I realized now that I had indeed heard it. I was in my own kitchen, washing the mug and plate I'd used for breakfast. I heard it and thought the building handymen were in the courtyard and had dropped something heavy, the way they do sometimes. You hear a bang, a thud, then voices as they yell at each other. What I heard was also a thud, but I would never have believed it could be a human body.

Now the medics returned to the lobby. They went outside to the ambulance, Vincent holding the door for them. He returned to his post, where I still stood as if paralyzed. Finally, the dreadful thought came to me.

"Was Mr. Morris there?"

It seemed minutes before he answered.

"No, no one else. Mr. Morris went out around six this morning. Andrew was still on the door then and the police called him at home to ask. They're trying to find Mr. Morris now."

I knew I should say something, some conventional phrase—"Oh, how awful," "I can't believe it"—and go out to the street as if on the errand that had taken me downstairs in the first place. Instead, I turned around without another word and came up here. I opened the door, threw myself on the couch, and howled.

What can have happened? How could she have done it? Was this why Greg didn't come yesterday? Was she threatening to kill herself if he left her? It must be. I think it must be. But why did he go out so early today? Did he think I might still be at the Waldorf? Was he coming to me after all? Where is he?

A storm of emotions whipped around inside me. Fury at her for hurting Greg. For hurting me! A wave of nausea as I remembered the thump in the courtyard and imagined what must have happened when her body hit the ground. Bizarrely, indignation as a Windrush resident: the selfishness of choosing to leap into a courtyard looked out at daily by scores of families! Now we'll all think of it every time we look outside our back windows. And what if it gets into the papers? What about our privacy? Our property values? What about the building's reputation? Not to mention poor Rodrigo, blundering into a mass of human smithereens— and Frieda Anhalt, who will remember the woman's falling body for the rest of her life.

But most of all, what it might do to Greg.

Why would she kill herself? That's the question I've been trying to figure out all day. For God's sake, thousands of women are deserted by their husbands every year, every week, every day, *and they don't kill themselves. They sue the bastards for all they're worth. They make them move out, they start a new life, they find a lover of their own. I think of her, cool and smug and superior in her leather jacket at Carnegie Hall. She was no fragile flower, that's for sure. How manipulative she must have been under that swaggering show of indifference, how spiteful. I haven't felt a moment's pity for her.*

Here, seeming to pull herself into the present from a place far away, Anne interrupted me.

"I suppose you're shocked by this."

I knew what she meant but tried to dodge it. "Well—it is shocking," I said. "Any suicide is shocking."

She hesitated before saying, "I don't mean the suicide. I mean my reaction."

I nodded. This was too true to deny. In fact, I had read that last paragraph with growing disbelief, struggling to keep my emotion out of my voice.

"I can tell you that I came to feel very differently," she said. "And not long afterward."

At the time, this didn't impress me much. We sat in silence for several long seconds before I took the initiative and began to read again.

Still, since she has done it, there's no longer any reason Greg and I can't be together. Here's the blessing of it. There's no need now for him to stay true to Susan. There is no Susan; she saw to that. Of course we'll have to wait to make our attachment public, see each other only covertly for some months, maybe even a year. But after that, there will be nothing to keep us from coming into the open, nothing untoward, no reason for gossip. We live in the same building. It's no secret that we're acquainted, and I'll soon be divorced.

Once I could get up from the couch, I thought about looking for Greg at his studio. I decided, though, that I'd rather not be the one to deliver the news. Surely the police would find him; he would hear it soon enough. I waited through an endless afternoon until I was sure he must have been located, told—and probably questioned—then finally left alone by the police. At seven-thirty, I called his apartment. (Did I ever write down in here that I found their home number? I got it from Information, listed under Susan's name, though of course I never used it before. I just wanted to have it.) But he didn't pick up. I know he must want to talk to me now and I feel I must talk to him—face him, own up to my part in what's happened. It struck me that he is likely not answering because it could be anyone calling, even a reporter—how could he know it was me?—so I made up my mind to go to 6C and ring the bell. To avoid being seen, I took our elevator down to the basement and crossed it to go up in Greg's.

I rang, knocked. If he was there, he chose not to come to the door. It occurred to me now that he probably wasn't there. Who would want to spend the night in the apartment where his wife had leapt to her death twelve hours before? Or he might have someone with him, a friend or a relative of hers he wouldn't want me to meet. We must keep our relationship secret, now above all. The connection between Susan's suicide and our affair, should it come out, would be obvious. I couldn't endure the gossip that would result, the accusing, contemptuous glances of friends and neighbors. I'm sure that as her husband—widower, now—and as a public figure, Greg feels this even more strongly.

So I came home and stayed here, as I had all day. Steve called half an hour ago. I picked up in hopes it was Greg and flinched at the sound of his voice. He said he won't be coming back; I can keep the apartment. I tried to argue—why should I have it?—but he ignored me, talked right over me, his voice conspicuously neutral, emotionless. I suppose he prefers not to live where our sham marriage (as I imagine he thinks of it) was lived out. He's already found a place to rent for now, he said, starting tomorrow. His lawyer will be in touch with me to start divorce proceedings. He hopes I'll be willing to admit to infidelity, since this is the only grounds available to us, but if I prefer it, he'll work out a way to make himself seem the guilty party.

If I take the blame, he added, I wouldn't have to expose whoever the—the man—is. (This is the only place where his tone gave way to the strain of his words.) He'd rather I didn't, in fact. He doesn't want to know who it is, to know any of the details. Instead, he'll set me up with a hired stand-in and a private eye to take pictures of us. As smoothly as if he were reading from a script, he added that he plans to come pick up some of his things tomorrow evening between six and seven and to please be out of the apartment while he'll be here. Then he hung up without saying goodbye.

Here Anne broke in to tell me she was "wrung out" for the day. She sent me away, saying that she'd have Marta let me know when she was awake and ready for another session tomorrow.

"It might be the last," she added. "We're near the end."

"However long it takes is fine with me," I answered, but she wasn't listening.

When I got back to my laptop, I found half a dozen new emails. One was from Petra, who sent photos of a client's kitchen-in-progress, including the burnt orange countertops she had tried to dissuade her from installing. Three were from students who wanted to meet with me, probably to argue about grades, or ask if they could hand in an assignment late. There was a very welcome one from Neat Trick, the leather goods company I sometimes wrote copy for. For once, they had substantial work to offer—a whole slew of descriptions of purses and wallets for me to write, plus stories about the artisans who made them. There was also a "thanks anyway" note from Pierce MacAuley.

The day passed. I taught, sat in my office, and went through the essays handed in by my students, returned to the Windrush, ate a dinner of canned tuna and a granola bar, got started on the Neat Trick assignment. But no matter what I did, my thoughts returned and returned to the morning's reading with Anne. Her reaction to Susan Morris's death seemed to me downright evil. "What about our property values?"!

And the death itself—the smashed, shapeless body so different, as her doorman had said, from what you see in the movies, the pain and despair that must have given rise to it, the poor handyman who'd discovered her. And so forth. Uneasy and restless, I treated myself to a nine o'clock movie at the Angelika, then returned to 10A, and carried on my own morally indefensible, scholarly pilfering into the night.

Early the next morning, I received another summons from Anne.

Eighteen

Anne's request for another reading came earlier than usual. When I went into the kitchen for coffee at eight, Marta told me she wanted me to go in to her as soon as I could.

I nodded. I was still waking up. I started to take some coffee and leave—Marta had a pot ready—but she put a hand on my arm to stop me and looked urgently into my eyes. Hers were already glassy with tears.

"You see how bad Mrs. Anne is—so much worse every day," she said. "I called the doctor and he says she should have nursing aides all the time, around the clock, even when I'm here. People who are trained. Her heart could fail, she could have a stroke, all kinds of things could suddenly happen.

"So last night I tried to convince her. I told her I would never forgive myself if something went wrong and I didn't know what to do, so for my sake if not her own...But she said she's ready to go. She doesn't want to fight anymore." Here the tears started to stream down her cheeks. Even I began to well up.

"I see how you're suffering," I said, "but I don't think you should feel responsible. I know you'll miss her if she—if she goes. But I think it's her decision to make, don't you?"

Head bent low, she nodded in silence.

"You wouldn't like her to live in pain if she doesn't want to, I'm sure."

"No. So...so maybe I am the one who is being selfish," she conceded.

"I know you love her. I'm sure she knows too."

She nodded again, then finally released my arm so I could pour myself some coffee. When I turned to carry it back to my room, though, she stopped me.

"Maybe you can change her mind," she said. "Will you try?"

Unwilling to tell her no, I replied with an ambiguous, "I'll see."

She hugged me. Awkwardly, I hugged her back. Then I sped up my morning routine to get in to Anne as soon as possible. At 8:45, I was there.

"I hope it wasn't too inconvenient to come so early," she said as I sat down beside the bed. "I fell asleep at five in the afternoon yesterday and slept till seven a.m. Apparently, even I don't need more than fourteen hours of sleep a night."

"It's no problem," I answered. I was dismayed to hear a chilly note in my own voice as I spoke. Some of my disgust at her reaction to Susan Morris's suicide had dissipated overnight, but I still felt prickly toward her.

She reached under the pillows next to her and took out the notebook I'd been reading from.

"Listen, I didn't mention it yesterday," I said, "but the entry we read was the last one in that journal. There's a blank page after it and that's the end. Do you want me to go get the next one?"

"I have them here," she said. She reached across to the Advil bottle on the nightstand, opened it, and shook a dozen pills into her hand. A moment later, I saw that the little key to the drawer was among them. She gave me a half-crafty, half-sheepish look as she funneled the pills back in and closed the bottle. "You don't mind if I'm a little secretive," she said as she unlocked the drawer.

I made a noncommittal "Mmm" sound, annoyed that she still didn't trust me—perversely, ludicrously annoyed, given how untrustworthy I was—and tried to get a peek inside. Except for when she'd opened it to get the photograph, it had always been closed while I was here. Now I saw that the notebooks we'd taken out of the bookcase weeks before were neatly stacked inside it.

"Put that one back and take out the next," Anne said.

I did this, noting that the framed photograph was tucked in behind the journals. She locked the drawer again and slid the key under the pillow.

As soon as I opened the new journal, I could feel something bumpy enclosed within its pages. Anne was waiting, though, watching me, and I didn't investigate.

Monday April 15, 9 p.m.

A harrowing night last night. Hours of lying awake in cold fear, then nightmares I thankfully can't remember. Ate an egg this morning and promptly wished I hadn't. I was brushing my teeth to try to get rid of the taste when Amy Reeves called. Susan Morris had died, she told me. Did I know?

I said I hadn't.

Well, she went on, she realized that our acquaintance with her and Greg was slight, but she and Len would be going to the funeral and they wondered if Steve and I would like to go with them. She thought we might already have heard what happened. Susan had killed herself, she said, trying in vain to suppress her excitement at having such sensational news to tell. She jumped out a window. That's why Amy thought the news might have gotten around the building. No one knew why, but some people were saying the loss of her concert career had finally made her want to end it all. And of course there were all those miscarriages, though not many people were aware of them.

My palms were sweating and my fingers almost numb with cold as I said "How terrible" and told her how shocked I was. But—when was the funeral? I asked.

"Ten o'clock tomorrow, up at Riverside Memorial. Amsterdam and 76ᵗʰ. Do you want to come with us?"

Tomorrow! Tomorrow, and I still haven't heard a word from Greg, not even to tell me this.

Vibrating with adrenaline, I said I would, as a gesture of neighborly support. Steve would be busy, though. He had to make an appearance in court. As before, I have no idea how I came up with the lie so quickly, but in this case I was surely inspired by my desperation for a chance to see Greg again. It occurred to me after I hung up that Len might mention the funeral to Steve, maybe say it was too bad he couldn't be there, but what would it matter, after all? Sooner or later, everyone would know of our separation.

"I imagine some other people in your building will be coming too," Amy said. *"Greg and Susan haven't lived there long, but they must have made some acquaintances by now. Len and I are going early, so look for us in the chapel. We'll save you a seat. It's definitely going to be crowded. Greg's so well known and well connected. People will want to be seen. And Susan had a career too,"* she added as an afterthought. *In her voice, I could hear her own eagerness to be among this "well connected" crowd.* *"Plus our book club, and other friends of hers, whatever family they have, and—you know. Anyway, Len and I will go early."*

I hung up trembling. Somehow, without realizing it, I'd been sure he would at least call me about the funeral. If I never see him alone again... But I can't let that happen. I won't let that happen.

I didn't bother to tell Anne she had left a line blank before adding a short paragraph.

Went to the White Horse at 5:45 to leave the apartment empty as Steve requested. Sat at the bar till 7:30, drinking Scotch after Scotch.

I looked up to say this was all she'd written that day. Her expression was anguished, eyebrows drawn together, lips quivering. She said, "Go on."

Tuesday April 16, four p.m.

A waking nightmare. Up at 5:30 a.m. and spent an hour lying in bed worrying about what to wear to the funeral. Black, of course, but silk or crepe? High heels or low? What to wear! As if it mattered!

I made myself wait till nine to leave so as not to be conspicuously early. Went to Eighth Avenue to catch a cab and ran smack into Maryanne

Birch, all in black, including a pillbox hat with a little veil. Her apartment is two floors below the Morrises'. Below Greg's. She saw my own clothes, asked where I was going, and then of course we had to go together. She was full of the suicide, almost unbearably garrulous about who had found Susan, who had been home that morning—she hadn't, she was glad to say, because what if she'd seen Susan falling past her own window?—who heard her fall, why she did it, how no one seemed to know if Greg had been there at the time or even if he'd been back since—she rang his bell last night but no one answered. How well did I know Susan? Very slightly, I said; I was going mostly for the sake of the friend who'd introduced us, a colleague of Steve's.

Bubbling on, Maryanne told me she thought Susan might have had a disease, something incurable. A rumor to that effect was going around the building. A woman whose name I didn't catch—another neighbor—had heard she'd been suicidal for years, even institutionalized after trying to kill herself once before. I murmured "Oh" and "Really?" and wondered if either of these stories had any basis in fact. Then she added another line of speculation, this time lowering her voice even though we were alone in the cab.

"I have a friend who's a violinist in the New York Philharmonic," she confided, "and she said she's heard that Greg fools around when he's on the road. I don't know if that's true. My friend—well, she's not really a friend, I don't like her much, because she gossips all the time. But I guess it could be."

My hands had already gone cold. I wanted to open the door next to me and fling myself onto the street. Somehow I managed to say, "I don't like gossip either," and I suppose she realized she'd been gossiping herself, because she finally shut up. We rode the rest of the way to the funeral home in silence. Once we were there, I was able to shake her off.

I hung my coat up on a rack off the lobby. My hands no longer felt so cold, but inside my chest was a kind of effervescence, a malign effervescence caused, I think, by a tremendous coming together of opposing feelings. Did Greg really cheat on Susan routinely? Of course I've worried about this before and told myself that, even if he did, our relationship was nothing like a quickie with a fawning fan. And it wasn't—that, I will go to my deathbed swearing. But still, the thought of it…

On the other side of my emotions was the solemnity of the occasion, the sadness on the faces on the attendees, whether real or feigned. And, of course, what this public ritual for his dead wife must be like for Greg.

Above all, though, I felt a lifting of my heavy (and by then agitated) heart. I had wanted to see him so much, and now I was about to. Grotesque, given the circumstances, I realize—but true.

The chapel was very large, with a high, arched ceiling. I found Amy and Len in the third row, no more than ten feet away from Susan's heavy, gleaming coffin, so much larger than Susan herself. I noted there were no flowers on its closed cover and remembered that this, like burying the dead as soon as possible, is a Jewish custom. I felt a tribal kinship with Greg that I somehow haven't before.

The coffin brought home what Susan had done with new force and vividness. What was inside it—what chaotic remains? And how, I *realized suddenly, could Greg feel anything but devastated? If it had been Steve—not that Steve would ever jump out a window, thank God!—I'd have been devastated. And Greg and Susan had been together far longer than we had. Whatever their marriage had been, only a psychopath could fail to be profoundly shaken.*

Eventually, a string quartet came into the chapel from a side door. The musicians seated themselves on four folding chairs I had failed to notice, readied their instruments, glanced at one another, waited for the room to quiet down—by now the chapel was full, with an overflow standing at the back—and began to play something slow and sweetly sorrowful that I didn't recognize. Maybe a favorite of Susan's, maybe something she played. They continued as a line of grief-stricken people, plainly family members, began to enter from the opposite side of the room.

Greg came in first, followed by an elderly man who looked as I imagine he will look forty years from now. Then a bent, crumpled, sobbing woman I presume was Susan's mother, on the arm of a large, pale man, no doubt her husband. (A fine time they chose to show up for her, if what Amy had told me about their cutting her out of the family was true.) Then three people in their forties or fifties, one of them certainly Susan's sister. She wore the kind of wig Orthodox women wear. All the men had yarmulkes on, Greg included. The sight of him filled me with such a desire to go and walk beside him that I had to clutch the edge of the bench I was sitting on to stay put. The relatives took seats in the empty front row, heads bent, silent. Then a rabbi who'd come in behind them went to a lectern on the platform behind the coffin.

He wore a yarmulke and a prayer shawl but nothing else to mark him as a rabbi: clean-shaven, in a dark suit like any dark suit. He stood waiting until the music ended before starting to speak, then read Psalm 23. He was young—too young to have known anyone in the family for long—but he talked about Susan with intimate familiarity. I can't remember most of what he said, only that her character was as fine as, or even finer than, her superb musical talent. She was quiet and kind, generous, and beautiful as well. She bore bravely and without bitterness the cruel condition that had put an early end to her musical career, instead taking pleasure in her husband's rise to prominence. This was in keeping with the closeness the two had always shared, meeting as students, performing together, supporting each other and—and so on and so on. After this, a few tactful words on the tragic mystery of any person who "ends his or her own life," the reasons for which we can never fully know.

Then he called her sister, Leah, to the lectern and sat down. Despite her downcast eyes, Leah stumbled on a riser on her way up. She recovered and lowered the microphone the rabbi had used. Too close to it, so that her words exploded over the room, she talked about the childhood she'd shared with her sister in Chicago, she the elder daughter, Susan the younger. She told a little anecdote about how Susan had outshone her by mastering the violin at five, almost without instruction.

But this story, evidently intended to be both touching and amusing, was too garbled by the amplification to be clear. She cried as she finished with a few sentences about the joy and pride Susan had brought to the family, how they cherished her and would, like her many fans, mourn her always; how they would treasure the celestial recordings she'd left behind. On these last words, her voice broke and she hurried down to her seat.

She was the only member of the family to speak. Afterwards, the rabbi rose again and read a short prayer in Hebrew, to which we all said Amen. Then he announced that the interment would be private and the family would sit shiva at the Morrises' home from seven till nine tonight, and tomorrow and Friday from five until eight. The musicians played again, the same sad, beautiful music as before, while Greg led the others out the way they'd come in. Soon a hum of voices filled the chapel. People stood and said to each other how simple and moving the service had been, craned their necks to see what celebrated musicians might be there—I noticed several without trying—then clogged the aisles as they stopped to talk with other mourners while those behind them tried to weave their way out.

Len and Amy said to each other that it was remarkable how well the rabbi—a stranger suggested by Riverside Memorial, Amy happened to know—had depicted Susan, how deftly he had handled the—the way she died. Len echoed her praise and I agreed, then fled at the first opportunity. I couldn't even think of an excuse. I just gave each of them a perfunctory hug and wormed my way up the aisle, then through the ruthless mob around the coat rack, and left.

Not a glance over his shoulder to scan the room for me! Not a flicker of an eyelash! Agony. Agony. I tell myself it's only discretion that guides him, but how can he be so unfeeling as not even to ask me what happened when I told Steve? I would never do the same to him.

"There are a few blank lines here," I told Anne, "then it starts again at 8:30 that evening." I didn't wait for her to tell me to go on.

Back from the shiva gathering at Greg's apartment. All afternoon, I argued with myself about whether or not to go. I knew I shouldn't, I knew he wouldn't want me there, but in the end I couldn't help it. I lied to myself. I am a neighbor, I said, one who had been introduced to him and Susan through friends. I had a right to attend.

I waited till seven-thirty to be sure others would be there when I arrived. And indeed, some dozen people talked in quiet twos and threes even in the foyer, the overflow from the already jammed dining room. The living room, visible from the foyer through a set of closed French doors, was dark, the curtains drawn to hide the windows. I wondered how Greg could bear to hold a gathering in his apartment so soon after his wife leapt out of it.

Most of the people who'd come, I assumed, were musicians—Greg's colleagues, but also former classmates of the deceased, teachers she'd had, perhaps, people she'd played with. I recognized one well-known conductor. I didn't see Amy or Len, a mercy for me, but Maryanne Birch was leaving just as I came in. We nodded to each other and moved on.

I stayed far away from Greg, which was not hard to do since he sat at the center of the room on a plain wooden stool facing away from the table. Around him stood ten or fifteen people waiting to pay their respects. The old man who was surely his father sat next to him talking to Susan's sister. The rest of the room was packed with a milling, murmuring crowd.

As far away as I stayed, though, he spotted me. I saw it—something lit briefly in his eyes. It could have been love, it could have been mere recognition, but I think it was a warning.

Can't write any more. Too broken.

"Is that all there is that day?" Anne asked as I paused.

"Yes. Would you like to rest for a bit?"

"Not now," she said, then muttered, "We don't have far to go."

"So this is from the next night."

Wednesday April 17, 9:30 p.m.

Drowning in a sea of pain. My mind keeps flipping—one minute I know it's over, the next I can't believe it is. The way you know but can't believe someone you love has died. How I will live now I have no idea.

What happened: Like an idiot, I went this evening to the second night of shiva. I knew it was the wrong thing to do, stupid to do, but again my longing to see him overcame my reason. I opened the door and found the apartment much less crowded. He caught sight of me at once, stood, and calmly came over to me, a hand out, as if I were someone who'd traveled to be here, someone he particularly wished to welcome. It was obvious he'd prepared for this contingency, and had made up his mind what he would do.

At the open door, he squeezed my arm lightly, as you might to thank someone for coming, then drew me out into the elevator vestibule as if to have a quiet word with me. And this was indeed what he wanted. The moment we emerged from the apartment, he closed the door behind him and dropped my arm.

"Go away," he said, his voice low. "Don't ever come here."

"I'm sorry," I said. "I know I should have waited. I just wanted to see

you so much." I looked into his face for understanding, even pity. *"I've been losing my mind,"* I said. *"We haven't been in touch at all since—since we decided on our plan."*

"Did you think I would get in touch?" he demanded, pronouncing the words *"get in touch"* with burning scorn. *"Why? What do we have to talk about? I told Susan I was leaving and she told me she'd kill herself. We argued all night and I went out before dawn and left her alone. Because I was angry at her! Because she wouldn't let me have my way! And she did it. We did it, you and I. We killed my wife."*

I wanted to say that she'd killed herself. I wanted to say he might at least ask what had happened to me, how Steve took the news, whether my life had also been shattered. Instead, I blurted out, "So you did tell her?"

"Of course I told her. What do you think drove her out the window?"

I stopped reading.

"I suppose that's all I wrote that day," Anne said after a long silence.

"Yes."

"Yes." In a flat, humorless voice, she added, "I always had a gift for ending chapters."

Following this, she was quiet again for a long time. Her face was unreadable, her gaze seemingly focused on something outside the walls of the room.

"There's one more section to read, I think," she said at length.

I had skimmed the next entry during her silence. It was only a few paragraphs, and I was certain it was the last of what she called the "episode."

"Yes. From the next day."

"Yes."

Thursday April 18, 7 p.m.

I must be insane. I left a letter for Greg with the doorman this morn-ing. I pleaded with him to reconsider. I tried to refute his claim that we "drove his wife out the window," naming all the less extreme, more prac-tical paths she could have taken, the paths every other woman takes—the path Steve is taking. I said her choice was vindictive, made with the knowledge that it would sentence him to a lifetime of perpetual guilt. I begged him to deny her that satisfaction, even if only for his own sake, even if he never wanted to see me again.

I closed with a declaration of my love and a plea in the name of mercy to give me five minutes alone with him.

An hour ago, after I'd gone out and come back twice in hopes the door-man would have a reply to give me, Vincent did indeed hand me a letter. I carried it up here, sat at my desk for a long time just holding it—holding the heavy cream envelope he had touched, running a finger over my name written in his handwriting. Finally, as careful not to rip the flap as if it were a precious relic, I unsealed it.

In its way, it is a precious relic. In its deadly, excruciating way. It said, "Do not contact me again."

Nothing more was written on the page. When I turned to the next one, I saw that it was blank. So was the next, and the next, and all the rest. Pasted onto one of the empty pages, though, was the cause of the bump I'd felt when I opened the notebook. It was the letter whose message I'd just read aloud, still in the envelope marked "Windrush doorman, please give to Anne Taussig Weil."

NINETEEN

I never read to Anne again. The day after we finished the "episode," she had a stroke. It happened at nine in the morning; Marta happened to be tidying her room at the time. She recognized the signs and called an ambulance at once, but considerable damage had already been done. I later learned that Anne had a health-care directive with a DNR order, but the EMTs never saw it and they saved her life. And so she was left to endure the slow death she'd so much wished to avoid.

She returned from the hospital to the Windrush cruelly diminished. She had lost much of her memory and, it seemed, her ability to think. It was hard to know the extent of this, since she couldn't talk properly, not only because the right side of her body was paralyzed but also because she had aphasia. Incapable of refusing, she finally had round-the-clock nurses, arranged for by Marta and covered by a long-term-care insurance policy she'd maintained for years. It was the best help available, but the strangers in her bedroom appeared to frighten her, and she couldn't communicate even her simplest needs. Mercifully, she slept a lot.

As for me, I moved out of 10A four days after the stroke. I had lived there less than a month, but it was obvious I should leave; I had no business there now.

The god of rental space was with me. Petra asked Justin (they'd broken up by now but stayed friends) and Justin knew someone with a Chelsea apartment who suddenly had to spend three months in Sydney. Subletting wasn't allowed in her building and she needed a cat-sitter, so Kristin—that was the name of this lucky woman—wasn't asking for rent. She had a great job and a fat salary and was far more concerned with Tigerlily's welfare than money. So I left the Windrush—but not, I am sorry to say, before taking advantage of the four days in between.

I made good use of it. I took the journals I hadn't yet had time to photograph to a copy shop and also a number of mildly interesting papers I'd missed in my earlier raids on her file drawers, then carefully returned each item to the place I had found it. Thus, I departed with a great deal of useful material, even if none of it could compensate for the frank interviews that had been my original goal.

Temporarily installed in Tigerlily's very pleasant apartment, I started sorting through my trove. I woke each day electric with energy. With all I had now, I knew for sure I could finish my dissertation. That certainty fed me, speeded me up, imbued me with an almost manic ability to focus. I told Professor Probst I had rounded a corner, solved the "more material" problem, and would soon have new chapters for her. I worked hour after hour, from early morning till after midnight, while Tigerlily walked over my papers. Grudgingly, I crammed my teaching duties in when I had to.

My stash was so large, I found, that it took nearly a month just to organize. Once I finally started reading the journals—flying through them, really, dashing in and out of the various decades they covered, trying to get an overview of their contents and make at least a sketchy timeline of the turning points in her life—I found that they did indeed contain much of value, even more than I'd expected.

For one thing, the later notebooks documented what I'd already guessed: that Anne had never stopped loving Gregory Morris. Out of "loyalty" to him, she kept their affair secret even from her closest friends. For a long time, despite bouts of fury at him, she harbored a wistful hope that they might somehow join their lives together after all. This was one reason, if not the only one, that she never remarried.

Then came a summer afternoon, almost fifteen years after Susan Morris's suicide, when Greg, contrary to his usual habit of cutting her dead when their paths happened to cross, caught up with her on purpose as she walked, "thinking of this and that" (as she noted in the journal) in Washington Square Park.

"I hope you've forgiven me for—for all that in 1963," he said quietly, without preliminary ("not even a hello," she wrote). "How it ended, the way I left you hanging that unspeakable night. You probably think I've been heartlessly cold to you, hateful. But it isn't that. It isn't that," he repeated, looking not at her but down at the asphalt path they stood on. "I just can't forgive myself. I knew Susan was unstable. She'd suffered from awful depressions—long, long spells of them. She'd even tried to kill herself once before. And still I told her I was going to leave her. She said very clearly that she'd take pills or jump out the window if I did—and then I left the house at dawn! As if to give her some privacy so she could do it! So you see . . ."

He stopped, shook his head in silence. "I try not to think about it. I never talk about it. But that's why."

"Then he hurried away before I could say anything," Anne's entry finished. If they spoke again, I didn't find any record of it in the journals.

She wasn't a nun. As I read along through the 1970s, I found entries documenting a lackluster but prolonged liaison with a history professor named Carl Hauptmann. After this ended, she wrote of several other dalliances, most of which provided more companionship than romance. There were details from the time when, five years after its astounding success as a book, the film version of *Vengeance* was finally put into production and, eventually, released. A professional screenwriter had been hired to write the script and, perhaps inevitably, Anne was incensed by its deviations from her novel.

In the later '60s, after the spate of publicity *Vengeance* had brought settled down, came three long years dominated by the writing, selling, and publication of *The Balance*, her last and sadly unsuccessful book. Following its release, she had scrawled floods of angry entries about reviews that praised her style and wit in the first paragraphs, summarized the story in the next five or six, then ended with "and yet it somehow doesn't work." After these entries came frustration about its miserable sales, crying jags as copies were shipped back from the stores to the publisher, then remaindered, and, eventually, a grim resolution to try again.

Over the next two years, the journals centered on the writing of *The American Tour*, the ill-fated novel born of this decision—the one, as I have already mentioned, that I found in her file drawer along with the rejection letters it received. Writing it after so much pain and disappointment from *The Balance* was a grueling affair. Eventually, of course, I read it, and I think some of that hard struggle shows in the manuscript. It tells the story of a teenaged girl who manages to attach herself to a British band touring America. The band is young, just starting out, and the tour is on a shoestring budget. The girl, Maddie, hears the group live on a New York radio station and falls in love with them at once. She goes to their show at a tacky downtown venue and, after eyeing the lead singer and being eyed back, presents herself at the stage door. Soon, she drops out of school and is off on a bumpy road trip with a quartet of Brummies.

It was quite a funny book, I thought, with some of the dry wit of her early novels and a certain amount of satire—gentle, affectionate satire. All the same, Anne was very far from the generation she was trying to explore. She knew nothing about the world of rock and roll, and the youth culture of the time was, for her, another universe. I would argue that she made a brave choice in taking on so contemporary a story, and a game attempt at getting it right. Still, she wasn't at ease with her subject, and it isn't surprising the book failed to find a publisher.

After a full year of bruising rejections, she decided to withdraw the manuscript and quit writing novels altogether. She'd realized by now that the cause of her failure after *Vengeance* was the very success of that book itself. *Vengeance* was what had brought her to the attention of the general public, and another book like it—a novel no less wrathful and sweeping, shocking and extravagantly dramatic—was the only book readers would ever want from her again.

Though she'd given up on novels, Anne remained a presence in the literary community into her early eighties, until the damage to her vision irreversibly sidelined her. Within a year of the failure of *The American Tour*, she began to poke her head up here and there. She moderated panels and spoke on panels. She taught writing seminars, as she sometimes had in the past. She wrote blurbs and reviews and letters to the editor. She served as a judge for book awards and as a member of the Board of Directors of the Authors Guild. Summer after summer, she went to Bread Loaf to mentor fledgling writers. She contributed essays to literary publications, supplied prefaces to new editions of classics, among them, as I've mentioned, *Pride and Prejudice*.

Even with the income stream *Vengeance* continued to produce (and still produces, by the way), none of this would have been sufficient for her to live on comfortably. But unlike other writers, Weil didn't need to earn a living by her pen. Because Stephen Pace died so soon after the couple separated, they were still married, and he hadn't yet changed his will. And so, along with Apartment 10A, Anne inherited his considerable fortune.

The legacy came with a heavy price. I have seldom read lines as wrenching as her journal entry the day she learned of his death. She grieved for years, with a grief complicated by guilt for her "brutal" treatment of him. Under the circumstances, she felt she had no moral right to accept her good luck—the money and the apartment. Still, of course, she managed to accept them.

For all this, she never quite came to the point of regretting her affair with Gregory Morris. She continued to treasure it as the greatest romantic adventure of her life. And, she unwaveringly believed, of his.

As for her earlier journals, they contained other sorts of useful information: clues to the childhood events that had fed her creativity, including her many fantasies about her mother, who had died young; accounts of intellectual—and sexual—awakenings in her college years; a portrait of herself as a fresh young arrival in New York, desperate to find a job and thrilled to be hired as a copyeditor by Simon and Schuster; an intimate record of her development into a published writer; and the various flirtations and affairs she had in the years before she married.

When she entered her thirties and Steve began to appear in her entries, it was soon apparent that he was as "exotic" to her as she was to him. As she had written after her 1963 visit to his estate lawyer, she had never been involved with anyone so "grown up." For his part, he was "mystified" by her ability to make up characters and stories. She enjoyed how marvelous her gift seemed to him, and soon, although she wondered if it was wise, decided to allow him to fulfill his plainspoken desire: to shelter and protect her. "Rescue me," she wrote, describing his intention. "And why not?"

Their time together really was congenial, as she had told interviewers. As I made my way through the months and years, it became clear that the luster of his "solidity" wore off, and her imaginativeness came to fascinate him less, but he was proud of the two books she published during their marriage. They did, as she'd maintained, share pleasures and bring each other new ones; she had never played tennis before they met, and, despite her previous scorn for athletic diversions, she found she loved it.

It amused her to learn that he hated wearing suits and, especially, ties. On the weekends, he dressed "like a teenager," in "dungarees" and flannel shirts. He left affectionate notes for her in unexpected places. "You are my spice," said a tiny one slipped into a jar of cinnamon sticks. She made sure not to repeat the errors of his first wife (already remarried), which included poor cooking, indifferent housecleaning, and reluctant sex.

Though I'm ashamed of it now—ashamed and chastened—I had inured myself to the moral unease that stealing so much material initially provoked in me. I confess I was also much relieved to know that, with Anne incapacitated, Patrick Quigley would be most unlikely to pursue my violation of the non-disclosure agreement by the time evidence of my thefts could surface in my dissertation. (Not that I expected anyone outside of academia ever to know about, let alone read, my dissertation. I did not.)

There is, however, one thing I took from Anne that has troubled my conscience ever since: the snapshot of her with Gregory Morris on their last day in Philadelphia.

It was easy to steal. After her stroke, Anne stayed in the hospital almost a week. This interval overlapped with my last three days in residence at the Windrush. On the second afternoon, Marta came in to clean as usual, and in particular to remove the traces of the frantic medical drama that had taken place in the master bedroom. When she'd gone home, I saw that she had found the key to the night-table drawer and left it in the lock. So I had only to go to the bedroom that evening and take out the journals still inside—and, along with them, the photograph. This I removed from its silver frame. I brought my loot to a copy shop, where the four journals that had eluded me for so long were finally Xeroxed, and the picture reproduced on photo paper. They did a very good job.

Then I returned to Anne's bedroom. I restored the journals to the drawer and put the duplicate picture into the silver frame, keeping the original for myself. I knew it was a vile thing to do— such an intimate, cherished image—but I couldn't resist it. At the time, I could think only of what a coup it would be to use it in my dissertation, not only to illustrate but also to document irrefutably the affair between Weil and Morris. I have never confessed this until now.

I was at my desk working on the timeline of Anne's life—the period when she was in college, as it happened—when Marta phoned to let me know she had died.

It was pneumonia that finished her off. For two months, she had lingered, not yet dead but not quite alive. Then her lungs became congested, and this time, under Quigley's orders, the stipulations in her health directive were followed: she received only palliative care. Marta was with her at the end, she told me, holding her hand.

Her call hit me with a visceral sense of loss I hadn't expected. Since my departure from 10A, I'd phoned several times to ask how Anne was doing, even visited once to see if she might still be able to talk to me about her work. Of course, I found her far too impaired to do anything of the sort. My ten-minute stay left me both frustrated and very sad.

Now, hearing of her death, I thought of all she had suffered in the second half of her life. I remembered especially her remark about the effect Gregory Morris's passing had had on her: that no matter how long expected or merciful, death is a shock to those left behind. I called Petra for some comfort, and she comforted me. By now she knew I had acquired enough new material about Weil to finish my dissertation, though we never discussed exactly how. I think she was relieved to know I'd developed some affection for Anne after all.

Two days after her death, the *Times* ran a short obituary alongside one of her early book-jacket photos. The writer identified her as "the author of the blockbuster novel *The Vengeance of Catherine Clark*," gave a thumbnail summary of its plot, mentioned that despite unenthusiastic reviews, it had soared to the top of the *Times* best-seller list and stayed on it more than a year. He went on to note that "some critics" saw it as a precursor of Erica Jong's *Fear of Flying* and other popular novels with "strong female protagonists." There was also the usual fleeting mention of where and when and to whom she'd been born, as well as her marriage. The writer barely noted that she'd published other novels and did not think it necessary to give a cause of death.

The day after that came her funeral, arranged by Marta. Despite all my thefts and deceptions, I attended the service for Anne with a feeling that I was a qualified mourner. It was held in a small chapel at an undistinguished, nondenominational funeral home in the Village and was very poorly attended. The only child of two only-children, she had no relatives. Half a dozen mostly elderly people came as a group. From their look of mild, almost touristic interest, I took them to be neighbors from the Windrush. There was a fiftyish man I suspected of being Kenneth Fitzhugh and a few others who might have been former students or other surviving literary contacts. Patrick Quigley also came.

Her coffin was simple, nothing like the massive one she'd described as holding the shattered remains of Susan Morris. The director of the funeral home conducted a very short service during which no one else spoke. At the end, he noted that, since Anne was to be cremated, this marked the conclusion of the day's ceremonies.

Only Marta cried.

I hugged her before I left and teared up myself in the face of her grief. I asked what she would do now and learned that Anne had left her some money, more than enough, she said, to keep her afloat until she found another job. I considered suggesting that we go to the Windrush together for a cup of coffee, since the service had been so brief and so abruptly ended, but decided against it. I had already taken the whole morning off.

As I came out into the fresh day, I heard someone call my name and turned to see Quigley. He'd been waiting for me to emerge. Without explanation, he asked if I could spare a few hours tomorrow; if so, he would like me to come see him at his office. Of course, I said I could, and we made an appointment for ten a.m.

I left with a head full of questions. Had Anne, as I once fantasized she might, left me something to reward my better-than-expected readings? The photo of her with Greg sprang to mind. It was only a wish, and an ill-founded one—but how ironic if it turned out to be legitimately mine after all.

TWENTY

The day after the funeral, I woke up an hour before my alarm went off. It was a relief when the time came to leave for my appointment with Quigley. I had searched online the previous day and learned that the midtown firm where he practiced was small but solid. Quigley was a partner. He received me punctually, coming out to the handsomely furnished waiting room to shake my hand.

I couldn't quite read his face. The cheerfulness I'd seen in it when we'd first met was absent, but his expression was pleasant and his aura of exceptional well-being intact. I greeted him as Mr. Quigley. He said to call him Patrick. We shook hands and he ushered me into a corner office.

Here he waved me into one of the two leather chairs across from his desk. He offered coffee or tea, but I was much too anxious to know why he wanted to see me to waste time on refreshments. He seated himself at the desk and put his folded hands atop a manila envelope. I could see it was addressed to me.

"About three months ago," he began, "Anne asked me to come to her apartment. You may remember my visit to her then."

"Yes, of course."

"Well, the reason she'd asked was that she wished to amend her will. We took care of this, and at the same time, she dictated quite a long letter to be given to you after her death. That's what this is," he added, lifting his hands to tap the envelope. "I'll give it to you in a moment. I suggest you read it here and now, so I can answer any questions it raises in your mind. But first, I want to let you know that, when she revised the will, Anne left you three bequests. For one, the sum of two hundred thousand dollars."

Disbelief and confusion left me unable to say more than, "Really?"

"Very much so. The second is whatever royalties her books earn in the future."

This revelation brought tears to my eyes. The money was a staggering, almost incomprehensible surprise, but the legacy of her royalties was even more meaningful. It tied me forever to the story of her most passionate creation. It was a show of personal attachment to me, goodwill toward me—and she had arranged for it at a time when my own feelings toward her were not admirable. It was an intimate gift, and in that way more valuable than the munificent lump sum.

Quigley waited while I struggled to regain my composure.

"The last bequest," he said, after a long moment, "is the use for your dissertation of all her papers, including her journals, of which I gather there are several hundred."

For a moment, I couldn't speak. Then, "Three hundred," I told him.

"Ah. Yes. Well," he went on, "her letter will explain why and with what hopes she has left these writings to you. I wouldn't have known the contents of the letter if she'd been able to write it herself," he noted, "but of course she wasn't. She had to dictate it to my assistant during our meeting with her. My assistant—Amber Waring, you may remember her—typed it up and read it back to her over the phone for corrections. And now, here it is."

He picked up the envelope and handed it to me.

"I can give you a conference room to sit in while you read it," he said. "Again, I do advise you to read it while you're here."

I said I would. He stood up and I stood too, on wobbly legs. Then he escorted me to a room with a very long polished mahogany table and a view of the Chrysler building. A pitcher of ice water sat next to a large glass. I seated myself in one of the wheeled leather chairs.

"I'll leave you," he said, adding as he closed the door, "I've cleared the next few hours of my calendar, so come back to me any time if you have questions."

I sat without moving for at least a full minute, literally slack-jawed. I thought of all the lies I'd told Anne, my flagrant intrusions into her file drawers, the papers I'd taken without permission, and, most of all, my raids on the glass-fronted cabinet. Finally, I opened the envelope, my movements mechanical. Astonishment had knocked the curiosity out of me.

It was indeed a long letter, eight typewritten pages. I read it, then reread it.

"Dear Elizabeth Miller," it began.

I think you will wonder very much at the news Patrick Quigley has just given you. Here I will explain.

The first thing you should know is that I recognized your name the moment I saw it in your answer to my ad. Your email address indicated a link to Columbia University and although you signed yourself "Beth," I soon realized you had done so as a means of ensuring that, in the improbable event that I would remember a name on letters received and ignored years before, I would all the same fail to connect you with the Elizabeth Miller who requested an interview with me.

But I did remember your name, because I never threw your letters away. Although I turned you down at the time, it was with more ambivalence than you could have guessed. No writer wishes to be forgotten, and I have been forgotten. The prospect of being resurrected in even a scholarly treatise destined to reach an audience of half a dozen people tempted me. After all, who but a scholar would think of writing about me now? And no such person had approached me before.

I declined then because I didn't know how you would portray me. Despite the admiration implied in your letter, I thought it more than likely that you thought ill of my books, particularly my famous one, and were planning to attack, not immortalize, it. Your view might be that it did more harm than good, that it somehow undermined the cause of women more than advanced it. You might disparage its style—justly, I think, since even I am embarrassed by that aspect of it. Unlike my other books, it was written in a white-hot heat. I dashed down whatever words served my urgent feelings and was done with it in six months. I also felt there was a whiff of surprise in your stated dissertation subject; I wondered if you planned to argue that *Vengeance* was the result of some lucky accident, as when a kitten scampering over a keyboard plays the theme of *Für Elise.*

In sum, I had learned from my long-ago experiences with journalists—so respectful when requesting an interview, so flattering during it, so venomous in print—to regard requests for interviews with a lively mistrust. Still, with such a dismal, obscure end to my literary career looming as I plowed toward the tail end of old age, I thought now and then of contacting you and offering to meet with you after all.

For whatever interest it holds, I don't think I was far wrong about your take on my literary worth. This suspicion is based not on anything you've said but rather on the ingratiating manner you've so assiduously cultivated even as you lied to my face. The fact that you did lie to me, I might add—and that you do still—was also clear to me from the start. You are not as good a liar as you seem to think.

Moreover, as I mentioned to you once, in spite of the

state of my vision, I can still read enlarged words on my computer, and so I was capable of searching "Columbia University Ph.D. candidates" to confirm that the account you gave me of your education was far from complete. If all this had not been enough, your recent assertion that you know *The Aspern Papers* only as a title you've heard somewhere—well, I need hardly say more. These are just a few examples of your many deceptions, as you know better than I.

To return to the matter of my recognizing your identity from the time you emailed me: At first, I thought it was all a grand coincidence. Fate had sent me a deeply literate scholar just when I was in need of someone to read my journals aloud. But after the first few minutes of our initial meeting, during which I saw your sharp mind and your obvious efforts to present yourself as a quiet, modest nobody, I realized that my post on Craigslist contained some clues to my own identity. First and most important were the initials and birthdate embedded in my email address. But there was also the "pre-war doorman building in Greenwich Village with river view," a description of the building to which you had sent your letters.

Still, it truly was a coincidence, wasn't it, my placing the ad just when you needed a room to rent? For this, I thank the gods.

You will now be yet more confused as to why I wish to leave you my royalties, the free use of my journals and papers, and the money that accompanies these legacies. There are several reasons.

For one, although I've been startled by the extreme lengths to which your ambition has driven you, I myself have been driven and ambitious in my day. I've found your lies more amusing than disturbing, as I'm afraid I may have revealed once or twice by smiling at them. To be honest, I've quite enjoyed toying with you. It's provided a diversion from brooding over Greg's death, as well as a distraction from my own worsening health. In fact, it's been more fun than I've had in years.

Apart from this, and despite all I know of your selfish motives, I am grateful to you for the sensitivity of your readings, for making yourself available to me at will, and especially for your steadfast attempts to hide whatever shock, disapproval, or embarrassment my story has provoked in you. I also believe you've come rather to like me, as I have you.

And now to why I am willing to let you reveal the contents of my journals: As you are well aware, I never intended them to be read by anyone other than myself. In fact, until today, my will instructed Patrick to have them pulped. But as you continue to read to me the story of my affair with Gregory Morris, I find that I think it's quite an interesting one, and not badly told. At least so far; at the time I am dictating this letter, we are still some distance from the end.

I also believe the story as written strikes you as engaging, however little you may think of my published works. (If I have died before we finished reading the "episode," as I have called it, please ask Patrick to let you read the remaining pertinent journals and do so now. This letter will make more sense to you if you have. You will know the end when you reach it.)

Another reason for my willingness to allow the journals to survive me is that since Greg's death, there is no one left to be embarrassed or shamed or angered by the revelations in them. He has no children, I have no children. To the best of my knowledge, the few other parties who might once have been harmed or offended are also gone.

This matter of the journals' revelations brings me to a very particular point. For all that's been written about it, reviewers and the reading public have never understood the true origin of *The Vengeance of Catherine Clark*. They could not. At the risk of spoiling the end of the episode for you (that is, again, if we haven't yet gotten to it) "Catherine Clark" was not some avatar of myself, nor a composite of women I'd known, nor even a wholly imaginary character conceived expressly for the purpose of demonstrating the rage and power of women. "Catherine Clark" was Susan Morris.

Susan killed herself (as I hope you already know, since that means that we made it through the whole story before

my death), whereas Catherine Clark of course does not.
Quite the opposite. It is her unfaithful husband who
commits suicide after she destroys his life. You know how
deep my love was for Greg. You know that it survived for
many years, despite (as you'll remember from your very
first reading to me) his taking things so far as to pretend
not to see me when we bumped into each other after his
wife's death.

So you may be surprised to learn that very soon after
the end of our affair, my estimation of him began to
change. This alteration started when, a month or two after
Susan's funeral, Amy Reeves told me that Greg had indeed
been a serial cheater, just as I myself had sometimes feared
he might be. She'd had this information from Susan
herself, who for all the disdain she had shown Amy when
we happened upon her that night at Carnegie Hall, had
confided it to her some years before.

The confirmation of my suspicions shook me to the
core. I have reason to know that our case was different, of
course. Greg did indeed love me, did announce to Susan
his intention to break up their marriage for me, and so
precipitated the disastrous sequel. Still, to have been
persistently, repeatedly unfaithful to her over a period of
many years—and none too discreetly, either—that was a
low, selfish, dishonorable thing to do. As such, it greatly
diminished my scorn for her violent and unnecessary
reaction to the news that he planned to leave her.

(Elizabeth, I do hope we've read the whole story by now!) Indeed, it was largely the reason I developed so much sympathy for her—the sympathy that led me to write *Vengeance*. At the same time, it led me to accept my own role in her death, to acknowledge that I had betrayed my natural ally—a woman like myself—in favor of a man.

I also felt more and more horrified by the pain I'd caused Steve, so trusting and so blameless. He was still alive when my feelings about Susan began to evolve, and you can be sure that his sudden death so soon after the blow I had dealt him only deepened my already piercing sense of guilt. Many people assumed the fury of *Vengeance* stemmed from some willful harm he had done me, and I longed to correct this injustice to him. Soon, I came to carry my perfidy around as a heavy stone.

Shortly after Amy told me about Greg's infidelities, a whirlwind of fury began to rise in me—fury on Susan's behalf, fury at him, and fury at myself as well. This is the fuel that burns in *Vengeance*. Not my vengeful anger at some man who did me wrong, but the rage I wished Susan had turned on us instead of herself. In a way, the book was a tribute to her, an act of penitence, a stab at allowing her to come out the victor after all. And I think it succeeded in this, because Catherine Clark became a touchstone for thousands of women who had allowed the men in their lives to dominate and mistreat them.

And so it is that, in the book, Susan has her revenge,

not at the cost of her own life but at no cost to herself at all. In my reimagining, it is Catherine who makes her faithless husband pay for his actions, her husband whose life is crushed by loss after loss: her own violent, public departure, the respect of his employer when she tells him of Howard's abuse of her, the friendship of his colleagues when his growing sense of victimization erupts into bellicose outbursts at the office, and finally, after Catherine's visit to his ex-wife, his right to custody visits with his children. And, of course, he is the one who kills himself.

After *Vengeance* came out and I found I could no longer succeed as a writer, I realized I had also enabled Susan to take her revenge on me.

With regard to my papers, I believe that some of these—contracts and other professional documents, for example—may provide names and dates etc. that are missing in the journals. Once you've made use of them and the diaries, I'd appreciate your looking into whether some institution might be interested in acquiring them. The Browne Library of Popular Culture at Bowling Green University may be able to direct you to an appropriate collection. I doubt you'll succeed, but I'd like you to make an attempt.

And now, Elizabeth Miller, I am going to toy with you one last time—and toy more like a lioness than a house cat, I fear.

I have asked Patrick to tell you about the bequests I've provided in my will. However, I've also asked him to omit a key piece of information: that they are contingent on a condition.

That condition is that you must prepare, and prepare to the satisfaction of my agent, Kenneth Fitzhugh, an edited, market-ready manuscript of my journals before you make any other use of them. Unless and until you have fulfilled this condition, Patrick will see to it that you abide by the non-disclosure agreement you signed, which requires, among other things, that you keep in strict confidence any information learned from the materials you were then about to read.

To clarify, you now have two options. You may write your dissertation immediately, without these materials, and permanently forfeit all of my bequests. Or you may accept the bequests and promptly start work on the edition sketched above. I must warn you that the 290 or so notebooks you haven't seen aren't nearly as exciting as the ones we've been reading. Combing through them and culling an edited, salable version will be a mammoth, time-consuming, and often tedious task, and this is why I am leaving money to sustain you during the necessary effort. Patrick will fill you in on how your progress would be monitored and the funds meted out.

When it is done and approved by Kenneth, you may turn over the business of selling it to him. (He is optimistic about finding a publisher, given that it solves the longstanding mystery of why a world-renowned pianist left the stage at the very height of his career.) You may then go on and use any and all of the legacies— journals, papers, whatever remains of the lump sum, and, of course, the royalties from my existing books—as you like.

Why have I set this condition? It is not from spite, to thwart you, or "get you back" for deceiving me, as you may imagine. It is simply because I suspect that, once you'd made use of my private writings to achieve your own ambitions, you would not trouble to fulfill mine. I may be wrong in this—forgive me if I misjudge you—but knowing your capacity for self-serving underhandedness, it's a risk I prefer not to take.

To encourage you to choose what I will call Option Two—accepting the legacies and editing the journals—I have instructed Patrick to make Option One just a little less appetizing. Once apprised of your decision to refuse the bequests, he will send your review committee department a copy of our non-disclosure agreement. He will suggest that, in order to avoid the necessity of a lawsuit that might cause Columbia University some embarrassment, he be allowed to read your dissertation before you are permitted to defend it.

If he finds that you have included information you could only have learned from your time with me, Patrick

will bring a suit against you for breaching the terms of our
NDA. He will also inform your advisory committee that
you gained access to my home under false pretenses. As
documentation, I have forwarded him a printout of your
emailed answer to my ad. He will leave it to them to
decide whether your irregular (to say the least of it)
behavior disqualifies you as a candidate.

Should you choose Option Two, as I hope you will, it
does not escape me that in taking these rather extortionate
measures, I am likely to incur your anger, and with it,
perhaps, a most unflattering portrait of my character in
whatever preface, afterword, or annotations you may add
to my journals. I would remind you that you did gain
access to me through false means and I am therefore not
unjustified in taking these steps.

At the same time, since the revelations of such a
collection must inevitably reveal my own moral failings
anyway, the prospect of any harsher portrayal of me on
your part does not particularly trouble me. Nor does my
own conscience: For one thing, should an edition of the
journals be published, you will be the recipient of any
money it earns.

Also, because I believe that publishing such a book
would start you off nicely as a writer—a career in which I
think you would do very well, whereas, quite honestly, the
capacity for deception you have demonstrated does make
me wonder about your suitability as a scholar—I feel that,

at the same time as I jeopardize one professional path for you, I offer another. That opinion notwithstanding, if you still have enough energy and desire to complete your dissertation after the years it will take to edit my journals, I wish you the very best of luck.

I believe I have now said all that needs to be said. I trust that your common sense, if not any warm feeling you may harbor for me, will persuade you that the better course for you is to accept my bequests. Please do, and may they bring you pleasure and success.

Yours with affection,
Anne Taussig Weil

The letter dropped from my hands. I sat, head spinning like a T-boned car. "Be careful what you wish for," I heard Rod Serling intone, as the camera dollies back from the greedy fool on "The Twilight Zone" who sees too late the trap he's made for himself. How rich the English language is in idioms for comeuppance!

A taste of your own medicine.

Hoist with your own petard.

The shoe on the other foot.

Serves you right.

Just deserts.

He who laughs last laughs best.

Or, in this case, she.

Book Club Discussion Questions

1. How did your opinion of the characters change as you read the book?

2. What do you think happened to Liz after the book ends?

3. Which character did you like the best? Which did you like the least?

4. How did the setting of the book impact the story?

5. Did you agree with Liz's decisions? Have you ever been in a similar position?

6. How did you feel after reading Anne's response to the death of Greg's wife?

7. Who did you most relate to in the story?

8. Are there any passages that stand out to you?

9. Were you satisfied with how the story ended?

10. Are there any books you would compare this book to?

11. Were you rooting for Anne and Greg to stay together? Why or why not?

12. How did this book make you feel?

13. Did this book make you think differently about lying?

14. Who would you cast to play Anne and Liz in a movie?

15. Have you ever met someone you idolized? Did your meeting change the way you felt about them?

16. How would you react to Liz's dishonesty if you were Anne?

17. Did any songs come to mind when reading this book?

18. Why do you think the author chose to tell the story from Liz's point of view, and not Anne's?

19. Do you think there are any strong symbols in the book?

20. If you could ask the author one question about the book, what would it be?